LIFEBOATS AND LIES

JULIA ROBERSON

Contents

CHAPTER 1

Sometimes I'll be standing somewhere and realise that everyone around me will be dead one day. I'll be looking in on a crowd from the outside, and they begin twisting and morphing into blurs of colours until they barely resemble human beings anymore. The idea of them having any emotions or personalities seems absurd because they aren't people. They're just unrecognisable masses, filling up space until they die.

Holy shit, I need to lighten up.

'Hello? Mia?'

Aiden's voice snaps me out of my thoughts, and I suddenly remember where I am: standing outside a stranger's house at ten o'clock on a Friday night.

'This is a lovely door and everything--heck, I wouldn't mind having a door like this myself one day,' Aiden continues. 'And that window. Are those mahogany frames? But I do fancy--and this may stun you now, so be prepared--I do fancy entering the place at some point.'

I glare at his sarcasm, but he's too busy bouncing with excitement to notice.

I don't blame him. School is officially out for summer, and this is the biggest party there's been since, without a doubt, the dawn of time--well, okay, that may admittedly be a slight exaggeration, but point is, it's a big deal. The only downside is the host, Robbie Morrissey: a boy whose life revolves around basking peasants such as myself in his superficial beauty to remind us of how irrelevant we are, and how magnificent he is. Aiden would walk the earth to be given a chance to be in the same room as the guy. I, on the other hand, think he's an egotistical arsewipe, so am only here to offer my services as Aiden's moral support.

I step onto the porch with Aiden standing so close that I can practically feel his breath on my neck, and as we walk through the open doorway and enter the house, the sound of an intense dubstep song almost deafens me. Aiden pulls me inside while he pushes his way through the crowd of people I was gazing at moments ago. The house is huge, and even when cluttered with the sweaty bodies of hormone imbalanced teenagers, it's impressive.

The walls are all neutral colours, which I'd usually chalk up as dull and boring, but paired with the simplistically modern furniture, all of which looks like it was handpicked directly out of the latest Ikea catalogue, it somehow becomes quite mesmerising. With a bright pillow here and an abstract painting there, it all comes together to create something oddly genius. We duck our heads into several doorways, but none of these rooms appear to be what Aiden's looking for. I can't help wondering how big of a death wish Robbie must have to open up this place for parties.

Aiden stops when we find the kitchen, and yells in glee as he leads me into the room. As we enter, a few recognisable faces catch my eye, but none of them are friendly. All of my friends besides Aiden think parties like this are just an excuse for the Neanderthals of society to wreak havoc. While I generally agree with that statement, I've never been all too close to any of them, and so here I am.

It's only now I realise Aiden has left my side, but it doesn't take a second to spot him standing inside Robbie Morrissey's fridge. He's rummaging through it as if he's lived here all his life. His mouth is seeping with some kind of pinkish coloured foam, turned even more vivid against the contrast of his dark skin. I'm just about to question my own sanity when I notice a packet of marshmallows in his hand.

'Want one?' Aiden asks me absentmindedly as he shoves another bunch into his mouth.

'Aiden, you can't just let yourself into a stranger's house and eat all of his marshmallows!' I hiss. 'Who keeps marshmallows in the fridge anyway?'

'Yeah, yeah, sure.'

I'm confident he heard none of that. I follow Aiden's gaze, but see nothing of interest besides a couple flirting with each other so vulgarly that I sort of want to throw up. The girls lingering in this room are dressed in expensive dresses and fashionable playsuits, and the boys stare at them with desperate, hungry eyes. A flutter of self-consciousness arises within me because it didn't even occur to me to dress up. I don't dwell on that thought for too long, and notice Aiden still scanning the room. I know what he's searching for--or rather, who.

I sigh. 'You're already looking for him, seriously?'

'Calm your mackerel, I'm just curious is all,' he mutters. I hardly manage to hear him over the music in the air and the marshmallows in his mouth. 'I'd swear you'd never seen Zack Maddox in your life. I mean, dang, I'd tap that. I wouldn't mind a bit of Robbie too.'

'Aiden, you'd probably make love to a toaster if there wasn't a risk of your dick being frazzled.' I shake my head as he continues searching the room. 'Besides, Zack Maddox and Robbie Morrisey are complete arseholes. They use people like disposable toys.'

'They can use me any way they want,' Aiden mutters with a smirk.

Ugh.

While I've never actually met Zack Maddox, if I ever did, it sounds like I'd want to ram his head down a toilet bowl and repeatedly slam the lid down onto it. I've not met Robbie before either, but I imagine I'd stop at ramming his head into the bowl. I don't think he quite warrants the lid slamming because from what I've heard, Zack is a whole other level.

'I'm going to use the bathroom,' I announce to Aiden, who's still hopelessly scanning the kitchen for Zack Maddox as he drowns his lack of success in marshmallows. 'You might want to move on to the next room.'

Aiden only just hears me. By the time he responds, I'm already heading towards the kitchen door. The electronic music is still pumping loudly around the house, so Aiden shouts his reply.

'Don't forget to wipe!'

I immediately disassociate myself from him, naturally.

It's only when I leave the kitchen that I realise I have no idea where I'm going. I peer around the hallway in hope of spotting any indicator of a bathroom, but have no such luck. There are crowds of people surrounding me, and it's impossible to hear myself think, let alone figure out where to go. The slightly stale stench of sweat, alongside my bladder feeling like it's about to burst isn't helping.

'Nice shirt, babe.'

I spin around to see a tall figure leaning against the wall behind me, and I immediately recognise who it is from the countless photos and videos I've seen of him.

There's a subtle smirk on Zack Maddox's face as I gaze at him, and his green eyes are noticeably bloodshot from what I figure is alcohol and I dare not question what else. His light hair is messily shaped into a quiff, and the only glimmer of tidiness to it is the way it's trimmed on the sides. He's dressed in a pair of distressed jeans accompanied by a baggy white shirt at least three sizes too big for him, and covering that is an equally oversized plaid shirt. We match. How vomit-inducing.

'Sorry,' I reply dryly. 'The dress code here isn't really my style.'

Zack snorts. 'Not like other girls, are we?'

'Where's the bathroom?' I snap, ignoring his stupid comment.

'Last door on the left,' Zack says as he nods his head behind him. 'Or I could show you to the empty bedroom I've got up-stairs.'

Or I could saw off my own limbs.

'I think I'll pass, thanks.'

I don't give him a chance to respond. Instead, I rush down the hallway because, quite frankly, what Zack just said to me makes me a little sick in my mouth.

Before I enter the bathroom, I peek inside. It's small with just a toilet and a mirror above a sink, but it'll do. The lock on the door is jammed, disabling me to shut it properly, so I have to stretch my arm out and shove one of my hands against it in an attempt to keep it closed. Hardly ideal, but I'm too desperate to care.

Once I'm done using the toilet, I turn to the mirror and cringe. My hair makes me look as if I've been standing in the middle of a wind tunnel for an hour, and geez, Aiden could've told me how much this shirt resembles a tent. He was probably too busy looking for his fantasy boyf--

The bathroom door bursts open, slamming shut seconds later. Just when I thought I'd gotten rid of him, Zack Maddox is inches away from me, his back shoved against the door as laughter spills from his mouth.

'What the hell is wrong with you?' My mouth drops open in disbelief.

Zack's eyes flash to me, and they widen as if I'm the one who's appeared out of nowhere.

'Shit, sorry, babe, thought it was free.'

Before I have a chance to remind him of our conversation minutes earlier, he starts explaining his sudden appearance as if I asked him, or care.

'Someone's trying to hit on me. Real ugly, we're talking a low three at best.' He's still pushing himself against the door. 'I can turn around if you need me to,' he says, nodding towards the toilet.

How thoughtful.

All of a sudden, Zack erupts into another round of ear-shattering laughter. He's still shoving all of his weight against the door, and I don't think he realises there's no one pushing against it. He hasn't stopped laughing by the time I ask him to move so that I can leave.

'Nah, c'mon, stay here for five. This party is shit, I wanna have fun,' is his slurred reply.

He doesn't budge. His face is inches away from mine, and he reeks of alcohol and cigarette smoke.

'Move,' I demand through gritted teeth.

My stomach is twisting as I stare at him. His eyes are deeply bloodshot, his dry lips parted slightly. Both of us are silent, Zack's face vacant of emotion, and the dark shadows underneath his eyes are enhanced by the dim lighting in the bathroom. He glances at me, and his skin is so pale that it looks transparent.

He looks ill. Really ill.

Zack's face suddenly contorts, all traces of vacancy vanishing from it, and he sniggers. His pale eyes scan every inch of me, and not in the way a boy looks thirstily at a girl, but in a way that's dripping with ridicule. He laughs. He laughs even more loudly than he did earlier, so much so that it makes my ears ring.

'God, what's wrong with me? You're not even hot, I must be more wasted than I thought.' He's still laughing.

'Move!' I hiss at him.

My voice cracks as I feel a hard lump forming in my throat. What's wrong with me? If I even dare get upset over this, I'm being stupid. Ridiculously stupid. This boy is a complete arsehole, and I know that every word he speaks has as much substance as thin air. I realise I'm still clenching my jaw, so try to relax it. It doesn't work.

Zack holds his hands up defensively. 'Hey, don't get pissy with me for being honest. You shouldn't be so fucking miserable.'

He laughs again, but this one sounds more hollow, and for a moment, the emptiness returns to his face. My palms are sweating as they shake with frustration, my heart's rapidly being swallowed up by my gut, and the lump in my throat is growing. Zack throws another insult at me, mutters something inaudible under his breath, and finally, he turns away. He disappears, leaving the door open behind him.

All I can think about when I step out of that bathroom is finding Aiden and getting the hell out of this place. My hands are still shaking with anger as I shove past a crowd of people standing in the middle of the hallway and run into the kitchen. He's not in there. I run into the next room and find nothing. The same goes for the next room, and the next one, and the next one. Once I've checked every room on the bottom floor, at least half an hour has passed and I'm no closer to finding Aiden. I don't even have my phone to try and call him.

I have no choice; I'm going to have to leave here on my own.

As I make my way through the crowds and head towards the front door, all I can think about is Zack Maddox. Why didn't I punch his lights out? I bloody wanted to. How dare he speak to me like that? Who does he think he is? I'm sweating, and the heavy dubstep music is giving me a headache. There's a choking sound, and it isn't until my eyesight becomes blurred that I realise it's me.

Why am I letting Zack's words stab themselves into me so bluntly? I bite my lip and try to swallow the lump in my throat. No, I'm not upset. I'm not. I'm just angry. I don't get upset, I just don't.

So why is the world whirling so violently that I feel like I could fly off any second?

As I finally reach the front door and go to grab its handle, something barges against me, almost knocking my heart out of my throat.

'Mia! There you are.' I've never been so thankful to hear Aiden's voice in my life. He pauses as he scans my face. 'Are you all right?'

'Can we get out of here?' I choke.

Aiden doesn't ask any more questions. He nods, grabs my hand and leads me outside.

I need to stop this. I'm embarrassing myself. I need to distract my thoughts from Zack, and so I gaze down at my feet as they stumble down the long driveway.

'Hey!'

We've only been walking for a minute or so when the sound of a deep voice makes us stop in our tracks. Aiden has his phone in his hands, and the voice forces him to look up from it.

'Excuse me, hey!'

Aiden glances at me before narrowing his eyes, and we both search the darkness around us. I'm about to say something when a figure emerges from behind some bushes a few hundred yards away, and starts jogging towards us. As the figure approaches, as well as noticing that he's running really damn fast, I acknowledge his striking resemblance to Zack Maddox.

It's him. It has to be.

The figure's yards away now, and I realise I was wrong because it's not Zack. It's Robbie Morrissey.

'I need to use your phone!' he's yelling before he even reaches us.

Robbie doesn't stop, let alone wait for an answer. He grabs Aiden's phone from his hand, and sprints back towards the shrubbery he came from. What the hell? Aiden's stammering, and before I even realise I'm doing it, I'm chasing and shouting after Robbie. As I make my way behind the bushes to find him, I spot another recognisable figure. Zack Maddox is half-lying, half-sitting against a big, green bin.

I stop as Aiden arrives behind me, gasping for air. 'Holy mackerel, you should study sport science or something at uni, Mia, that was--Oh shit, what's wrong with him?' he questions as he looks down, immediately spotting Zack.

As my eyes grow accustomed to the light, I notice how Zack's appearance is even worse than it was in the bathroom. His eyes are shut so I can't see if they're more bloodshot, but they're drowning in the dark shadows underneath them. His face is pale, his lips scaly. He's eerily silent, and as what previously happened in the bathroom replays in my mind, I realise the lump in my throat has gone. Now I'm just angry. Really bloody angry.

'The screen isn't working, it's frozen, I--Argh!' Robbie snaps, turning to Aiden. He pulls at the golden brown hair at the back of his head. 'I think he's taken too much of something. He's not--'

'Uh, it does it a lot, you just have to --'

'What's wrong with your phone?' I interrupt Aiden, then turn to Robbie questioningly.

'I don't--I can't find it,' Robbie stammers. 'God knows where Zack's is, and in case you've not noticed, he's not really in a state to look for it, so stop being an idiot and--'

'Here,' Aiden says, taking his phone back from Robbie. He begins tapping at the screen to get it to work.

'Aiden! It's his fault if he's gotten himself completely wasted, and he deserves the crap he gets into because of it.' I don't even try to hide the frustration in my voice. By this point, Robbie has the phone pressed to his ear. 'Seriously, guys?' I continue. 'He doesn't need a bloody ambulance, he can just sleep it off and--'

'He's not breathing!'

With that, Robbie finally gets me to shut up.

CHAPTER 2

It feels like I'm underwater. Robbie's blabbering on the phone, but I can't hear a word he's saying because I've been staring at Zack so long that it's disorientating me. He's progressively looking worse and worse, and Aiden's staring as emptily at him as I am. Robbie's muffled voice rings in my ears, and I slowly turn my eyes to him. I lock them onto his tanned face for a few seconds before wavering back to Zack, who's still lying lifelessly on the ground. I exhale a lungful of air.

'No,' I mutter to myself. 'No.' I say it louder this time.

This is a joke, isn't it? The two most heartless human beings known to mankind thought it'd be hilarious to fake something as serious as this, and they figured it'd be even more hilarious to make an idiot out of two nobodies. I clench my teeth. The anger that had settled is bubbling up all over again. This isn't funny. This is really not funny.

I bend down and kneel next to Zack, then shake him. Nothing. Robbie's talking on the phone above me as I shake Zack even harder. Has he actually called emergency services? I begin tapping Zack's cheeks, so much so that Robbie snaps at me for hitting him so hard. I ignore him and start shaking Zack again. Still nothing. This is all a joke, it has to be. I hiss Zack's name. No response.

What's happening?

'Is he still not breathing?' Robbie asks me so quickly that he nearly trips over his words. I don't respond, I just stare. 'For God's sake, is he? They need to know!'

I hover my hand over Zack's mouth expecting to feel a warm breath, but the air is still. More nothing. I turn back to Robbie and shake my head as a stutter escapes my mouth. He's not. He's actually not breathing. This can't be real. He has to be breathing. As Robbie continues talking on the phone, I carefully place index and middle finger onto Zack's neck.

'A pulse--He's got a pulse,' I announce, although I'm not sure to who.

'Shit, Mia, we did this at school, remember?' Aiden is kneeling beside me. I hadn't even noticed. 'First aid, recovery position, y'know? I don't remember, I can't... I don't know.'

He places his hands under Zack's arms, then hesitantly maneuvers him onto his back. He proceeds to move his arms around in different directions, none of which are anywhere near correct, not to mention the fact that CPR is supposed to come before the recovery position. The music blasting from the house is deafening, and the smell of the humid summer air is intoxicating.

This is happening. This is as real as the flesh on my bones.

Before I can think about making any moves, a loud swear leaves Robbie's mouth from above. I look up to see him bashing Aiden's phone screen with his fingers. He swears again, dives onto the ground beside us, and starts shaking Zack with way too much force.

'Stop! It'll make him worse!' I shout.

'You were just doing the exact same thing!' Robbie growls back, and while he has a valid point, now is really not the time to be arguing.

'Why aren't you still on the phone to emergency services? What the heck are--'

'It just died on me!' he exclaims. 'Where's your phone? We'll use--'

I shake my head. 'I don't have it! I'm meant to be grounded, my--my dad took it away because I let the dog--I mean, ugh, it doesn't matter, I just don't have one.' I'm swearing now. 'They're on their way though, yeah? Did they say what we should do?'

'Something about CPR, but I--I dunno!'

I turn back to Zack, who's even paler than before. The prospect of performing CPR on him makes Robbie visibly squirm, but as I turn to Aiden, I don't think I've ever been so grateful for his obsession over dickheads with quiffs. If there wasn't an eighteen-year-old kid dying in front of us, it'd proba-bly make me laugh.

'Ah, shit... Shit, shit, shit,' Robbie mutters. 'My folks are going to kill me. What if his parents sue me? Can they do that?'

Is Robbie kidding? His best friend is dying in front of us, and all he's worried about is how much of an inconvenience it might be. Jesus. Aiden's in the middle of performing CPR, which he's doing surprisingly well, but it's not working. I don't think it's working. Before long, Aiden's struggling to breathe himself.

'I can't--I feel really light-headed,' he mumbles as he sits up, then drops his head into his hands.

I barely waste two seconds before taking over. I'm not giving up. As shitty as Zack was to me earlier, I'm not giving up. I mirror Aiden's technique, and by the time I'm starting to feel dizzy myself, Aiden has recovered enough to take over again. It feels hopeless, like we're playing some messed up tag team game where we're running in circles, but I'm not giving up.

I'm in the middle of catching my breath after giving CPR for the third time when there's a splutter, and I'm so dazed that it takes me a second to realise who made the sound.

Zack.

Aiden pulls away, and we all turn silent. Zack splutters some more, but his eyes remain closed.

'Check if he's breathing,' I order Aiden.

He does what I tell him. 'I think so, I--I don't know... I mean, I can't really hear because the mu--'

I shove Aiden aside, and check for myself. It's barely distinguishable, but as I lower my ear to Zack's mouth, I feel hot air gently blow against it. He's breathing. It worked. The CPR actually worked. All of a sudden, I become my father and develop an intense need to tell everyone exactly what to do.

'Robbie, get everyone out of your house. It'll be ten times easier if they're all gone when the ambulance gets here, and turn the bloody music off while you're at it. It's awf--'

'What does the music have to do with--'

'Just do it!' I snap before turning to Aiden. 'The ambulance won't be able to get into here because of the electric gates, so go and open them.'

Aiden nods, and unlike Robbie, does exactly as he's told by jumping to his feet and sprinting down the long driveway. Robbie still hasn't moved. I give him orders again, and he mutters something under his breath, but eventually heads towards his house.

I use the boys' disappearance as my opportunity to remember how to place someone into the recovery position. I've got no idea how accurate the end result is, but I hope it's enough. That's all it has to be.

'Zack?' I gently shake the limp body in front of me. 'Hey, can you hear me? I will be so pissed off if I never get the chance to tell you how much of an arsehole you are, so don't you dare die on me, okay?'

There's no response. I check if he's still breathing. He is. His chest rises slowly, and I release a shaky breath. I continue blathering on as I grasp onto the belief that it'll actually help him, but there's still a part of me that can't accept this as reality. This is Zack Maddox, and Zack Maddox can't just... He can't just die. He's invincible. Everyone knows who he is, and his presence is a hurricane. People like this don't just die.

My hand brushes his face as I try to stir him awake, and I hadn't noticed before, but he's freezing. I whip my shirt off and drape it over him as I try to cover as much of his bare skin as possible, leaving myself shivering in nothing but a grey t-shirt. I gently shake him again, and as I'm about to speak, the music emanating from the house comes to a sudden stop.

I must've forgotten what silence felt like because as it comes crashing down, it stuns me. My heartbeat has never been so loud. I'm about to try and rouse Zack again when I notice his eyelids fluttering slightly.

'Zack?' I shake him. 'Zack, hey, wake up.'

His eyelids flutter again, and his lips part.

'I... I don't, it--it was an accident. She didn't--He's... I don't--he's bleeding. She said--I--'

'Is that Zack?'

I whip my head around, and about ten feet away from me stands a young girl with blonde hair. Before I can respond, she shouts in the direction of the house.

'Shit,' I mutter under my breath.

A few more people emerge and stand next to the blonde girl. More follow, and there's soon a small group beginning to form. Some start gossiping, some begin laughing, some look like they're on the verge of crying, and some even pull out their phones to take a photo. I can't believe what I'm seeing. This isn't a show.

As the group expands even more, some come forward and kneel next to Zack, just as I'm doing. I'm suddenly barged aside by a frantic girl wearing some glittery abomination of a dress, and before I know it, I can't even see Zack anymore. I stumble to my feet and look around me. Shit. Almost everyone who was in the house now seems to be crowded around Zack. Robbie did a cracking job then.

'Oh my god, someone call an ambulance!' one of the younger crowd members yells.

Already done that, hon.

'I just found him here! No one was around to help, it's disgusting!' someone who's now kneeling beside Zack shouts.

Well, that's complete bullshit.

'I swear I just saw him, like, five minutes ago!'

'Where's Robbie?'

'Has anyone called an ambulance?'

'He's dead!'

As I barge people out of the way to try and get back to Zack, I notice the first girl who appeared earlier. She's hesitantly moving him out of the recovery position I placed him in.

'Stop!' I shout at her, but she can't hear me over the chatter of the crowd.

I charge forward until I find myself beside Zack again, and move the girl out of the way. As I place him back into the position, I hear sirens, and an overwhelming sense of relief washes over me. He's still breathing. It's shallow, but it's there.

The second I see reflective jackets emerging through the crowd, I step aside and hide myself among the mass of teenagers gathered in Robbie Morrissey's front garden. As the paramedics order the crowd to back away, the space where Zack lies opens up. I spot my shirt still draped over him on the ground, and for a moment, curse myself for leaving it.

It's strange seeing somewhere that was once so full of life so empty. There are deserted cups spilled over the kitchen floor, and next to the fridge lies a packet of pink marshmallows. There's an uneaten pizza sitting on the marble counter, and it feels like it's staring at me, like it's questioning where everyone disappeared to. I'm staring back at it when I hear Aiden's voice for what feels like the first time in forever.

'There you are! Holy mackerel, Mia, I've been scouring the garden looking for you, almost filed a missing person's report.

Have you been in the house the whole time? You don't half know how to stress a guy out.' He pulls up a chair next to me. 'This is insane! Can you believe it? Like, I hope Zack's fine, but how exciting is this?'

Is he serious?

'I can't wait to tell everyone about how we were Zack's saviours, I mean, think of the rep we'll get. And hey, I technically kissed Zack Maddox. If anyone questions you about it, just say I did, oka--'

'You're just as bad as them!'

Aiden freezes. Zack could be dead. He could be dead, and all anyone seems to be interested in is gossiping about him. The boy made every last inch of my body tremble with anger just hours ago, yet I seem to be the only one who's even the slightest bit considerate of what's happened to him. I know how engrossed Aiden can get into this kind of thing, but this is just wrong.

'Sorry,' Aiden mutters. 'I've just--I got caught up in all the...' He gestures to the space around us. 'Sorry.'

Aiden scratches the back of his neck, and we both fall silent. The ambulance must've gotten here close to half an hour ago, and most people have left. I've got no idea where Robbie has vanished to, but I don't really care.

'Hey, what was wrong earlier?' Aiden's voice brings me back to the present. 'When you wanted to leave, before we found Zack?'

After all of the hype tonight, what happened in the bathroom has taken a backseat in my mind. Zack wasn't well then, was he? It was so obvious. He was deathly pale, his eyes were so bloodshot that the veins in them were almost popping out, and he was all over the place. A trickle of guilt gnaws at my mind. I should've spotted it then. I could've helped him sooner.

I shake my head. To be frank, he should be grateful I helped him at all after the way he treated me. It's pretty obvious that he overdosed on who knows what, so if this does end badly for him, then it's his own fault. I shouldn't feel guilty.

'Mia?'

'Oh sorry,' I say, remembering Aiden's question. 'Just some guy is all. He was creepy with me, and it freaked me out a bit.' I pause. 'You don't know him.'

Aiden says something else, but I don't hear it. All I want to do is crawl into bed. I called Mum from Robbie's landline to explain what happened, so she's on her way to pick us up. Despite the fact I'm going to be even more grounded considering I lied and sneaked out to a party, I don't really care. I just want to go home. I'm staring at the pizza again when I hear a voice that isn't Aiden's.

'D'you mind leaving? I need to clean up.'

I turn to the doorway to see Robbie standing there. He's pulled a jumper on over the t-shirt he was wearing earlier, and his brown hair has fallen flatly onto his forehead. 'Sorry for being a dick earlier, I was kinda stressed.'

I nod and get up from the kitchen table, and Aiden follows. Robbie is clearly still drunk. He's leaning against the door as if he'll crumble to the floor if he doesn't, and he's blinking at an unnaturally frequent rate. There's a trickle of sick running down his jumper.

'That pizza needs eating,' I mutter as Aiden and I leave the room.

It's not long until Mum arrives to pick us up, and with her arrival comes endless questioning. It doesn't bother me because the familiarity of her voice eases my mind after this disaster of a night, although I decide to leave out any details on finding an unconscious eighteen-year-old lying beside a bin. Luckily, she agrees with me that Dad grounding me over forgetting to clean the dog's paws after taking him for a walk in the forest was a bit absurd, so she's not angry with me.

'Your dad's not too happy with you,' Mum says softly.

A tsunami of nerves crashes into my stomach. Dad's going to kill me tomorrow. I didn't necessarily lie to him, I just didn't tell him the details of where it was I was going tonight, or that I was going out at all. While grounded. But, I mean, I could be a lot worse. I could've been rushed to hospital after passing out in someone's front garden.

'Don't worry, sweetie,' Mum continues. 'He's at work until the morning now, and I'll make sure to soften him up when he gets home.'

As we drop Aiden off at his house, a thought hits me. Zack spoke. When he was lying on the grass, he spoke, didn't he? Before that first girl arrived, he said something. I scan every detail of every memory I have from tonight in an attempt to recall what it was he said. It was weird. Something really weird. What was it? Something to do with blood. Bleeding? Yeah, that was it; he said that someone was bleeding, that something was an accident.

I know I should shrug this off, that chances are it was something he said in a complete delusion. I can't, though. I don't know why, but all I can think about for the rest of the journey home are the words Zack Maddox spoke as he lay dying on the damp grass outside his best friend's house.

CHAPTER 3

'That's why I didn't go with the pink one. Might as well have grabbed all of the unicorns, sparkle and glitter in the world, shoved them into a blender until they were reduced to liquid form, and then written 'gay' on my forehead with the concoction.'

'Mhmm,' I murmur absently.

I'm trying to listen to Aiden, I really am, but there's only so much Aiden talk I can take, and he's been rambling on about the colour of his school bag for the past twenty minutes. We're waiting in our new sixth form college's reception for the head of the maths department, who was due to meet us ten minutes ago.

I managed to fail maths last year, so have organised free tutoring sessions within the college to resit an exam and boost my grade. College itself has been a lot easier than I expected. It's way more relaxed than school, and thanks to Aiden's awe-inspiring ability to make friends, it's not as lonely as I feared it to be.I should be solely thinking about this stuff at the moment, but I keep getting distracted. The events of Robbie Morrisey's party keep replaying in my head, and the longer I sit in the middle of the college reception, the more the blur of crowds surrounding me remind me of that night.

The whole thing makes my head ache. No one's seen Zack since the party five weeks ago, not even Robbie, and everyone I know has come up with theories. Some people even think he's kicked the bucket. Stone cold dead. People's reactions to the whole thing are amusing really: some who've never met the boy before in their life are acting as if it's the biggest tragedy of the century, while others think he deserves whatever has happened. Some even say they hope he's dead.

That sends a shiver down my spine. Sure, he's a monumental dickhead, but I'd never wish death upon anyone. I'm just relieved no one knows that Aiden and I helped him that night because I don't think I could deal with the attention it would bring.

'...and that's the problem. Dogs could read minds but we'll never find out because dogs can't speak English, and we can't speak do--'

'Sorry,' I finally interrupt Aiden mid-ramble. 'I love you and everything, but I'm really not listening.'

He winks at me. 'You're just jealous because I got a bonerific B in maths, while you couldn't even scrape a D.'

Ugh, the worst part is that I was two marks off that D. I don't want, or expect, an A or anything. I just need a C because that's what most universities ask for. Dad performed his usual routine of telling me it's okay, but then ranting to Mum when he thinks I'm asleep, while Mum reminded me every passing minute that she was proud of me no matter what. I sometimes think I could strangle a cat and leave it on our doorstep, and she'd still tell me how proud of me she is.

'I'm going to fail the resit as well at this rate. The head of maths was meant to be here ten minutes ago,' I mutter.

I search among the cluster of youths as if it will make the person I'm looking for magically appear. Aiden's started a conversation with himself again, but I'm somewhat thankful as it distracts my mind from wandering into places I don't want it to go. He could tone it down a bit, though. It's times like this I wish he wasn't pretty much my only friend. I turn my full concentration back to Aiden in hope of it looking like I'm deeply fascinated with whatever it is he's saying.

'Apparently though, someone spiked his drink or something, and it was extra bad because he had an allergic reaction to it, which probably explains why he was in such a state when we fou--'

'Euphemia!'

Oh God, no.

'Euphemia, I'm sorry I'm so late!' The blonde-haired woman bouncing towards me shouts my full name out again, making every other student in reception turn and look in my direction. 'First week back and everything, you know? Busy, busy, busy!'

The woman who just shred away any chance of me making new friends at this college reaches Aiden and me with an enormous smile on her face. She has an overall plumpness that makes her resemble a rounded fruit, but I'm still reeling after the mortification of losing my dignity to concentrate on that for long.

'You are Euphemia, aren't you?' she says, finally stopping for breath. 'Your hair looks darker on your file photo, but then I know what you teenagers are like with your hair and your clothes, so--'

'Yeah, that's me,' I interrupt. 'It's Mia, though.'

'Right, perfect, I'm Angela. I better take you straight to Preston,' she continues. 'He'll be the student tutoring you--lovely lad, very well spoken. Hopefully you'll get that C this time round, eh?'

Before I have a chance to respond, she's already walking again. I almost have to jog to keep up with her, and I'm not sure she's even noticed Aiden yet, which is a first by all accounts. We follow her through the crowds and along the hallways until we eventually come to a stop in the college library.

Delyth, who's sitting in front of one of the library computers, briefly catches my eye as she manically waves at Aiden and me. She's a girl from Aiden's English class who's latched onto us since their first class together, but she doesn't do much besides sit there grinning as she watches Aiden with admiration. I'm a little afraid she might not realise he's gay. Angela's shooing Aiden away, and once he's gone, she leads me to a door in the corner of the library.

'He's straight through there,' she says joyfully, nodding at the pale blue door. 'I'm supposed to be in a meeting right now, so I'll leave you to go in and sort out lesson times and what not, okay? Apologies again for being late, Euphemia!'

Before I can decide if that is in fact okay, or remind her that I refuse to go by that name, Angela rushes away. I roll my eyes, pull open the door, and drag myself through. Before I have a chance to notice anything about the room I just stepped into, I hear a voice that stuns me so much it almost leaves me winded.

'Miss Euphemia Evian, punctuality is evidently not your forte.'

All I can do is stare. After all of the rumours I've heard, the questions I've been asked, and the confusion I've dealt with over the past five weeks, to see Zack Maddox sitting at the desk in front of me with a casual smirk on his face is incomprehensible. I begin stammering. My thoughts are sprinting laps in my head, and it's as if the bag on my back has become ten tons heavier in the matter of seconds. He can't just... I don't... How can he just appear like this as if nothing ever happened? Where's he been? Does he recognise me? Is it actually him?

Am I going insane?

Zack laughs. 'Out of curiosity, has anyone ever told you that your name sounds like an STD?'

'Don't you remember me?' I ask, ignoring his question. He shakes his head. 'From the party?'

'Some elaboration would be useful.'

'Robbie Morrissey's party,' I reply. 'Where have you been? Do you have any idea how screwed up some of the rumours are about you? What happened?'

'The college's maths tutoring is--'

'Don't ignore what I just said!'

'I've only got a few minutes, and if we've failed to establish an arrangement by then, your future grades aren't looking too great.' I can't figure out if Zack's voice is cold, or simply robotic. 'I've analysed your timetable, and we both share free lessons on

Thursday afternoons, so I thought that would be a good time. Is that feasible?'

'It is feasible, yes,' I mock. 'But let's face it; you're not reliable as a person, let alone as a maths tutor.'

The only response I get is a smirk and an amused look surfacing in Zack's green eyes. I'm trying to pull a reaction out of him, but he just seems amused by me. Does he genuinely not remember who I am? I sigh. There's not even any point trying to argue, is there? The college's tutoring is free, and my parents sure as hell can't afford an outside tutor.

'Right, I need to head off,' Zack says as he stands up with a small pile of papers in his hand. 'See you in here on Thursday at two o' clock.'

He brushes past me, making me turn around as he reaches the door. I still can't believe it's him. I really, really can't.

'Wait, Zack, do I need to bring my own stationary?' I don't even bother sounding snappy this time. I need to figure out a better way to get answers out of him because being rude clearly doesn't faze him. 'Calculators and stuff?'

'Nah, I'll have all of that. Call me Preston, by the way. Zack's my middle name.' He pauses as he holds the door open. 'And the ideal pseudonym to use whenever I feel the need to behave like a narcissist intent on vigorously crushing others' vast expectations.'

With a wink, he leaves, and the only trace of him ever being in the room is the door shutting behind him. I don't think I've ever been so confused in my life.

As the day moves on, my concentration is lost. I can't even try listening during lessons because all I can think about is my meeting with Zack--Sorry, Preston Maddox this morning. The amount of brain cells he seems to have developed over the past few weeks is bewildering enough, and that's only the tip of the iceberg. To make things worse, the entire college is talking about him because it's the first time he's surfaced in over a month. What's baffling people even further is the fact that he's so chilled about it.

Preston isn't really speaking to anyone, and when he does, he's apparently not acting like the person I briefly met this morning, so I figure it's best I don't mention my bizarre interaction with him. Otherwise, I'll have pubescent teenagers pestering me like bloodthirsty fleas. That's probably why I'm so relieved when I'm released last lesson, albeit ten minutes later than when the class was meant to finish. It's only my fourth day of college and I'm already swamped with stress and confusion, and the fact it's nothing related to my education is irritating.

I'm jogging down the building's main staircase when I feel my phone vibrating in my pocket, and when I manage to pull it out and answer, Aiden begins screaming in my ear.

'Mia! Where the mackerel are you? The bus is leaving!'

'What? Really?'

As if I'm waiting to begin a track race and the starting pistol has just been fired, I turn my light jog into a sprint. I get some baffled looks from the students left inside the building, but I easily disregard them while Aiden shouts into my ear.

'I've been so worried! Delyth here has been in tears, listen!' Aiden yells. I hear a girl muttering, who I assume is Delyth, but it's Aiden who speaks next. 'Please? For me? Mia has to know how distraught we all are at her disappearance, even you, Deltyth. You're meant to be a drama student, just fake it.'

Aiden's still speaking as I run outside into the pattering rain, but I'm too busy desperately hoping to find the bus to take much notice of what he's saying. I run alongside the building towards the parking area, and to my horror, catch a glimpse of it turning the corner at the end of the street.

'I missed it!' I say over the phone.

'Don't worry, I'll sort it!' Aiden replies.

For once in his life, Aiden stops speaking. His voice is replaced by the sound of mumbling in the background. I wait ten seconds or so until I hear his voice again, mixed with an unrecognisable one.

'C'mon, be a babe, I'll pay you,' I manage to make out Aiden saying.

The other voice replies, but it's too deep and too rough for me to understand it. I figure it's not a satisfying reply as it's followed by a groan from Aiden.

'Uh, okay then, I've got twenty-seven pence, a coupon for a head massage...' There's a muffling sound. 'A strand of cotton, a handmade bracelet, a button--it's a lovely baby blue colour--and a... What the hell is that? My God, seriously, what is that? Is it even--Oh! I know, it's... uh, no, you don't want that.' Aiden pauses. 'That's everything. Do we have a deal?' Seconds later, I hear a loud swear. 'My granddad was a bus driver once. Do you know what makes you different to him? He never ripped my heart out and threw it onto the ground.' There are even more muffling sounds, followed by a slumping one. 'Yeah, you're screwed.'

By now, I've found shelter under the bus stop's metal roof, but there are still droplets falling onto my head from somewhere. I'm going to have to walk home, aren't I? I swear, thank Aiden for trying, and then hang up. I don't have an umbrella and I can't wait for the rain to ease because they lock the college gates by four thirty, and it's coming up to twenty-five past now. Can't things just go right for five measly minutes?

A mile or so into my walk home, I begin doubting my sanity. I always do when I'm alone. It's not that I start running around the place going crazy, or slump into a state of depression. I just have a tendency to do these weird things when I lack company. Things like shutting my eyes and seeing how far I can walk without crashing into anything, and gazing intently into passing car windows to try and read drivers' minds. Come to think of it, maybe I'm not insane. Maybe I'm just horrifically immature. Or maybe I just need something to distract myself from the pouring rain that's falling onto me as I drag myself through the trek home from college.

Once I've passed enough lamp posts to last me a lifetime, I've lost the will to even try and distract myself. I glare at my feet as if to scold them for not getting me home yet, and step off a curb. I knew I should have brought money with me today. I could have gotten a public bus home then, but no, I had to be stupid and assume I--

There's a sharp tug on my backpack. I'm yanked back onto the pavement, my hands flail, I yelp, I swear, my heart catapults against my rib cage, there's an ear-shattering beep, and a car zooms straight past where I was standing moments ago.

Chapter 4

I'm shaking. Another car swipes along the road, whipping my hair into a frenzy over my face. I was just on that road. Right in the middle of it, and I didn't even realise. I was so busy sulking that I didn't even realise I'd stepped onto a road. How could I be so stupid? I'm still shaking. I can't stop. My heart is trying to smash out of my body, and I've forgotten to breathe. How long have I been holding my breath? I release it, and it comes out as unsteady as the rest of me.

A hand clutches my sleeve, and I scream.

'Whoa, it's just me. Are you okay? Not too wise of a move back there.'

I spin around. I don't even process who it is at first, but when I do, my shaking turns into stammering. Zack--No, Preston. His hair is drenched, his usually wavy quiff stuck to his forehead. Did he just pull me out of the road? No way. If anything, he would have pushed me into that car, then skipped all the way home.

'Yes, I'm fine, I've got to go,' I mutter, the embarrassment over what just happened creeping in.

I turn away from Preston and try walking on, but my legs feel like they could cave in any second, and I'm stumbling. What's wrong with me? I'm soaked. My clothes are sticking to me, and I'm freezing. I'm still shaking, and I've got no idea if it's because of the cold or the shock. I glance at my phone to check the time: almost five o' clock. Dad should be on his way home from work soon, so I could try ringing him to see if he can pick me up. I'm about to stop stumbling onward to dial Dad's number when I hear footsteps jogging after me.

'Hey, wait!' Preston again. He nudges me under the shelter of a bus stop. 'You're going to fall back onto the road at the rate you're going, and it would be rather traumatic on my behalf if you got trampled.'

'It's fine, I can manage.' I try to sound snappy, but sound about as threatening as a kitten. 'I'll call my dad to see if he can pick me up.'

Preston nods, and he seems satisfied. He unnecessarily waits with me under the bus stop as I call Dad, who picks up after the first ring.

'Hey, Dad.' I clear my throat as I realise my voice is still wobbly. 'Could you pick me up, by any chance? I missed the college bus so I'm walking home, but it's raining really heavily and I'm a little freaked out because I crossed a road without looking, and a car--' Dad says something, but I cut him off. 'I'm fine, don't worry, I just need a lift home.'

'Things are hectic here, Mia, I don't think I'll be able to pick you up until six at the earliest. Who are you with? Are you alone? Do you have any friends who live close by you can stay with? I don't want you on the street alone, especially not in the rain.'

'My place is only five minutes up the road,' Preston, who I almost forgot was even here, interjects.

Dad must have heard him because he begins interrogating. 'Who's that? Is that your friend? Go to their house for a bit, darling, don't wait on the street.'

'No, don't worry, I'll just walk home instead or some--'

'You're not walking home alone, Mia, just wait at your friend's, and I mean that. If I find out you've walked home or waited on the street, you're in deep trouble. I've got to go, okay? Text me the house's address.'

Before I can even say goodbye, Dad hangs up. Well, I just made that situation ten times worse. I'd really rather not be alone with Preston for an hour, so when he tries leading me away from the bus stop and towards his house, I don't follow. I'm still shaking a little.

I raise my eyebrows at him. 'If you think I'm going anywhere with you, let alone a house that's probably empty, you may as well find the nearest brick wall, ram your head into it, knock yourself out, wake up, and then repeat the process several times over.'

Instead of answering, Preston shoots me his signature smirk. He bends down and begins untying one of his Dr. Marten shoes until the shoelace is pulled out completely. He stands up, black lace in hand, and places his arms out in front of him. Both wrists are aligned against each other.

'Tie my hands together.'

'What?'

Jesus, he's weird.

'I can't harm you if my hands are tied.'

Preston passes me his shoelace, and I stare at him with it in my hand. With a smile still on his lips, he nods at his wrists as the shoelace starts feeling rough against my fingertips. This guy does owe me a hell of a lot... Plus I know for a fact that if I stay here and wait, Dad will just about kill me. With a sigh, I wrap the lace around Preston's wrists and fasten it, tightly. In a triple knot. All the while, he hums an unrecognisable tune that has a beat perfectly in sync with the pattering rain.

Preston's hands are still tied as we arrive at his house. He's clearly lost all kinds of common sense because he left his front door wide open whenever he left earlier, so we're able to casually stroll inside. It's nowhere near as big as Robbie's house, but it's still impressive with a long, narrow hallway on the bottom floor leading to at least six open doors. I'm walking fairly steadily now, minus the occasional stumble, and I've text Dad the ad-dress. Since I tied his hands together, Preston's not said a word to me. The only sound he's made is that tuneless humming, and he carries on doing just that as he leads me up the carpeted stairs.

Once we've reached the landing, I'm led into a large bedroom with walls covered in colourful posters of what would be a small boy's dream, from pictures of threatening dinosaurs to Power Rangers battling each other. The double bed's duvet has an image of some cartoon car on it, and there are curtains to match.

'This isn't your bedroom, right?' I ask, concerned about the reply I'm going to get.

I don't have to be wary of the answer though because Preston doesn't give me one. He says nothing.

'Has anyone ever told you that you're really weird?' I ask him.

'Has anyone ever told you that your name sounds like an STD?'

'You've asked me that already, remember?' I snap back at him.

'I didn't receive an answer, so I'm asking again.'

He doesn't get one this time either, and instead, I shoot him a glare. He ignores it and wanders over to a silver stereo in the corner of the room. Rather awkwardly, as his hands are still tied, he fiddles around with it until he manages to pop a CD into the machine. All the while, I'm sitting on the bed with my wet hair dripping over the cartoon car. I wish I at least had something to dry off with.

'I'll fetch you a towel now,' Preston says as if he just read my mind. 'And leave you with the soothing sound of Nirvana's Lithium.'

I roll my eyes. How edgy.

I look up to see him turning away from the stereo as a song begins to play, and I don't take my eyes off him until the back of his worn denim jacket disappears out the doorway. Unless my perception of normality is upside down, Preston's a tad strange, and certainly not the Zack Maddox I met the night of Robbie Morrissey's party. Any annoyance I have towards Zack is being slowly melted away by my curiosity towards Preston.

By the time Preston returns, I'm tapping my knees in rhythm to the song playing in the background, but quickly stop to catch the cream towel he throws to me. As I'm rubbing my damp hair, I realise that he doesn't have a towel himself, but he's just as soaked as I am.

'Aren't you going to dry your hair or anything?' I ask.

'I like rain.'

As if that's a satisfactory answer, he shuts his eyes and sits against the wall opposite the bed. I scrub at my hair for another five minutes, and when I'm done, he's lying on the carpet with his eyes shut as he lights a cigarette. The Nirvana song is playing for the third time, I've dried myself off, the rain outside has fizzled out into nothing but moist air, and I'm questioning Preston's trustworthiness. I really hope Dad gets here soon. Before my thoughts can develop further, Preston begins muttering.

'Birds scream at the top of their lungs in horrified hellish rage every morning at daybreak to warn us all of the truth, but sadly we don't speak bird.'

'What?'

'It's something Kurt Cobain wrote.' Preston nods at his stereo. He takes a drag, and then stares at the smoke he breathes out.

'Oh, right,' I say slowly.

Is he intentionally trying to embody a tumblr's wet dream, or is it an accident? I open my mouth, but quickly realise I have no idea what to say, so I just sit there with a gormless look on my face. Preston is silent as well, and if it wasn't for the song playing in the background, the room would be deathly quiet.

'Sorry, you don't want a cigarette, do you?'

I shake my head. 'I don't smoke.'

'Despite what everyone claims, it won't kill you.' His eyes are shut again. 'Not even the parts you won't miss.'

'I'd rather take advice on that from a medical professional, thanks,' I mutter.

Preston begins laughing quietly, then sits himself back up against the blue wall. He stands, then places his burnt out cigarette into his pocket, and I'm extremely tempted to inform him of how there's a good chance he'll soon be on fire. I leave him to it though, and he mumbles something inaudible. I don't even get the chance to question him because before my mind can conjure up anything to say, he's left the room again.

Well then, as lovely as this has been, I think I should maybe wait outside the house for Dad. As the temptation to do just that arises, a completely different temptation overwhelms me. I could always have a little look around, couldn't I? This is the home and possibly even bedroom, though I dearly hope not, of the famous Zack Maddox, after all

I quietly lift myself off the bed, and scan the room from corner to corner. My only guess is that Preston has a younger brother, but then why on earth would we be in his room instead of Preston's? Questions dance around my head as I wander around the room, and I become more and more confused at every colourful childlike poster and ornament I pass. When I reach the other side of the bed, something metallic catches my eye. As I approach it, I realise that it's a silver photo frame. I take the frame from atop the wooden bedside cabinet as I sit back down onto the mattress.

Encased in the silver border is a young woman with eyes like green-tinted crystals, and standing beside her is a young blonde boy who shares them. On the woman's lap sits an olive-skinned toddler. The blonde boy must be Preston. Does that mean this is his room? Is that his mum? Who's the other boy? They seem to be in some kind of children's play area in this photo, but--

'I think your dad's arrived.' The sound of Preston's voice behind me makes me jump out of my skin, and I slam the photo frame onto my lap. 'I hear a car engine.'

I stammer a little as I stand up, then put the photo frame back into place as subtly as I can, all the while praying he didn't catch me looking through his stuff. When I turn to face him, Preston's eyes are shut, and the small smile on his lips implies anything but anger. He's sitting against the wall with a cigarette in-between his fingers again as if he never left in the first place, his wrists still tied together. When did he come back?

I glance out of the bedroom window to see Dad's indistinguishable four-by-four parked at the end of Preston's street. How the hell can Preston hear the engine from here? It's making a faint humming sound, but that could have been any car for all he knows.

'Do me a favour,' Preston says from the floor as I reach the bedroom doorway.

I look at him questioningly, and he responds by nodding at his restrained hands. I bend down, which I immediately regret because his face is now inches away from mine. Our eyes meet for a split second and he's got that goddamn nonchalant, yet somehow smug, look on his face. I shift my eyes away, and his breath smells of cigarettes as I quickly untie the laces from around his wrists. Preston thanks me as I stand back up.

'I suppose I'll be seeing you in the foreseeable future,' he mutters. 'Goodbye for now, Euphemia.'

I turn to him to see his eyes closed again. 'It's not--I mean, it's Mia,' I reply.

'Mia,' he says simply.

'Uh, yeah... bye,' I mutter.

As I make my way back down the stairs, I can hear the same Nirvana song replaying in the background for what feels like the hundredth time. It's only now I actually remember why I came here in the first place. The car whizzing past me--literally inches away--replays in my mind. Did Preston really pull me back? It's the only logical explanation, and now that my mind is actually functioning properly, I realise that he must have.

A wave of guilt almost knocks me over as it strikes me how much of a bitch I've been. I didn't even thank him. I still want to throttle him for being such a dick to me before, admittedly, but I feel bad. Maybe we're even now that he's stopped me getting splattered by a car. I hesitate and consider going back upstairs to say a thank you, but quickly dismiss the thought. It's probably best I just leave. As I reach the bottom of the stairs, I notice a plaid shirt draped over the banister that wasn't there earlier. When I pass it, I freeze, then turn back. It looks like one of mine, one I got for my last birthday, but I don't--I freeze again. It is mine.

There's a tiny chunk missing from the sleeve where Maxxie, my dog, had his way with it. It's the shirt I was wearing the night of the party. The same shirt I draped over Preston when he was unconscious, the one I didn't take home with me. Does this mean he knows who I am? Or is it just a coincidence? Should I take it? I reach my hand out, but hesitate. Should I? I shake my head. It's my shirt, of course I can take it. Without giving myself the chance to change my mind, I grab the shirt, and finally leave the house.

The front door's still open, so I make sure to close it as I step outside the building. I can still see it when I'm standing at the end of the street a few minutes later. Dad's car hums beside me, but I don't get into it for a while because as I stare in the direction of Preston's house, it's impossible not to notice that the front door is, once again, wide open.

CHAPTER 5

After visiting his house, I've decided against getting to know Preston on personal terms. It's not anything he's specifically done, and it's not even necessarily a bad something, but a something that makes me scared of what I might find if I dig deeper. That's exactly why I need to get this over with as quickly as I possibly can.

'Is this it?' Aiden questions, bouncing beside me as we stop at the end of a driveway.

I notice the house's front door is open, and nod. 'Yep, definitely it.'

I had a maths lesson with Preston this afternoon, and he left a half finished assignment behind, which is due by the end of the Christmas holidays. Considering said holidays start today, unless I personally hand him the work, he's got no chance of passing physics. I better get some good karma for doing this.

With Preston's incomplete work in my grasp, I trudge down the empty driveway, followed by Aiden. As I approach the open door, I'm not sure whether to knock or just stroll in as the latter seems to be Preston's desired approach. I decide to knock, and as we stand and wait, we hear an indistinguishable One Direction song echoing from upstairs. I furrow my eyebrows. This is a flashing red light of why I've chosen to avoid getting to know this kid on personal terms.

'D'you think he'll let me use the toilet?' Aiden asks as I hear a door open upstairs. 'You know I've had pee anxiety since the incident when I was eight, and before you say anything, I know it was a long time ago and I should be over it. It's not as easy as that though, Mia, and I really need to go. If I pee myself in front of Zack Maddox, I will literally have to disembody myself right then and there.'

Footsteps barrel down the stairs until Preston is standing in front of us with a one-sided smirk on his face, and a lit cigarette tucked behind his ear. He seriously needs to start storing those things in safer places. I hand him his work before he has the chance to begin any small talk, and I'm about to take my opportunity to leave when Aiden opens his mouth.

'Can I use your toilet?' There's a hint of panic in his voice. 'Uh, please, I don't want to pee myself,' he jokes, but begins stuttering. 'Not that I've ever done that before, like, not even on a waltzer in a fairground when I was eight or anything. That would be mad, right? Imagine that, kinda hard to having not done--'

'Down the hallway, turn left, and it's straight ahead.' An amused glint dances in Preston's eyes as he laughs.

The second Aiden enters the house and runs for the toilet, I want to chase after him and flush myself down said toilet because that sounds far less risky than having to be alone with Preston. It's irrational because I see him every week for our maths lessons, but there's a massive difference between Preston the maths tutor, and Preston the boy who made me tie his hands together with a shoelace. Then there's the peculiar case of Zack Maddox, of course.

I relax a little when Preston doesn't say anything to me and takes a drag from the cigarette behind his ear. As he places the paper I gave him down onto the stairs, it's hard not to notice the irritating, bouncy sounds of One Direction pulsating through the house. Why is he even listening to such crap?

'You shouldn't take music so seriously.' Preston's voice snaps me out of my trance, and I'm beginning to worry he can genuinely read my mind. 'Enjoy it for what it is. Don't get caught up in what it isn't.'

I wonder if he writes down his pretentious quotes beforehand. I bet he does. I bet he gets giddy when he manages to whip one out too.

Before I can reply, Aiden emerges into the hallway behind Preston, and shuffles himself back beside me. He thanks Preston for the use of his toilet, and rambles on about something nonsensical for a few seconds. I don't think I've ever seen the poor boy so nervous and embarrassed, all at once. As I try to say goodbye to Preston and turn away, he stops me.

'Are you two up to anything tonight?' he asks. 'I'm throwing a small party here, so if you fancy it--'

'Sounds awesome!' Aiden replies before Preston even finishes his sentence, let alone before I have enough time to decline the invitation.

I open my mouth to speak, but Aiden shoots me a pleading look. Either due to me becoming momentarily crazy, which I can honestly see being the case, or due to the feeling of Preston's eyes on me, I don't say a word.

'Great, come whenever,' Preston replies. 'Bring some friends if you want, go wild.'

Several hours later, when darkness has swallowed up our surroundings, Aiden and I are standing in the same spot we were hours before. Preston's detailed invite of come whenever wasn't exactly comprehensive, so we decided on nine o'clock as a safe option. Not too late to miss the fun, but not too early to look overly eager, according to Aiden's logic. Delyth and a freckle-faced girl, Samantha, who I've never met before in my life--someone else from Aiden's English class, apparently--are also lingering beside us. Aiden thinks bringing more people along will be more impressive.

As all four of us stand on the porch, I cannot express my shock at how the front door is actually closed for once. I knock on it and wait. Aiden's fidgeting beside me, and he hasn't stopped rambling on about how stupid he made himself look in front of Preston earlier. This is his chance to redeem himself, so he says, and I don't have the heart to remind him that he isn't really Preston's type anyway, with him being a gay man among other complexities.

We're let in by an unfamiliar short girl, and as the sudden re-alisation hits me that I probably know absolutely no one in this party besides the people I'm with--well, two of the people I'm with, anyway--I ask the girl for Preston's whereabouts. I have to clarify I mean Zack. She raises her eyebrows and scans me up and down in a manner which suggests I share the same worth as a pile of decaying shit, and then asks for my name. I give it to her, she disappears upstairs for a minute, and then returns having replaced the look of disgust with one of confusion.

'Upstairs, first door on the right,' she mutters.

There's a small crowd of people in the hallway as we move towards the stairs, but it's pretty quiet. It's all a lot calmer than Robbie Morrissey's party, and I don't even think there's any music playing. I glance around the hallway just in case, but no one looks familiar, so we begin making our way up the stairs.

'This is so exciting!' Delyth chirps from behind me.

'We're hitting the big time now, Mia,' Aiden squeals as he turns around to face me, his deep brown eyes set alight. 'Before we know it, Zack will have fallen madly in love with me.'

I roll my eyes at him, then glance behind to check Samantha is still here because she has about as much presence as a dead fly. It's pretty unnerving. I catch her light eyes, and she shows a nervous smile that sparks a pang of guilt inside me for comparing her to something so gross. As we approach the doorway, an overpowering stench overrides my senses--one that's instantaneously recognisable from parties I've attended in the past. The urge to turn back and head home hits me like a brick to the face. Before I can say or do anything about it though, Aiden and Delyth have entered the room. Samantha is still behind me.

I hesitantly wander in to see Preston lying on a king size bed with some ginger girl attached to his neck via her lips. Sort of like a leech. Another girl at the end of the bed watches on in misery as if her sole purpose in life is to also develop leech-like qualities and suck on Preston's neck. There's grime music--Stormzy, I think--playing faintly in the background, and disregarding the six teenagers slumped onto the cream carpet, there isn't much furniture besides a wooden wardrobe and some bedside cabinets. The majority of people in the room are holding a spliff.

When Preston notices our entrance, he jumps up, almost throwing his leech off the bed, and clambers over some limp bodies to reach us. I stare at the perfectly rolled, and more importantly, illegal contraption in his hand.

'Hey!' Preston grins as if he's been best friends with each one of us all our lives, and turns to me. 'Didn't think you were gonna come, babe.'

His eyes are bloodshot, his smile uneven.

'Um yeah, I'm not sure about this. Preston, I--'

'Zack,' he snaps at me. 'It's Zack.'

Right, okay, so the personality disorder's playing up again.

'Zack' nods towards the massive bed he was previously sprawled across as a gesture for whoever to sit on it, and Aiden jumps at the chance with such excitement I fear he might explode and disintegrate into a million glittery pieces. Samantha and I stay standing, but Delyth follows Aiden onto the bed. Preston finds Aiden's excitement absolutely fantastic, and begins giggling like a schoolgirl. I knew I'd regret coming here, but I had no idea I'd regret it so soon into the night.

'Robbie, you ugly little shit, hand these guys a smoke,' Preston shouts as he flops back onto the bed in-between Aiden and Delyth.

I hadn't even noticed, but sitting next to my feet is Robbie Morrissey. He lifts his head at the sound of Preston's voice, throws him some rolled joints, and then looks questioningly at

Samantha and me. I shake my head, whereas Samantha nods enthusiastically, catching me off guard. Robbie hands her one, and she scurries away to the empty corner of the room without saying a word to me. She sits down and lowers her head, her red hair hiding her pale face, and then begins smoking the thing as if it's the sole substance keeping her alive.

Robbie's not smoking anything himself; he's just sitting against the wall with a bottle of beer next to him. For whatever reason, that comforts me. I'm glaring so hard at Aiden that I could start burning a hole into his head, but he ignores my stare and takes a lit spliff from Preston. He's taken a drag within seconds. Everyone else in the room is either unconscious or uninterested in me, so I slump myself down next to Robbie.

I glare at Aiden one more time as I mutter to myself. 'I am going to kick that boy where it hurts so hard that his balls will end up touching his tonsils, I swear to--'

'Ouch.' Robbie begins laughing beside me, and my cheeks flare as I realise he heard every word I just spoke. He's still laughing when he says, 'Mia, right?'

'Yeah, hey,' I say with an awkward smile as I wonder if he recognises me. Surely, he must do? 'How come you're not smoking?' I ask as I notice a pile of neatly rolled joints in front of him.

He shrugs with a slightly crooked smile. 'I just roll the stuff, don't smoke it.'

Robbie then demonstrates how to create both the quickest and neatest joint I've ever seen, not that I have much experience in that line of work. I'm admittedly impressed. It's hardly a quality that will lead him on to achieve great things in life, but hey, it's something. Zack's laughter suddenly cackles out, and it catapults me right back to the night of Robbie's party. He may have redeemed himself since that night, but right now he's Zack, and Zack sends shivers down my spine.

Judging by the wary look in Robbie's icy eyes, every emotion I'm feeling is painted across my face. He nudges me and nods towards the bed where Preston's leech is once again suckling on his neck. Aiden, on the other hand, is staring deeply at Preston's blonde hair, caressing his fingers through it. Delyth's just sitting there having an in-depth conversation with the lampshade above her, which is nothing new. That image in itself alters my mood ever so slightly, and I giggle. Too bad it's irritatingly short lived.

Aiden's laughing now, and it's almost as grating as Preston's laugh. I don't think I've ever wanted to smack my best friend so hard in my life, and as every second passes, the laughter from the bed increases. My stomach acid bubbles as Preston shoves the ginger girl off him and tells her to piss off because she's boring him. The girl protests, calling him an arrogant dickhead in the process, but Preston disregards her entirely and begins chatting to Aiden. With her face red with what I can only assume is anger and embarrassment, the girl gets off the bed and storms out of the room.

Who the hell does Preston even think he is? What does he think gives him the right to treat people like crap? If I hadn't been brought up to be so polite, I would pounce onto that bed and--A loud, sharp whistle interrupts my thoughts.

'Hey, babe!' Preston's grinning at me. He taps the empty space beside him. 'It's your lucky day!'

That does it for me. I can't do this. I don't even care how stupid I look, or how much I'm overreacting. Before anyone can blink, I stand up, bolt out of the room, and head straight for the only other room I've ever been inside in this house. The door's closed, but I don't care. Screw the door, it's a stupid door anyway. I jump onto the childish bed with its childish bedding, and slam the childish door behind me. Within minutes of me entering the room, I hear a quiet knock.

'If that's you, Aiden,' I snap with my eyes locked onto the textured ceiling. 'Please piss off and get back to your pissing marijuana with your new pissing friends and your new pissing boyfriend.'

I stay glaring at the ceiling as I hear the door open and close again.

'Contrary to what some people claim, I can't say homosexuality has ever especially appealed to me.'

I turn my head to see Preston, whose previous sloppy demeanour has been replaced with a noticeably more sophisticated one.

'Jesus Christ, we're Preston now, are we?' I sit up on the bed. 'I don't know who you think you are--neither do you, apparently--but you have no right to be such a massive dickhead to absolutely everyone. People are still people, regardless of what name you feel like giving yourself, I mean, you just... just, ugh!'

'Look, I'm sorry, I occasionally get carried away.'

He shrugs, and something I've never seen before surfaces in his eyes: sincerity. He suddenly starts laughing again and destroys the whole thing, but hey, at least it was there for a moment. A groan escapes my mouth as I lean back onto the bed and lie down. No wonder I don't want to get to know Preston on personal terms, it's just so much... effort. And confusing. Really damn confusing. I sigh.

'Okay, whatever,' I mutter. 'Seriously though, have you ever had yourself tested for a personality disorder? I'd highly recommend it.'

Preston sits beside me on the bed, and chuckles so lightly that it almost becomes a faint, girlish giggle. 'If only it were that simple...' He shuts his eyes and lies down. 'The more simple we are, the more complete we become: Auguste Rodin.'

I don't respond, primarily because I haven't the slightest clue who Auguste Rodin is. After a minute or so, I begin thinking a response would have been pointless anyway because Preston's chest starts rising and falling more slowly. I think he's asleep. That is until I hear a soft mumble.

'By the way.' Preston sighs. 'Has anyone ever told you that your name sounds like an STD?'

'Shut up!'

The only reply I get is a light chuckle disguised among another tired sigh, and within moments, Preston is fast asleep.

CHAPTER 6

'Mia!'

I turn my head at the sound of a deep voice, but it's impossible to see much of anything through Cardiff's crowded high street. Flashes of colourful clothing surround me as eyes glance in my direction, but nobody's face seems familiar. Mum, who eagerly informed me that we were going shopping to buy new towels this morning, bobs her head in all directions to find the identity of the voice. She's beginning to resemble an excited chicken, and I'm about to dive into the nearest alleyway to escape the humility of being seen with her when the voice calls again.

'Hey, Mia!'

A group of teenagers ahead of us are split through the middle by an unseen force, and within seconds, I spot a recognisable face emerging. They initially look agitated by the boy who just shoved himself straight through them, but when they realise it's Robbie Morrissey, their annoyance is replaced by curiosity.

'Hey, sorry, I just saw you and figured I'd come say hi.' Robbie smiles as he stops in front of us.

'Oh, hey,' I reply. It's strange to see him out in public in the middle of the afternoon. Up to now, Robbie Morrissey's only existed in the realms of late night parties. 'I'm, uh... We've just bought some really nice new towels.'

Oh dear God, please tell me I didn't just say that.

Mum's face suddenly lights up, and before I can even blink, she asks for Robbie's name, how old he is, if he goes to school, if he has a job, and around fifty other unnecessary questions. She doesn't do any of this in an interrogative manner, but in a way that would make every onlooker think she's known Robbie since he left the womb.

I try distracting myself from the embarrassment by focusing on the warm scent of hot dogs cooking in the distance, but it's proving to be a pretty useless distraction with Mum nattering in my ear. I'm slowly melting into a puddle of shame, and half-heartedly wanting Mum to vanish into thin air, when I feel her eyes on me.

'That sounds like a fab idea, what do you think, Mia?' she says, but as I was busy conjuring up an escape route, I have no idea what she's on about. 'We're done with what we needed to get, so you may as well.'

To not look like a total idiot, I smile and say, 'sure.'

Mum responds by grinning giddily at me, winking, and then practically skipping away to leave Robbie and me alone. Wait, what? What did I just agree to?

Robbie holds up the white plastic bag in his hand. 'I've got everything I need, so do you want to find a coffee shop or something?'

'Uh, sure... Sounds good,' I reply slowly as I pray I didn't just agree to a date with Robbie Morrissey.

The coffee shop we find is crammed by the time we've bought our drinks. Robbie solves the problem of finding seats using an admittedly admirable method. He approaches two girls sharing a table, and somehow encourages them to leave with their half swilled hot chocolates. He turns to me, grins, then nods at the armchair opposite as he slides into his own. It's as if he and Preston have this supernatural power that allows them to control people, specifically females, between the ages of around fifteen and twenty. I'm not sure if I should be in awe of it, or hate it with intense passion.

'Sorry about my mum,' I say as I sink into the black leather chair. In an attempt to seem calm and collected, I destroy any shred of pride I have by saying, 'she gets like it whenever I acknowledge anything with a penis. I think she worries I might be a lesbian. I always assure her I'm not, but she never looks convinced.'

As the realisation of what I just said hits me, I want to die. I literally want to dig a hole through the tiled floor below me, lie in it, cover it back up, and die. Robbie, on the other hand, has never looked so amused in his life. He bursts into laughter and swipes a loose strand of his light brown hair back into place. I can't help noticing that his hairstyle mirrors Preston's.

'How's the iced coffee?' he asks as he nods at my drink. 'I don't buy just anyone drinks, so you should appreciate it.' He winks.

'Pfft, I bet you say that to all the girls.'

I say it in a jokey manner, but judging by the way Robbie widens his blue eyes and stammers, he's not used to this kind of reaction. He rubs his neck, and once again, I envision myself burrowing a hole into the ground. It's a good plan actually, maybe I should follow it through. Come on though, that was a pretty self-indulgent pick-up line. That crap can't actually ever work, can it?

'Sorry, I was joking,' I say. 'My humour's a little warped, so making an idiot out of myself is a daily occurrence for me.'

Robbie's eyes soften. 'No, it's nice.'

A pause of slight awkwardness follows, and neither of us says anything for a short while. I begin staring at the raindrops as they collide with the window to my right, and Robbie adjusts the sleeves of his leather jacket. He slurps at his smoothie. The fruitiness of his drink is mixing with the aroma of fresh coffee, and it's beginning to make me wish I'd gotten a smoothie myself.

As I turn back to Robbie, it looks like there's something dancing on his tongue that wants to waltz out of his mouth, but he takes a while before actually saying anything.

'So hey,' he begins. 'This has been bugging me since we met at Zack's the other day, but you're the girl who helped at my party, right? With, y'know, the Zack situation?'

I reply with a nod, and the drizzling rain outside now seems far less interesting than it did moments ago. A million and one questions attack me from all angles, and I try to summarise them all into one.

'What actually happened that night?' I ask.

My drink is cold in my hands, and as I await Robbie's response, the tips of my fingers begin turning numb. Tiny droplets run down the plastic cup and splash onto my skin, but I'm too busy biting my lip in anticipation to wipe them off. Intense chatter and laughter is exploding all around me, but as I watch Robbie and wait, all I hear is a monotonous buzzing noise. He leans back in his chair, takes another sip from his orange smoothie, and scratches the back of his head before finally answering.

'He overdosed, I guess. Once you and your friend left, the ambulance guys seemed to think that was it, so I guess that's what it was. I didn't see him take anything that night, but he's always pretending he doesn't take shit when I know he does. Zack's not mentioned that night since it happened, but who gives a crap, really? He obviously pulled that stunt for attention; he's enough of a dick to do something like that.'

The bluntness of Robbie's reply catches me off guard, and it strikes me that he seems to know nothing more than I do about what happened to his best friend that night. I draw away from him as his harsh words circle the air, and I find myself wondering if Robbie knows that Zack isn't his real name. I wonder if Robbie even knows Preston at all, and if Preston Maddox's best friend doesn't even know who he is, then who the hell does?

'Thanks though, for helping.' Robbie snaps me out of my trance. 'I wanted to say something at Zack's the other day, but I wasn't sure it was you, and I didn't want to confuse the hell out of you if I was wrong.' He laughs. 'Sorry I was an arsehole to you that night, I was kind of panicking. My folks would have played hell with me if someone died in their front garden.'

'It's cool,' I say reassuringly. 'You don't seem like the biggest fan of Pre--Zack though, considering you guys are best friends.'

Robbie picks at his plastic cup and shrugs. 'Nah, we're good mates, I just... I don't get the hype around him, y'know? Everyone sees him as this massive deal, and even girls who want his head rammed onto a stake are interested enough in him to hate him so much. He's a dickhead to everyone, not just girls.' He stammers a little. 'Like I said, we are good mates and I'm not saying I'm perfect, but y'know...' He shrugs again. 'I just don't get it is all.'

'Well, if it makes you feel any better, I'd rather eat broken glass than go anywhere near Zack in that way.'

Robbie laughs, and leaves a knowing smile on his thin lips. 'Yeah, I noticed.' He stares out the window next to us and begins muttering. 'I just don't get it.'

I'm beginning to think I was wrong about Robbie. Maybe he isn't just an arrogant eighteen-year-old whose life revolves around reveling in the admiration he gets from strangers. Somewhere inside of him is a meek little boy wanting to grab everyone's attention, and show them how great he can be. He's so desperate just to be seen, but he's trapped in the shadow of his more alluring ally, who's always one step ahead of him. I soften my eyes as I watch Robbie pick at his cup again, and I sort of feel sorry for him.

On my way home, I struggle to form a solid opinion of Robbie Morrissey. He's no longer the narcissist who throws house parties where everyone can gather to admire him, but someone else I can't quite grasp a hold of. As with Preston, I've got no idea why I have this compulsion to define him, but I do. The darker side of Robbie still lingers in the back of my mind, but an array of other traits are starting to surface.

My head aches as I try to figure out which version of him is real, and which ones are fronts, but it's an impossible task. Maybe he really is the sensitive boy who desperately wants to be noticed. But maybe that's fake, and maybe he's actually an enormous arsehole whose way of getting into a girl's pants involves charming them through sympathy. By the time I reach my porch, my head is fried. I briefly notice how my sister's car is on the driveway, but I'm too busy trying not to think about Robbie to take much notice.

As I open my front door and enter the house, there's mumbling coming from the living room. I don't pay much attention to it, but as I'm about to jog upstairs, Mum calls me from behind the door.

'Mia? Mia, is that you?' Her voice is strained, and she only just manages to shout. 'Come in here a sec, baby, I need to talk with you.'

My heart freezes. I rewind my memories and frantically search for anything I've done wrong, but nothing clicks. I suddenly realise that she referred to me as baby, and when Mum refers to me as baby, it's a guarantee for bad news. Without a second thought, I head straight for my living room.

For a moment, I think the room's empty except for my Jack Russell Terrier, Maxxie, because it's dead silent. That original uncertainty is dismissed by the sound of someone clearing their throat. As I turn my eyes to the corner of the room, I notice my mother and older sister, Livvy, huddled up on our worn out sofa. The television beside it is switched off. Mum's eyes are glassed over. Absent. Livvy, on the other hand, has tears streaming down her face.

What's going on?

I stand still, frozen. I don't know what to do, how to stand, where to look, what to do with my hands. Should I sit? Should I move from the doorway?

'Come here.' Mum pats the empty space next to her. Her eyes finally focus, and she's looking at me.

I do as I'm told, give Maxxie a stroke on the way, and sit down next to Mum. I've never noticed before, but there's a scuff on the end of our sofa. I gaze at it.

'I was going to call you, but I didn't want to interrupt your date.' I open my mouth to tell Mum it wasn't a date, but snap it shut when I realise that now would be a grossly inappropriate time to do so. 'But everyone's fine, don't worry, it's just that...' She's stammering. I'm still staring at the scuff on the sofa. 'When your father come home today, he told me that he was... that he's been--'

'He's been shagging some slut from the football club, and now he's ditching us.'

Livvy speaks with such bluntness that if it wasn't for Mum's arms around me, her words would knock me off the sofa and onto the rough carpet. Maxxie barks.

'Don't speak like that, Livvy! Listen.' Mum hugs my sister and me as tightly as her strength will let her, and all of a sudden, she's spewing out words. 'Your dad loves you so much, okay, he just... he just loves me less than he used to, but he still loves you just as much, I promise. Just because he doesn't love me anymore, he still loves you. Okay? He still loves you.'

Mum carries on speaking about how much Dad loves us, how she won't let this affect my A-Levels or Livvy's university degree, how we've done nothing wrong, how much Dad loves us again, how she was just as clueless as we were to the affair, and how much Dad loves us once more, but all I can do is stare at the scuff on the sofa. Livvy's still crying. Maxxie barks. And I feel nothing.

In fact, I've never felt so much nothing.

I want to scream, I want to cry, I want to laugh, I want to phone Dad and tell him he's a disgusting pile of shit, I want to smash the entire living room up, or laugh and say that he was an idiot anyway, but I can't. I can't because I don't feel it, any of it. I shut my eyes and try to squeeze something out--anything--but nothing comes besides a hollow emptiness. I had no idea. How could I have no idea? He's my dad. I live with him. How could I not have noticed what was going on?

I watch Maxxie as he stretches his legs, and in that second I wish I could be him because then it would be okay for me to feel nothing. But I'm not a dog. I'm a seventeen-year-old girl who's just found out that her dad has been having an affair with some woman she's never met before in her life, a girl who feels nothing when she should be feeling everything.

Chapter 7

As I discover over the next few weeks, Christmas isn't the ideal time of year for a family to be ripped apart. When I woke up the morning after Mum told Livvy and me what had happened, I thought I'd made it up. I didn't think it was a dream; it felt too real, but that maybe I'd misheard or misunderstood. That Dad hadn't been having an affair. I was wrong. I'd understood perfectly, and I still felt exactly the same. I still felt nothing. Initially, I thought I was in shock, that the reason I felt so numb to the whole thing was because I couldn't comprehend it. As the days of nothingness turned into weeks of nothingness, however, it occurred to me that perhaps there was something wrong with me, that I couldn't feel like regular people could.

The Christmas holidays are now creeping to a close, and I still feel no different. For the first few nights, Dad slept on the sofa at a friend's house, but has somehow managed to worm his way back into the family home, claiming he has nowhere else to go. He's agreed to stay out of Mum's way, that he'll give her space, and alongside the fact he has nowhere else, that he's only staying in the house because he can't bear not seeing me. I call bullshit, but whatever. I can tell that it's killing Mum to see him every day. To see him every morning and act like he hasn't destroyed every shed of her self-worth.

It's funny, really, how our parents are human. How it takes something drastic to realise that. I'm a clever enough seventeen-year-old. I'm mature, I'm inquisitive, I'm open-minded. Yet until this revelation, I was still living in the delusion that my parents are different to every other human being on earth. That they don't feel emotions like we do, that doing the right thing is instinctive to them, that they don't have their own lives and secrets. It's embarrassing, actually, how deluded I was.

Livvy's gone back to uni for good until Easter. Before everything went to shit, she was meant to be staying home for three whole weeks. Instead, she was home four days. What I did see of her over those four days makes me think I should be glad I have the emotional capacity of a table. While Livvy spent Christmas Day curled up on the sofa, refusing to speak to anyone, I spent it getting on with things easily enough. Alongside how short her visit home was, the fact she spent most of it in a sad silence means we barely got an opportunity to speak, let alone figure this whole situation out together. We've never been especially close, so I'm not sure what I was expecting, but I'd hoped this could actually bring us closer. Now I feel like this is going to drive us even further apart.

I figure I'm just going to get on with things as normal. I feel normal, so might as well act it. There's no point faking misery, although sometimes I consider it. Mum can no longer look at me without an expectant gaze in her eyes. I've not shown anything near the degree of pain Livvy has, so she's waiting for it, and I don't have the heart to tell her it's never coming. None of my friends know about what's happened either, not even Aiden. It's primarily because I've not physically seen much of anyone, but I'm not sure I'll say anything when I do, anyway. I don't think there's much point. I don't feel like I need to vent to anyone about the whole thing, and I'd rather avoid the attention.

In celebration of acting normal, I'm attending a house party tonight. It'll be my first big public outing since the family shitshow went down, so I'm viewing it as a test. Maybe seeing everyone will spark up something inside me. I've decided that if after tonight, I still feel nothing, then I might just be heartless. The party is at the house of someone I've never met before in my life. It's Robbie who invited me. His friend who studies at Cardiff uni is throwing it, and I agreed to join so long as Aiden could tag along.

He and Delyth are practically attached at the hip by now, or at least she's chained herself to his, so she was able to get an invite too. We've won ourselves a space each in Robbie's car, which Aiden was ecstatic about because he thinks that means we've made the big time. He's decided that Robbie and I are star-crossed lovers or some shit, but I frequently assure him we're not.

When Robbie arrives to pick me up from home, Preston--of course in Zack formation--is riding shotgun because in his own words, he's the most important. Consequently, Aiden, Delyth, and I find ourselves squished into the back of Robbie's small car. Preston is playing an old Clubland CD, which is slowly driving me insane, but other than that I feel fine. I sure as hell don't feel sad, and I wonder if that's confirmation enough that I truly am incapable of feeling anything anymore. I try not to dwell on the thought.

Once we arrive, we park down a side street--illegally, I'm pretty sure--and I escape the cramped car as quickly as possible. As I do so, someone nudges me into Robbie. He stammers an apology just as I do, but mine is cut short by the shrieking laughter of Preston.

'Oh, piss off,' Robbie snaps at him.

I guess Preston's the one who pushed me then. I should probably stop underestimating how much of an arsehole he is as Zack. Preston responds to Robbie by raising his eyebrows, then winking at him before taking a cigarette out of his pocket and lighting it. He hands one to Robbie, then offers one to the rest of us, but we all decline. Aiden wavers, but I shoot him a harsh glare of warning. Though these cigarettes are straight tobacco, I don't want a repeat of the party at Preston's where Aiden spent the whole night playing the role of Zack's doting lapdog.

I've only ever been to this area of the city once before, and that was to help Livvy move into her student accommodation a few miles away. We're in Cathays, a place quite obviously occupied primarily by uni students. As we walk along the road, takeaway shops are dotted at every corner, and the terraced houses that form this neighbourhood look a little worse for wear to say the least. As we turn a street corner, our destination comes into view, and it sticks out like a sore thumb.

Music is blaring from inside the terraced house, and groups of friends sit and stand on what was at one point likely a front garden, but is now just a slab of concrete. Preston, who had previously been bragging to Robbie about one of his female victims from the other night, is quickly recognised by a group of people outside the house. They call him over, and like a puppy being let off its leash for the first time ever, he rushes towards them.

By the time we catch up with him, he's already sitting on the brick wall that frames the house's porch with a girl on his lap, her arms wrapped around his neck. I'm legitimately impressed. That must be a record or something.

'Gross,' I mutter as I pass him to enter the house.

As we step inside, all ability to hear myself think vanishes, and flashes of Robbie's party last summer jolt into my head. People dance, drink, sing, laugh around me, and before I can process much of anything, there's a bottle of vodka being shoved in my face. I turn to see Aiden, his face lit up by a massive grin.

'Shots?' he asks.

Well, it'd be rude not to.

With the help of Robbie's persuasion abilities, we manage to steal ourselves a corner of the living room sofa. Minus a bathroom and a bedroom at the front of the house, the layout of its ground floor is open plan. The kitchen sits at the far back of the building, where patio doors lead to a long, narrow back garden, and in-between that and the hallway is an impressive living room. Nothing like Robbie's lair, of course, but still a good size. The TV that hangs on the wall above the living room's coffee table is turned on, but I'm not sure why because it's impossible to hear over the music pumping from some speakers on a kitchen countertop.

Once we've made our nest on the sofa, Aiden pours us a shot each, and the clear liquid is soon burning itself down my throat. I still feel no different about the whole parent situation, nor do I feel compelled to discuss it with anyone, so I figure I'll drink more and see if that works.

'It's cool that you came,' Robbie says over the music.

Aiden is currently distracted by Delyth's attempts to seduce him through constant physical contact and exaggerated laughter, so I give my full attention to Robbie. I'm quite taken aback that he's stayed with us instead of chosen to go gallivanting with Preston and be a dick somewhere.

'Oh, thanks,' I reply, and I quickly realise how that response makes little sense, so I hastily attempt to cover it up. 'How come you're not off hunting with Zack?'

Robbie responds with a perplexed look on his face, and a slight stammer, and I realise that all my cover attempt did was solidify the likelihood of remaining single forever. Then it occurs to me that I'm thinking about Robbie in that sort of way, which makes me stammer even more, and then cringe slightly.

'Sorry. I mean looking for girls, entertaining the teenage population of Cardiff, being a general lad and, y'know, all that fun stuff,' I joke.

'Oh, yeah, nah... That's always been more Zack's thing. The girls always end up going for him anyway, so y'know, not much point.'

I swear, everything this guy says to me makes me feel sorry for him. There must be some sort of sympathetic look on my face because before I can respond to Robbie, he starts laughing like he meant what he said as a joke.

'D'you want to fetch some mixers?' He asks, nodding at the vodka Aiden has placed on the wooden floor below us. 'So we can make something that doesn't physically hurt to drink.'

Now that sounds like a good idea. Robbie jumps up from the stained sofa, and manoeuvres his way through the crowd into the kitchen area, while I follow the path he makes. He stops at a cupboard near the patio doors, then turns to say something, but I can't hear him over the music I'm surprised no one is yet to be rendered deaf from.

'Hey, Tush!' Robbie yells over my shoulder, and I turn to see a group of guys standing over the kitchen table playing some drinking game. 'Turn that shit down!'

The tallest of the group, an unnecessarily shirtless guy, turns to face us. He responds to Robbie's request by laughing, then proceeds to turn the music's volume up via his phone. Robbie rolls his eyes, opens a cupboard above him, then moves a sandwich toaster that looks like it's been used to death to bring out some supermarket branded lemonade. The perks of knowing the party host, I guess.

'It reeks of smoke here,' I comment, more to myself than Robbie, but he responds with an apology and then closes the patio doors.

'Thanks,' I say with a laugh.

Robbie replies with a smile, and two small dimples appear on his cleanly shaved face. I watch him as he pours our drinks, and go to comment on how strong he's making them, but don't want to make an arse of myself, so say nothing.

'Name a really bad song,' he yells over the music as he hands me my drink.

I respond with a questioning look, so Robbie nods at the speakers on the kitchen counter, which are soaked from spilled drinks by this point. I have no idea what to suggest, so raise my shoulders in an I don't know motion. Robbie leans back against the kitchen counter, pauses for a minute, then starts grinning madly.

He begins typing something into his phone, then draws my attention to the group of guys standing over the kitchen table again. Seconds later, the song that was playing is abruptly cut off, and replaced by what I can only describe as the worst collaboration of noise I've ever heard. I don't know what the song is, or why it was ever created, but it's horrific. Suddenly, the group of guys burst into hysterical laughter.

'I--I didn't put it on!' the Tush kid stammers as he frantically begins typing into his phone. 'I wouldn't put this on the playlist!'

The song changes once more, this time to a cheesy Boyzone tune I couldn't even stomach when I was in primary school. I start giggling. Most people are laughing by now, other than Aiden who's singing along from the sofa, which makes me laugh even harder.

'It's not me!' Tush demands. 'Look, the song won't change when I--' Suddenly, the song flips to the same generic house music that was playing before the speaker was sabotaged, and Tush is stammering all over again. 'It wasn't working before, I swear! I--Shut up!'

As Tush strops in the corner of the room, I turn back to Robbie as he's shoving his phone into his pocket. He takes a sip of his drink, then shoots me a wink. That's more like the Robbie Morrissey I'd heard so much about. I'm about to comment on his impressively executed plan when a short, slender girl falls into me, spilling half the contents of my drink over the floor. She laughs what I think is meant to be an apology, then pounces at a blonde guy a few feet away, and starts sucking his face.

Robbie swears at her, not that she pays any attention to it, then goes to grab a tea towel hanging from a counter. I'm about to yell at the rude bitch herself when she turns around, and I freeze.

'Mia! Oh my god!' Livvy detaches herself from the guy whose mouth she was attached to seconds ago, then lands a sloppy kiss on my cheek with that same mouth. 'James!' she yells back to the guy as she drapes her arm over my shoulder.

'Uh, it's Josh,' the guy replies.

'Yeah, James, this is my sis--'

I yank Livvy away before she reduces me to the point of embarrassment where I can no longer form coherent sentences, and drag her through the crowds into the ground floor hallway.

'Who are you here with? Oh my god, this is so cool, I thought all you ever did was sit alone in your room with your emo angst, and like, one friend!'

I don't think she intends on being insulting, but I mean, she is. She pulls me into a suffocating hug again, and this is honestly the most affectionate she's been since I was about six. I'm about to tell her to down a jug of water and restrain herself from embarrassing me any further when mid-hug, she screams in my ear.

'Aiden!'

Livvy squeals and shoves me aside, and I turn to see Aiden standing in the doorway that leads to the living room area. My sister quickly traps him into the hug I was locked into moments ago.

'Aw, you're so cute! Are you still gay?' For the love of God. 'You should be my gay best friend, not Mia's, she's boring. Are you growing your hair out? So cute!'

'Uh, no, just haven't shaved it for a while,' Aiden comments as he runs his fingers over his hair, which is starting to form into tight curls.

He's clearly horrified over someone noticing he's between haircuts, and presses down onto his scalp to try and flatten it. The hair just flicks back up.

'He's not an accessory, Liv,' I snap.

Once released from my sister's grasp, Aiden turns to me and asks, 'hey, Mia, have you seen my vodka?'

Aiden barely even finishes his sentence when Livvy unnecessarily yells a reply. 'Oh, I have alcohol!'

She grabs Aiden's hand, and pulls him in the direction of the stairs. Aiden, loving both attention and alcohol, happily obliges. I groan, swear under my breath, and follow them up the stairs. They're charging ahead of me, and I have to nudge the sweaty bodies of shrieking university students out of my way to keep track of Livvy and Aiden.

I follow them into a bedroom to find Livvy almost fully inside a small wardrobe. Aiden is sitting on the double bed that barely fits inside the box-like room as he and my sister laugh about who knows what. It says a lot when your friend is closer to your sister than you are. When Livvy emerges from inside the wardrobe, she thrusts her arm into the air with a near empty bottle of gin, almost tripping over in the process.

'Huzzah!' she shouts

'Have you drunk all that yourself?' I question, wide-eyed.

'Duh,' she retorts as if I'm stupid.

'Jesus, Liv, maybe slow it down a bit, you--'

'Ugh, sorry, Dad,' she mutters, catching my eye for a moment.

I respond with gritted teeth, and she grins at me. She knows what she's doing. Is that what we're going to be resorted to? Backhanded comments about the mess at home? She throws the gin at Aiden, who barely catches it, and he takes a shot straight from the bottle. As he goes to hand the bottle to me, Livvy snatches it back off him, and pours far more than a shot down her throat. It doesn't take a genius to figure out this isn't going to end well.

CHAPTER 8

Not even ten minutes after being upstairs, Olivia's bottle of gin is empty. She pouts her lips as she inspects it, then stands back up to shuffle through the wardrobe again.

'Oh, hang on!' Aiden exclaims from the bed, but before I can question him, he's left the room.

Livvy is still searching the wardrobe when I ask her what the hell she's doing, and she responds with some rambled sentence about finding more alcohol. She's always been a bit of a party animal, but I'd be an idiot to believe our parents' situation has nothing to do with the fact she's drunk the majority of a bottle of gin to herself. This time, she's empty handed when she steps out of the wardrobe, and without warning, she slides down it and slumps to the floor.

I sigh as I kneel down in front of her. 'Do you want me to call a taxi for you?'

'No!' Livvy yells, suddenly perking up. She lifts her head, and she's grinning. 'I'm having fun!'

'I'm not,' I mutter under my breath.

'We've never been to a party together, c'mon! Have a drink!'

I go to remind her that when I tried to do just that, she snatched the bottle from me, but figure now's not the time to try and start an argument. She keeps blabbering on about how great of a time we could have together, while I internally beg for Aiden to return from wherever he disappeared to.

'Why didn't you tell me?' I hear Livvy say from the floor below me.

'What?'

'Why didn't you tell me about Dad?' she spits at me. She's not smiling anymore. 'You know that I know you--I mean, I know that you knew.'

I stare at my sister in disbelief. 'I didn't have any idea, Liv, what are you even talking about?'

She laughs, but it catches in her throat. 'You live there, how couldn't you know? And you're upset--No, I mean, you're not upset, you don't care. If you didn't know, why don't you care? You knew it was happening, stop acting like you didn't,' she mutters as her head bobs from side to side against the wardrobe door.

'Are you being serious?' I stare at her in disbelief. 'Fuck you, Olivia. Fuck you.'

She can pass out on a stranger's bedroom floor and choke on her own vomit for all I care. I stand up, and bolt out of the room. How dare she say that to me? Just because I don't constantly cry and get drunk out of my mind, it doesn't mean I don't care. I do, I must do. I have to. I'm barely out of the room when the last person I want to see right now calls my name.

I spin around, my teeth gritted and fists clenched. 'What?' I yell.

'Bloody hell, babe, calm it.' Preston laughs. 'Was gonna ask if you were feeling frisky, but I'll take that as a strong no.'

He's just emerged from the door opposite the room Livvy's currently being a bitch in with a cocky grin on his face. I open my mouth to snap at him, but am distracted by a skinny brunette girl emerging from the same room. She says something about seeing him later, but he doesn't even bat an eyelid in her direction, and when she stays put, he shoos her away. Literally waves his hand at her to disappear.

I'm about to call him out when I notice his flyer is down, and within seconds, the urge to throw up bubbles in my stomach. Preston must spot me looking because he's soon chortling.

He zips up his jeans as he says, 'chill out, it was only a bl--'

'Nope, stop right there, I really don't want to know,' I interrupt him before he can elaborate.

The last thing I'm in the mood for right now is this, so I go to continue on my way, but Preston stops me again.

'Hey, you all right?' he asks, his voice suddenly soft as his eyes dart towards the room I just left.

'I'm fine,' I mutter.

He glances over my shoulder, and must spot Livvy because his eyebrows raise. 'She your friend?' he asks with a nod in her direction.

'Sort of,' I mutter, not entirely sure why I don't correct him. Probably embarrassment.

'Ah, more of an acquaintance?' He moves past me and into the room, so I follow because like hell am I leaving him alone with her. 'Well, based on the assumption that she's the one who's recently emptied the contents of what looks like a severely mistreated stomach into a charming heap on the floor, I'd perhaps suggest not leaving her to it.'

Zack has left the building then. It takes me a good ten seconds to decode what the hell he's blathering on about, but when I see the pool of sick beside Livvy's feet, it makes a lot more sense. Give me strength. I groan for what feels like the hundredth time tonight, and shove past Preston to try and fix the mess that is my sister. Who is she even here with? Where are her friends?

'Mia! You came back!' Livvy squeals as I bend down to her, and as she lifts her head up, I notice a trickle of sick on her chin. Wonderful. 'I feel sick.'

A frown is slapped onto her face, and as she goes to stand up, I steady her and awkwardly place her onto the bed a few feet away. Preston steps forward to help, but I shake my head at him to leave it. I don't know why he's still here and not out flexing his personality disorder.

'Do you know if she lives close? Though it's looking unlikely, if she's able to walk, it might be wise to get her home,' he murmurs, to which I shake my head. She's nowhere near sober enough to walk the twenty minutes back to her place. 'Okay, well, ensure she's on her side so that her airways don't become blocked by any more vomit,' he instructs, and I'm about to snap at him for playing doctor when Aiden suddenly reappears in the doorway with some vodka in his hand, and Preston continues with, 'that shit is nasty, babe. She ain't getting pulled any time soon, I can tell you that.'

I roll my eyes.

'Holy mackerel... What happened?' Aiden asks in the doorway, swaying slightly.

Preston responds with a gagging motion, winks at Aiden, taps his shoulder, then disappears back into the party. Well, he was useful for about zero seconds.

'I take it vodka's off the menu?' Aiden asks from the doorway. I stare at him dumbly, and he raises his hands defensively. 'Hey, you know me, just trying to throw in some comedic relief.'

I spend the next hour or so trying to revive Livvy to the point where she can at least lift her head up unaided, and in fairness to Aiden, he stays with me the whole time. I think he feels guilty about encouraging her to keep drinking when she blatantly needed to stop. I shoo him out eventually, partly because this isn't his shit to deal with, and partly because I don't want him to catch Livvy saying anything about our parents' situation.

It must be at least midnight by now, and the party is still very much alive and kicking, yet here I am nursing my older sister as she lays on a stranger's bed on the verge of passing out. It's almost laughable.

'Why would he do that, Mia?' Livvy mumbles from the bed, and it's the first thing she's said in about half an hour. 'Why would he do that to us?'

She lifts her head, her fringe wildly out of place on her forehead, her eyes the biggest I've ever seen them. I don't know what to say, so I don't say anything. Instead, I stammer a little, then shrug my shoulders. I move my eyes away from hers. Why am I so shit at this kind of thing? She drops her head back onto the sick-stained pillow, and sighs. She sniffs, and I think she's crying, but I don't check.

'I'm sorry,' I hear her say, 'I didn't mean--I--What I said, I didn't mean it. I'm sorry. I love you, Mia.'

She sniffs again, and then it's silent. I want to say it back, but don't know how to, and the words get so stuck in my throat that they simply end up lost.

I wake up the next morning with a splitting headache. Not because I drank too much, which it should've been, but because I barely slept last night. I was too anxious over Livvy falling over, or being sick, or doing who knows what in her sleep-deprived, drunken state to get any shut eye myself. By the time it's a little before seven in the morning and I notice the sun breaking through the half-closed blinds of this tiny bedroom, I decide to get up.

Someone else joined Livvy in the bed mid-way through the night--the owner of the room, I figure, but I don't remember her entering so I guess I must've gotten some degree of sleep. Livvy seems all right now, anyway, so I make my escape. I clamber over a heap of unwashed clothes, manoeuvre my way out of the room, then emerge to complete stillness.

Everything is deadly silent. There are some rogue teenagers passed out along the hallway, and of the rooms whose doors are open, I peek inside to see people fast asleep on the beds. The faint sound of someone snoring in the distance is the only thing to be heard, and if it wasn't for the chaos in my own head, the quiet would be perfect. It's as if the world has paused, only briefly, to allow everyone in it to breathe for a moment. To take it all in. To let the sun creep up into the sky, and let the night's chill slowly melt away. Just for a moment.

Despite my tiredness and anxiety-riddled mind, I appreciate it for what it is while I can, then move on towards the stairs. Once on the ground floor, it's a similar scene; the carcasses of teenagers are lying limply around the open-planned area, creating the most inconvenient of obstacle courses, while empty bottles and food wrappers cover what's left of the floor. I spot Aiden lying on the sofa with Delyth by his head, and some bloke I've never seen before in my life embracing him. I press my lips into a thin line to stop myself from laughing.

I step over some more bodies to reach the kitchen, and am about to begin searching for a mug to make some coffee when I feel a chill. I turn to see the patio doors are open. The smell of tobacco circles the air, which churns my already nauseous stomach, and I reach out to close the doors when I spot Preston. He's lying on the garden's uncut grass, fully immersed in the weeds and dampness. A pair of glasses are resting on his face, and he has a thick university textbook and a cigarette in his hands. All the while he's playing some smooth jazz on the speakers Robbie tampered with last night because, well, of course he is.

'Here we bloody go,' I mumble as I step outside.

He doesn't lift his head, or acknowledge me in any way that would suggest he heard me, but he must've at least noticed my presence because he's soon speaking some nonsensical gibberish.

'Did you know Stalin suffered from atherosclerosis?' he asks. 'I had no idea. It never ceases to amaze me how you can genuinely learn something new every day.'

He finally turns his attention away from the book in his hand, and focuses it on me as if he expects me to turn around like, duh, everyone knows that! I just respond with raised eyebrows. As I stop by his side, Preston continues chatting on about some more dictator-related crap, but I hush him. My brain can't handle this shit right now.

'You talk too much,' I mutter as I sit down on the grass beside him, only to realise it's soaking wet.

I'd assumed it wouldn't be too bad considering Preston is lying on it, but that sure was a rookie mistake. I would stand up, but as well as the logic of what's done is done, I'm just too tired.

'Your name sounds like an STD,' he responds, ever so imaginatively.

'Why are you even awake?' I ask, lifting my hand to block the rising sun from my vision. 'Let alone reading what looks like the political equivalent of War and Peace.'

He laughs, then rolls his eyes when it occurs to him that I don't get the joke. 'Among other political routes, War and Peace is centred around the politics of the Napoleon era--Well, it's impact on Tsarist society, so referring to anything as the political equivalent of War and Peace is actually quite inaccurate and--'

'Sh... Please, just, sh. Forget I said it. Besides, piss off have you read that, it's like over a thousand pages long.' I sigh. 'You're way too energetic for seven in the morning, pal. Seriously, why aren't you asleep? You can't have gone to bed any earlier than three.'

'Sleep has a tendency to evade me,' he replies as he closes the book and drops it to the ground beside him. 'But I can't say I'm ever too eager to welcome it.'

'Right. Sure. How was your night, anyway? Catch any gonorrhea? Or was it just herpes this time?'

'Please, Euphemia, at least give me some degree of credit. I'm riddled with chlamydia at most,' Preston responds, and this time, we both laugh.

He sits up as he takes a drag of his cigarette, then props it behind his ear. The music gently seeping out the speakers that, merely hours ago, were blasting the most obnoxious sounds is having a strange effect on me. Despite the stress of dealing with Olivia, and knowing I'll be arriving home to a war zone, right now, I feel okay.

'They suit you,' I say, nodding at the glasses propped on Preston's nose.

'Thanks, I've not got the faintest idea whose they are,' he replies as he removes the cigarette from behind his ear to take a drag. 'They're far too strong, though I enjoy the challenge. How's your friend?'

It takes me a second to realise who he's talking about. 'Alive, as far as I'm aware.'

'That's always encouraging.' Preston rests his cigarette behind his ear again, and it's putting me on edge. 'Come on then, what's the source of your melancholy?'

'Huh?'

'Your facial expressions resembled those of a death row inmate's throughout the entirety of last night, and still does on this pleasantly crisp winter morning, so I'm curious.'

'I'm fine,' I mumble, and I don't think I've ever sounded more unconvincing.

I wait for Preston to press me for more details, but he says nothing for a while. Just sort of watches me as he dabs out his cigarette on the grass, which I'd usually scold him for, but find myself frozen from the weight of his gaze.

'Okay,' he says, and just when I think he's going to leave it at that, he speaks again. ''The spoken word is silver but the unspoken is golden'.'

He had to get one out there, didn't he? I can't help but wonder what would happen to him if a day passed without spewing out a melodramatic quote. I imagine he'd self-combust.

'Which great philosopher or whatever I've never heard of said that one, then?' I ask, my eyebrows raised.

'None. It's from War and Peace.' With that, Preston suddenly jumps up from the ground. 'Book eleven, if I'm not mistaken.'

He winks at me, then strolls back into the house without another word.

The second Robbie drops me home that day, I know something isn't right. It's nothing explicit; it's not like I walk in on my parents screaming bloody murder at each other, but a cloud of uneasiness stalks me as I stand in the hallway. In a flimsy attempt to avoid whatever's wrong, instead of wandering into the living room, I run straight upstairs. I've barely been in my room five minutes when I hear footsteps on the landing. Within seconds, there's a knock on my door. If it's Dad, I might scream.

'Hey sweetie, I didn't realise you were coming home this early.'

It's not Dad, it's Mum. I flash her a strained smile, and she responds by entering my room and sitting at the end of my bed. I'm about to ask Mum if she can give me a few hours to have a nap, leaving me to avoid whatever it is that's wrong, when she speaks again.

'Listen, Mia, there's something I need to tell you.'

There it is.

'I'm not sure you've realised, but your father and I living under the same roof is... difficult. I can't--Well, I can't do it. We've decided it's best we don't keep doing it, and--'

'Dad's moving out?'

'No, honey, I am.'

I couldn't stop my jaw dropping if I tried. What? What? Why the hell is Mum moving out? She's done nothing wrong. Where is she going? In what world is this fair? My confusion must be slapped straight across my face because Mum is quickly rushing through an explanation.

'He's not--Dad's not struggling with the current setup like I am, he's okay with it, and--Well, as far as he's concerned, it's okay, so he doesn't want to move. It's difficult to explain.' Mum's voice drifts off slightly as she must realise no amount of justifying the situation makes it okay. 'I just--Honestly, Mia, I can't stay in this house. With or without Dad here, it's... It's too difficult.'

'Can I come with you?' is all I can say.

She shakes her head, and I don't know if it's the exhaustion messing with me, but I think her eyes are misting up. 'I'm moving to Cerys's place for a little while, and it's only small, but the second I have somewhere of my own, you can move straight in.'

I don't know what to say, so I don't say anything. Instead, I stand up off my bed, and wrap my arms around my mother as she tries, and fails, not to let herself cry in front of me.

'I'm sorry, honey,' she whispers as I tighten my grip around her. 'I'm so sorry about everything.'

I'm doing it again. I'm imagining everyone around me being dead one day. I try shaking the feeling off as someone laughs, and a flurry of cigarette smoke dissolves into the dark sky. The cold gnaws at my nose. Mum's been out of the family home a few weeks now, and it's been as horrible as I'd expected. I barely speak to Dad anymore, not that we were exactly best mates to start with, and I avoid being home as much as possible.

Someone shouts in the distance, and my attention is snapped back to the present. It's freezing, and I'd rather not be sitting on the lawn outside Cardiff City Hall at midnight, but then I'd pick this over home any day.

'C'mon, Mia, give it a go!'

I blink as I fully return to reality, and focus my eyes in front of me. Robbie's sitting there with a grin on his face, while Preston lies on the grass beside him. The three of us are on the lawn, while the others are pushing each other around city hall's car park in an old supermarket trolley. The grass underneath me is a little moist, and there's a main road running along the edge of this large field, so it's far from the relaxed atmosphere I crave. Delyth's shrieking laughter emanating from the trolley isn't helping.

Aiden and I have been hanging around with Preston and Robbie a lot more recently, and it's proved to be a great excuse to get out of my house. It's usually Robbie who asks us.

'I'll push you, if you want,' Robbie continues as he nods at the group behind him.

Assuming he's asking me to do so, I can't really say I'm in the mood to sit in a trolley and roll around Cardiff all night. I shake my head with a shrug as the sound of Aiden cackling echoes around me. I think he's the one pushing Delyth.

'Go on, babe, live a little,' Preston says from the ground. I can almost hear the grin on his face when he says, 'do it and I'll let you make out with me afterwards.'

I roll my eyes. 'I'd rather not catch herpes tonight, thanks.'

The boys laugh, Preston seeming especially amused. 'Fine, I'll let you make out with Robbie then.'

Robbie playfully punches him in the stomach, but Preston only laughs harder. This is the first time he's acknowledged me all night, and he's already making me want to drown him in the fountain a few feet away. He doesn't pay much attention to me when his personality disorder decides to make him Zack, and I prefer it that way. The fact he can't even be Preston when it's just Robbie and me really makes me question what the hell his and Robbie's friendship actually is.

Preston is still laughing hysterically when Robbie turns back to me with flushed cheeks. 'Ignore him, he's an arsehole. C'mon, I'll push you.'

Nobody still has any clue about what's going on with my parents, not even Aiden. I know it's probably a stupid idea to keep it all to myself, but I hardly feel mentally damaged by it. I don't need comfort from others. Having the capability to feel sod all is a pretty good coping mechanism, and besides, it would feel wrong to tell Aiden. He's always so happy and bright, and even discussing bad weather with him feels too negative.

'I don't know...' I say, finally replying to Robbie. 'Maybe.'

'Okay then, fine, I'll raise the stakes,' Preston butts into the conversation again. 'Do it, and I'll keep guard for you and Robbie to have a quickie behind city hall.'

This time Robbie hits him in the crotch, and I don't think I've ever been so happy to see someone in pain. Preston's laughter catches in his throat, and he doubles over on the ground with his hands cupped around his groin. He's still somehow laughing, not that what he said was remotely funny in the first place.

'Screw it,' I say, turning back to Robbie. 'I may as well give it a go.'

What can I say? Seeing Preston writhing in pain has cheered me up.

Robbie grins. He stands up, reaches his hand out, and lifts me to my feet. Preston's still grappling his crotch as Robbie leads me towards the others, but he manages to call from behind us.

'I'm only friends with you because your surname's Morrissey and I like The Smiths!'

Robbie responds by lifting his middle finger into the air.

'Holy mackerel, you're not actually going to have a go, are you, Mia?' Aiden exclaims as he bounces towards us.

He's wearing a bright orange jacket, and I'm surprised he hasn't caused any car crashes yet. I nod with a shrug, and he literally squeals.

'Let me push you, I want to push you! Oh my God, it will be like our childhood all over again! Remember when you tried teaching me to skateboard, and I pushed you down that massive hill, and then you flew off it and landed on a cat.' He pauses. 'I won't throw you onto a cat this time, scout's honour.'

I turn to Robbie questioningly, and he shrugs with a smile. Taking that as a go ahead, Aiden grabs my hand and pulls me towards the group. A Blink 182 song blasts in my ears as we approach them, and it takes me a while to realise it's coming from wireless speakers in Samantha's hands. It's the closest thing to any noise she's ever made. Delyth's lifting herself out of the trolley, and as her eyes clasp onto where my hand is in Aiden's, she looks like she's about to eat me alive. Someone needs to tell her Aiden's gay. They really, really do.

I don't properly know anyone else in the group besides Samantha, but then all she ever does is stare and smile at me. She's doing exactly that as Aiden helps me into the trolley. Robbie's caught up with us by the time I'm sitting inside it, but Preston is still lying on the otherwise empty lawn. My heart's beating out of time to the song pulsating from Samantha's speakers, and there's not a car or a soul in sight. The car park must be several hundred yards long, and I don't think city hall has ever looked so threatening. It stands to my left, towering over me as if one little nudge could send it crashing to the ground.

I grasp onto the trolley's sides, its metal freezing against my clammy palms. I swallow hard. The music suddenly changes, and Pendulum's Witchcraft starts playing. Aiden grabs the trolley's handle. This was a bad idea. This was a really, really bad idea. My voice competes against the music as I try telling Aiden I've changed my mind, but he doesn't even blink. I clench my eyes shut.

The song's chorus kicks in, and Aiden starts pushing. My eyes are still closed, my palms are sweating. The trolley's speed is accelerating every second, and the uneven concrete below me is causing it to wobble. What if I fall out? Oh shit, I'm going to fall out, aren't I? I yelp. Aiden's running, the music's getting louder and louder, and the moment the beat kicks in, he lets go. I scream as a wave of emotion almost knocks me over. Fear floods my bloodstream, anger over Aiden letting go vibrates in my brain, and the frustration of having no control looms over me like a heavy mist.

And then I laugh.

I laugh because for the first time in what feels like forever, I feel something. I feel everything. I want to jump out of this trolley and charge after Aiden, I want to scream and cry in fear, and I want to laugh at my irrationality. I finally open my eyes, and the wind rushes into them. It stings, but I don't care because it makes me feel alive. It makes me feel human. I zoom past a parking meter as a discarded polystyrene box swirls into the air, and I'm charging towards blackness as I approach the end of the car park. I'm about to let go of the trolley's sides and lift my arms up when I come to an abrupt stop.

I spin my head around to see Aiden behind me again, the trolley's handle firm in his grasp. I hadn't even realised he was running after me. Everyone else is standing in the middle of the car park now, which probably explains the music getting louder. All I know is that I want to go again. I need to go again.

'Do it again!' I yell at Aiden.

He laughs, and being the true best friend he is, he does exactly as I requested. He reverses me back towards the group, and as we near them, he starts spinning around. The trolley and I spin with him, and the exhilaration comes rushing back over me like a tsunami. It dances around my body as Aiden pushes, pulls, and spins me around the car park. I lift my arms up and feel like I could fall out any second, but I don't care. Faces turn into blurs, and everything around me becomes less and less real. The only thing connecting me to reality is the music seeping into my ears.

I'm feeling nothing again, but this nothing is different. This nothing is good. It's as if I'm floating. It's as if the trolley is a fragment of my imagination, with everything else around me piecing together the rest of this fantastical world. Maybe I am floating, and maybe this is reality. Maybe what I thought was real--my parents, college, Aiden, Robbie, Preston, everyone else--are just illusions. Maybe all these people won't be dead one day after all because what isn't real can't ever die. Maybe I'm just a body floating aimlessly through space, content in the nothingness that surrounds me.

The music suddenly stops, the song changes, and I snap my eyes open.

'Earth to Mia... Hello?' Robbie laughs as he finally catches my attention. He's standing in front of the motionless trolley. 'Give someone else a go.'

'Sorry,' I say as my cheeks flush.

He helps lift me out of the trolley, and I jump onto the concrete with a soft thud. The ground doesn't feel real anymore. Adrenaline pumps through my veins, and it still feels like I'm spinning. Delyth grabs the trolley from beside me, but before she can do anything with it, a hand snatches it from hers.

'My go.' Preston winks at her.

Rude. I hadn't realised Preston had joined the rest of us, and neither did anyone else judging by the surprised looks on their faces. Instead of staying put, Preston pushes the trolley out of the car park, and onto the pavement framing it. He's heading towards the steps of the underpass, and knowing his distinct lack of safety awareness, he's probably planning to ride it down those. To my relief, he goes past the stairs. He must be heading for the ramp instead.

As he reaches the top of the ramp, Preston gets Robbie to steady the trolley, then effortlessly jumps into it. There's a dead end at the bottom, and you have to take a sharp right turn to follow the underpass leading to the other side of the main road. Otherwise you'll get a face full of concrete. Despite that, Preston asks Robbie to push him straight down the ramp.

'Zack, mate, you do realise there's a wall at the bottom of it, right?'

Robbie raises his eyebrows, his voice ringing with amusement, and his hands still grasping the trolley. I can only just hear him over the music blaring from Samantha's speakers.

'Yep.'

'As in a hard, concrete thing you'll crash into and probably get yourself killed with?'

'Yep.'

Robbie raises his eyebrows again.

'Don't sweat it, I have it covered,' Preston reasons.

Robbie laughs as he does the most idiotic thing I've ever seen him do. He pushes the trolley just enough for it to start wheeling down the ramp.

'It's your funeral!'

I gape at the scene before me. Is Robbie stupid? He's already almost seen Preston dead once, so why on earth did he just do that? Preston stands up in the trolley with his legs slightly bent. What the hell is he doing? Why is he standing up? Dear God, does he have a death wish? He's grinning. He's actually smiling at the fact he's about to slam head first into a concrete wall.

I stare, my face contorted into an expression of complete distress. He's seconds away from hitting the wall now. I'm biting my lip to stop myself from yelping, and I can't take my eyes off him. He's inches away. Centimetres. Just as I'm about to give in and scream after him, Preston jumps, flips backwards, and lands feet first onto the concrete, stumbling slightly. Meanwhile, the trolley slams into the wall with an ear-shattering crash.

Robbie runs down the ramp to high-five him while everyone else stares in admiration. I think I almost just spewed out all of my internal organs.

Now that Preston's done showing off, I turn away and sit on the metal railing beside me. I can feel the coldness of it through my jeans, and the blue colour it's been painted with is peeling off. I pick at it as I watch Robbie high-five Preston once more while the others watch on, some still looking amazed at what just happened. I shake my head. There is something seriously wrong with that kid.

I'm about to stand back up when Delyth breaks away from the group, and sits down next to me.

'So what's the deal with you and Robbie?' she asks in a casual but clearly delving for gossip sort of way. 'Not that I'm assuming anything, but y'know, it seems like you two are into each other or something. I was just wondering because, like, does that mean you're over Aiden?'

What? Delyth carries on rambling per usual, but I don't process a word she says. She thinks I had a thing for Aiden? Up to now, I've been half-joking about her fancying him, but the reality of my theory is slapping me in the face like a wet fish. Oh no, the poor girl... I should tell her, shouldn't I? No one else seems to have so far, and she clearly isn't figuring it out for herself.

'Don't worry, Delyth.' I interrupt her mid-sentence. 'I've never had a thing for Aiden, I can assure you of that.'

'C'mon, Mia.' She nudges me with a wink. 'You so fancied him. Are you sure you still don't?'

'Del, seriously, I've never fancied Aiden in my life.'

'You so have!'

'I really haven't--'

'You have!'

Delyth's voice is raised, her eyes narrowed. Her lip is curled, and her hands are grabbing onto the railing so tightly that her knuckles have turned white.

'I bet this whole Robbie thing is just a front to make me think you're over Aiden... That's it, isn't--'

'Delyth, Aiden's gay.'

That shuts her up. Her agitated look disappears, and her face turns blank. She purses her lips and swallows hard as guilt starts creeping in on me. I shouldn't have said that so bluntly. Bless her, she probably really likes him, doesn't she? She must be dead embarrassed right now. I mean, I take my hat off to her for not stereotyping and assuming Aiden's sexuality from the get go.

I'm about to comfort her--heck, I'm tempted to wrap my arms around her and give her a hug--when she smiles. Not the embarrassed smile I expected though. The kind of smile that says, let's be best friends forever and ever, and have loads of sleepovers so can I rip your limbs off while you sleep, chop them up, spit on them, boil them, and then feed them to all your friends and family.

'Look, you can say you don't all you want.' A strand of dark, wavy hair falls over her face. 'You obviously fancy Aiden, but no way am I letting you win him. You can make shit up about him all you want, but I am not giving up that easily. I've never lost anything in my life, and I don't plan to start now.'

Delyth shoots me her I will kill you in your sleep grin again, stands up, and struts back over to the group. Well, that was deeply unnerving. I'm not sure whether to burst out laughing, or to start sleeping with a knife.

Chapter 10

Throughout the next week or so, Dad begins acting strangely. I can't pinpoint what it is exactly, just that he's avoiding me, and when he does see me he turns all soft. I figure the guilt might be driving him insane, especially when on Wednesday night, he orders us a takeaway and allows me to eat it in the living room. Maybe he's found out that I've taken up rolling around in trollies in the middle of the city late at night, and he's not quite sure how to deal with it. It's not until the Saturday night that it all makes sense.

I stare blankly ahead of me, and I don't utter a word. I don't know what to say. I couldn't even conjure up a coherent sentence if I tried. He can't be serious. He cannot be serious. I lift my gaze to Dad, who's sitting on the sofa opposite the TV, and his lips are pursed as he awaits my response. His hands nervously rub against each other, and he's tapping his foot on the carpet. I run my fingers along the fabric of the sofa I'm sitting on. That scuff is still there.

'What?' I finally ask.

'The last thing I want to do is upset you, Mia, and you know I'd hate to make you uncomfortable in your own home. Gwen has nowhere else to go though, darling, and her husband's been awful to her after everything that--'

'No.' I grit my teeth. 'I'm sorry, but no way is that woman living here.'

'We don't have a choice.' The softness of Dad's voice makes me want to puke.

'Um, yes we do, Dad. She doesn't have to live here.'

What does he expect? He just told me his girlfriend---the reason Mum's life has been distorted out of shape--is moving into this house. My house. He can't honestly expect me to be okay with that. I scan Dad's face in hope of finding something that implies he's kidding, but I know all too well that he's dead serious.

Dad sighs. He drops his head into his hands, and his heavy breath is impossible to ignore. When he looks up again, his eyes are bloodshot, and for the first time in my life, I think I might see my father cry. He clears his throat, stands up, and moves across the living room to sit next to me. I shuffle away from him.

'Mia, I know all of this is my fault. I know I never should have cheated on your mum, and I know I should have just told her I wanted to separate before anything happened with Gwen.' I try to interrupt him, but he hushes me. 'But even parents make mistakes. Even parents can be careless, and stupid, and immature. I loved your mum. I really, really did. Something just went wrong along the way, and I was too scared to try and fix it. I let everything build up until it came crashing back down, and I cannot tell you how much I hate myself for that. I want to make everything okay again so desperately, and I'm trying, Mia. I'm really trying.'

'What part of Gwen moving in is trying, Dad?' I bite..

'She and I are in a relationship, and in the long run, you have to get used to that.'

I don't want to have to get used to anything. I just want everything the way it was before. Gwen has visited the house occasionally, but I've made myself scarce every time. I've never spoken to the woman before, and now she's going to be living in my home.

'Look, we'll stay out of your way as much as we can, and Gwen will be here as little as possible. I don't expect you to play happy families with her, and I don't expect you to even acknowledge her when she's here. I know that'll come in your own time.' Dad looks up at me, and there's a hint of desperation in his eyes. 'Gwen doesn't have enough money to get her own place, and her friends and family have no space in their houses for her. Please just try and understand why she needs to stay here for a while.'

I understand. Understanding isn't the problem. Accepting the fact that the woman Dad cheated on Mum with is going to be living in the same house as me is the problem. Accepting the fact she'll be cooking food in Mum's oven, watching the TV Mum used to watch, showering in the same shower Mum used to use, sleeping on Mum's side of the bed. That's the problem.

I need to get out of this house.

'I'm going for a walk,' I mutter as I stand up.

I hadn't noticed until now, but I'm warm. I'm really bloody warm. I'm even sweating a little. I leave the living room, and Dad follows. There are blank spaces on the walls where photos of Mum and Dad once hung, and it's impossible to ignore the space right next to the front door where their wedding photo was. The whole hallway looks empty, not just the walls.

'Mia, please just talk to me. Look, I'll--I'll call Gwen and ask if she can stay at a hotel for a few days or something until you get used to the idea, please just don't--'

'Dad, it's fine!' I don't mean to, but I shout. 'It's fine... I just... I just need to walk for a bit, okay?'

Dad says nothing. He nods his head, and I don't think I've ever seen him look so defeated. His grey hair looks dull, his face washed out. Dad's usually bright blue eyes are the one thing I'm glad I inherited from him, and it unnerves me to think mine probably have the same tired look in them right now. I force a tiny smile as if I'm trying to apologise to him--for what, I don't know--and head out the door.

I try keeping my mind clear of any thoughts throughout my walk, especially ones related to Dad. Mum texts me asking if I want to visit her at her friend's place after college on Monday, but I don't respond. I'm trying hard to shove anything parent-related out of my mind right now. Dad's still refusing to leave the house, so I only ever visit Mum for a few hours every other day at her friend's place. Every time I see her it's like she's waiting for me to break down, and I know I won't. I can't. And it's horrible because the expectant look she has on her face every time I visit her makes me want to visit less and less, just so I don't have to see it.

I'm on the outskirts of Pontcanna when I realise where I am. I stop beside a recognisable bus stop, and stare at a turn in the road ahead of me. Screw it, it's not like I have anywhere better to go. I pick up my pace and head for the turning that leads to Preston's house. As I turn into his street, there's a curly-haired boy riding a cherry coloured bicycle along the pavement. He has the darkest hair I've ever seen, and as I catch his eyes, he smiles at me to show a set of teeth as white as piano keys.

Preston's middle-aged neighbour is on the driveway washing his car, and as I approach him, he glares at me as if I'm the sole reason his car is dirty and needs cleaning in the middle of a cold January afternoon. I notice a man peeking through one of the house's windows, but he hastily closes his curtains upon the realisation that I've spotted him. Geez, friendly neighbourhood then. I pace down Preston's driveway, and knock on the front door. It's closed, and I'm not sure what to make of that.

I wait a few minutes, but there's no answer. There are two cars parked on the driveway, so I can't imagine no one's home. Whenever I've been here before, in fact, there hasn't been a single car on the driveway. I knock the door again. This time, I see movement through the glass panels, and I step back slightly as it opens. A middle-aged woman, who I can only assume is Preston's mother, stands in front of me with a puzzled expression on her face. Her hair looks like it's meant to be a blonde colour, but it's more of a dull grey.

'Um, hey, is Preston around?' I ask.

The woman raises her eyebrows and mutters something inaudible under her breath. 'Preston Maddox?'

I nod a reply.

'Preston Maddox doesn't live here, I can assure you of that.' Someone calls from inside the house, and the woman glances behind her. She turns back to me. 'If you're friends with that boy, I'd suggest you cut ties with him immediately. He doesn't have a good bone in his body.'

I open my mouth to say something, but the door is slammed in my face before I can get a single sound out. What the hell just happened?

I don't move for at least a minute. Instead, I stand perfectly still on the front porch, and stare at the white door. Of course Preston lives here. I've been inside the house twice, and I've collected work books from him here plenty of other times. He's thrown a house party here, for Pete's sake. And geez, what has he done to that woman to make her hate him so much? How does she even know him?

When I start making my way back up the driveway, questions are buzzing around my head like insects I can't swat. At least it's taken my mind off Dad, but I don't think I've ever been more confused in my life. I'm so lost in my thoughts that I don't realise at first when someone calls after me. It's only when I reach the end of Preston's street do I take notice of the voice. I turn around at the sound of it.

'Hey, lady!' It's the boy with the bike. He cycles over and stops beside me. His face is flushed, and he catches his breath for a few moments. 'Are you looking for Preston?'

I nod slowly.

The boy flashes me his pristinely white teeth again. 'Follow me. I'm Matty.''

Partly because I desperately need to make some sense of this craziness, and partly because I'll do anything to keep away from home, I do just that. Matty dismounts his bike as he begins leading me out of his neighbourhood.

About twenty minutes later, Matty has led me over the River Taff, past Cardiff's museum, and through Cathays train station. I don't know how the boy has so much energy. He can't be any older than ten, and I've got no idea where the kid's parents are. We've just entered Cathays when Matty rests his bike against the crumbled wall of a dreary looking house. There's nothing to see besides rows upon rows of terraced housing, and the overcast sky makes the bland colours of their bricks hard to ignore. The contrast between these dingy houses and the grand ones in Pontcanna is unmistakable, and the terraced one we're standing outside is boarded up.

The front door is wide open, but it doesn't look like a soul has stepped foot in it for years. Despite that, Matty cheerfully skips up the overgrown pathway, and heads straight into the building. I stare at the doorway in bewilderment without moving an inch. That is until I realise a small child has just wandered into a boarded up house that is creepy as shit, and looks like it could eat him alive. I curse under my breath. Why do I always manage to get myself into these stupid situations? I sigh, then run into the house after Matty.

Once I'm inside, there's no sign of anyone, or anything for that matter. The narrow hallway is completely empty. There's a window beside the door letting in some much needed light, but other than that, it's dark. I scrunch my nose as the bland smell of dust overrides my senses, and I notice a stairway to my left. There are four doors on this floor, all of which are closed. There are no decorations on the wall, no colours, and nothing that suggests any sign of life. Surely, Preston can't be here? My heart feels like it's beating in my head, and my breaths are slow and heavy. I swallow.

'Matty?'

Nothing but a slight echo, followed by silence.

'Matty!'

There's panic in my voice this time. I call again. Still nothing. I call again, and again, and again, but not a single shout gets any kind of response. I think I'm starting to sweat. I tuck my hair behind my ears, and wipe my forehead with the sleeve of my jacket. Maybe all this is just bad karma. I mean, I did follow a random kid to the other side of town, and I'm sure that can be classed as kidnapping in one way or another. I call Matty's name again. Nothing.

There's no sign of life on this floor, so my best bet is to try the stairs. I take a deep breath in preparation, but end up inhaling a load of dust. I cough until my throat's so dry that I can't splutter anymore. Focus, I think to myself as I gain back my composure. As I approach the stairs, I notice a small metal lamp tucked away at the bottom of them. It's hardly an ideal weapon, and if there was anything dangerous in here, it surely would have sprung on me by now, but I pick it up anyway. I take the lampshade off to make it easier for me to swing it at anything if need be. Ensuring not to inhale deeply this time, I make my way upstairs. Each step creaks as I begin my incline.

I pause when I reach the top. There's a muffling sound. Is that a TV? Radio maybe? I listen for a few more seconds. It's music. There are only three doors on this floor, and I figure the music is too muffled to be coming from one of the two a few steps to my left. There is as little decoration here as there was downstairs, although the smell of dust has almost vanished. The walls and floor don't look as murky either.

'Matty!' I call again, but as expected, there's no response. 'Preston?'

Still nothing. I've got to risk it. With the lamp tightly in my grasp, I tip-toe towards the door the music's coming from. I have to bite my tongue as I approach it because I'm scared that if I don't, my heart will catapult out of my mouth. I swallow. Just a few more steps. I'm struggling to keep hold of the lamp because my hands are so clammy. The music is loud, but I can't concentrate on what's playing. I hope to God this is Preston.

Once I'm inches away from the door, I lift the lamp above my head in preparation, and reach for the handle. I shut my eyes and breathe out slowly.

'Okay, after three,' I mutter to myself. 'One... Two... Th--'

The door suddenly swings open. I scream, clamp my eyes shut, and drive the lamp forward. It slams against something hard, and it's not until I hear a thud that I open my eyes.

I slap my hand over my mouth, and drop the lamp onto the wooden floor. It lands with a bang. Lying in the doorway in front of me is Preston. His eyes are shut and there's a small trail of blood running down his left temple. My hand is still covering my mouth when I lift my head back up, and standing a few feet behind Preston is a wide-eyed Matty. Shit.

I quickly kneel down. 'Hey?' I shake Preston's arm, but get no response. 'Preston? Hey? Wake up... C'mon, I--Oh, God. Preston?.'

CHAPTER 11

'So hey, I was just wondering,' I say with a shrug of my shoulders. 'Are you going to, y'know, tell me what the hell is going on?'

'And I was just wondering if you were considering answering my question any time in the foreseeable future?' Preston replies.

'What? What question?'

'Whether or not anyone's ever told you that your name sounds like an STD.'

'Oh, shut up!'

Preston laughs as he dabs his left temple with a piece of bloodied tissue. I wait for him to say something else, but his laughter just fizzles into silence. Matty's laying out some playing cards beside the mattress Preston and I are sitting on, and I've still got no idea who the boy actually is. The only sound filling my ears is the battery operated stereo beside the mattress playing a Motown album, which Matty mouths along to.

The room is massive, and it must take up the majority of the second floor. It's spotless, too. There are mismatching kitchen units in one corner, along with a small table and two wooden stools, but the majority of the room is empty besides a few random chairs dotted around the place. There's a half full clothing rail behind me, and a few boxes spread about, but nothing has any order to it. There's a mattress slap bang in the middle of the room, and the walls are decorated with childlike drawings and photographs, but there isn't a single light switched on. Instead, it's illuminated by candles.

They're dotted all over the place, most of them resting atop the disorganised furniture. Their flames create a soft glow over everything, and they must be scented because there's a fresh, woody aroma circling the room. It's oddly beautiful, and the glowing candles are having a peculiar effect on me. I feel calm. In fact, I don't know the last time I felt so relaxed, which is entirely irrational given the situation.

My eyes continue dancing around the room until Preston mutters something, and I turn my full attention back to him. He's gazing into the mirror opposite us as he slowly waves his hand in front of it, making the oversized jumper he's wearing drape off his arms.

'Reflections have always captivated--'

'Oh, for the love of God.' I groan loudly. 'For once, Preston, just once, please can you cut the pretentious bullshit and actually be straight with me? Tell me what's going on before I dive my face into this mattress and suffocate myself with it.'

Preston fights a smirk off his face as he lies down and shuts his eyes for a few moments. I'm about to seriously consider carrying out my threat when he reopens them, stares ahead of him, and speaks again.

'Matty's my brother, he's just turned eight, and he lives with his foster parents in Pontcanna. I live here, and stay at their house whenever they're away.'

I'm momentarily taken aback by his candidness. The house I've been to countless times before isn't Preston's? What, do Matty's foster parents just hand Preston their house keys and tell him to have fun while they're away? If the woman who answered the door to me earlier is anything to go by, they'd rather shove Preston face first into a blender than even dream of doing that. I guess Matty being his brother explains the childish room in Preston's house, least what I thought was Preston's house, but he's never mentioned a brother before. Why is his brother fostered, but not him? Where are their parents?

I watch Matty, who's humming to himself as he plays with his cards. He glances up at me and smiles, his dark curly hair falling over his eyes. How can he and Preston even be brothers? They literally look nothing alike, from skin-tone to eye colour.

Preston must notice my confusion because he starts chuckling. 'Different fathers.'

I nod slowly. 'Do Matty's foster parents really let you stay there while they're away?'

Preston's chuckles turn to laughter. 'I never said they let me. I just said I did it.' He shrugs. 'It's not uncommon for them to be absent from the house. They're away every school holiday, and most weekends. I simply use that to my advantage.'

He's basically telling me that he breaks into the house, isn't he? How he does that is beyond me, and I'm not sure I even want to know.

I nod again. 'So what, do you rent this place or something?' I ask, glancing around the room. 'I actually like it; it's bigger than it looks from the outside. Sort of like a dysfunctional TARDIS or something. Why are all the lights off, though? And what's up with downstairs? I mean, geez, a little polish wouldn't go a mi--'

'I don't pay rent, I'm a squatter.'

Preston is on his feet before I have a chance to respond. He throws his bloodied tissue into a black bin bag on the floor, and walks towards the makeshift kitchen area.

A squatter? Is that even legal? I guess that explains the lack of electricity and the murkiness of the rest of the house. It makes no sense to me though. Preston is someone with an easy life. He's always so casual about everything, which hardly gives off the impression that he's... well, homeless. I mean, that's what he is. He doesn't legally live anywhere. I gaze at Preston as he shuffles some cups around on a kitchen counter, and I suddenly feel bad for him--awful, in fact. I can whine about Gwen moving in all I want, but at least I have a good home for her to move into in the first place.

I still have a million questions swimming around my brain, but as I watch Preston silently move around the kitchen, I figure now's not the best time to spring them all on him. I've made a dent in his face with a lamp already today, so I'd rather not add fuel to the fire.

'Don't worry, he never makes sense,' Matty mutters, and I turn to him.

His playing cards are now in a neat pile beside him. I laugh a little as he nods at Preston, and rolls his eyes. I couldn't agree more.

'What's a squatter, anyways? It sounds like a fruit, is it a fruit?' He pulls a sour face. 'I don't like fruit. I like fruit flavoured sweeties, they're nice. Do they still count?'

Matty watches me with innocence pouring out of his eyes, and I kind of want to pull him into a massive hug. Unsure of how to respond, I start twirling some of my hair around my index finger, and stammer a little.

'It's not a fruit, no, uh...'

'As for your other question,' Preston suddenly chimes in. He's moved away from the corner of the room, and is now standing next to us. He sits down onto the mattress. 'I'd be careful, pal. Fruit flavoured sweets are the grown ups' way to make kids eat real fruit. They're made in factories where all the fruits you could ever imagine are shrunk until they're so small that--'

'Until they look like sweeties?'

'Please, that would be way too obvious.' Preston rolls his eyes as if Matty's question was the most ridiculous thing he's ever heard. 'They shrink the fruit so much that it becomes invisible, and then...' He pauses dramatically as Matty's eyes widen. 'Then they hide them inside the sweets so that all you kids will eat fruit without ever knowing.'

Matty's eyes are wider than ever, and his plump lips slowly curve upwards. Preston winks at him as if sealing a deal, and Matty winks in return. I can't not smile. He gazes at Preston with more admiration than I ever would have thought possible, and Preston grins back. His eyes focus on Matty's face as if trying to take in every single feature. It's like there's a sense of desperation there, like Matty could suddenly vanish and all he'd be left with is right here, right now.

'So, Euphemia.' Preston taps my arm as he stands back up. 'What brings you to my humble abode?'

The small smile on my face vanishes as thoughts of Dad and Gwen come crashing back into my head. I purse my lips together. Matty's not paying attention and is playing with his cards again, but Preston's eyeing me expectantly. I don't want to tell him anything, I'm not ready. Besides, my issues seem irrelevant now that I know the extent of his.

'Nothing in particular, I was just walking past your house--Well, you know what I mean, and figured I'd drop by.'

Preston nods. I wait for him to ask for a deeper explanation, or tell me I'm lying, or even just give me a funny look, but nothing comes. He nods again, as if he completely understands that the last thing I want are questions. It's times like these I realise how different Zack Maddox is to the young man standing in front of me. Sure, he's really damn weird, but I'd shove Zack out of existence any day for the person he is right now.

'Why do you do it?' The words leave my mouth before I even realise.

'Do what?' Preston replies as he heads back towards the kitchen.

'Why do you change yourself to become someone you're not, someone so much worse?'

'Control,' he answers simply.

'I don't--What?'

'Happiness is all about control. Happiness can only be real when we're pretending because when we're pretending, we're in control. You know how when we were kids, when we'd run around like idiots and play pretend, and it was impossible to feel bad because we became what we were pretending to be? That's it; that's happiness. We could be whoever we wanted, and do whatever we wanted, and it never mattered because we could be someone entirely different the next day.' He shrugs. 'We could start again.'

I watch silently as Preston turns around and reaches for a cupboard. What is he talking about? He brings out three cans of cola, and throws one to me. Having the hand-eye coordination skills of a blind sloth, I miss the can, and it lands in front of me on the mattress. Preston throws one towards Matty, and he catches it effortlessly. He flicks it open and begins glugging. Matty and I have full fat versions of the drink, but Preston's is diet. I watch him questioningly, and he shrugs.

'I've heard diet kills you quicker.'

I roll my eyes. 'Not everything has to have some existential meaning, you know.'

'I'm screwing with you,' Preston says with a laugh. 'Regular tastes like shit.'

The room is darker now, and it suddenly hits me that I should probably text Dad to tell him I haven't been abducted. I send him a quick text saying I'm over Aiden's house because I'm not sure how he'd feel about me sitting on a mattress in the middle of an abandoned building. When I look up from my phone, Matty's sitting at the small table in the kitchen area with his cards. Preston is lying down next to me, and he's staring at a lighter in his hands.

'Aren't Matty's foster parents going to be freaking out? We've been gone for over an hour now,' I ask him as he flicks the lighter on. 'I'm not even sure he told them he was coming here.'

Preston smirks. 'Oh yeah, of course. They're probably trying to initiate a warrant for my arrest as we speak. Accuse me of kidnapping or something.' He inspects the flame bursting out of the lighter, then blows it out. 'But I honestly couldn't give a flying shit.'

'Do you not see him often?'

Preston doesn't say anything. He just shakes his head. I'm really starting to wonder who the boys' real parents are, and where they are. I'm lucky. My parents may be all over the place right now, but at least they're there. My gaze follows Preston as he flicks the lighter on and off repeatedly, and through an episode of momentary craziness, I finally say it.

'It's my parents.' I speak more loudly than intended. I lower my voice. 'I mean, the reason I ended up looking for you was my parents. Well, my dad more specifically, but stuff regarding the both of them. They've... They're in the middle of splitting up after my dad had an affair, and I know you probably don't care, but I swear it's driving me crazy.'

I try to leave it at that, but before I even realise I'm doing it, more words are spilling out of my mouth like a broken faucet.

'It's driving me crazy because I'm finding it so hard to feel something. The only time I can say I actually feel anything towards it is when I think my mum's upset or my dad's being an arse, and it's like--it's like I'm feeling for other people's pain, but not my own, like inside I'm nothing. I want to hurt. It's like I'm craving to feel any kind of pain, and it scares me. It scares me that I want to feel that badly.' My throat's swelling up, and the last words leave my mouth in a squeak. 'What's wrong with me?'

I've got no idea if I made any sense, or if Preston was listening in the first place. I don't even know if I want him to have been listening. All I know is that my tongue feels like it's buzzing, and I sort of want to throw up. I've basically just laid out everything I didn't want anyone to ever know, and the thought is making me feel sick. I don't look at Preston because I'm afraid of what his response will be, and I wait. At least a minute passes.

'There's nothing wrong with you.' His voice is so soft that I believe him without question. 'Everyone wants to feel hurt. Nobody admits it, but we do. It makes us feel important, like we matter enough to warrant something so strong. It reminds us that we're alive, and when it's not there, we crave it.'

The Motown song seeping through the radio's speakers suddenly alternates, and the irrefutable sound of S Club 7 begins filling the room. Matty flips his head up to look at his brother, and an enormous grin grows on Preston's face. He leaps to his feet, discards his lighter onto the wooden floor, and within moments the two brothers are jumping around the room like lunatics.It's as if the conversation Preston and I just had never even existed, and I realise exactly what he meant about becoming another person. I watch the boys dance from the mattress, and even as the gloomy words Preston just spoke echo in my head, I can't help laughing a little.

They're still dancing along to the god-awful pop music when I lay down and rest my head onto the mattress's pillows. There's a blanket on the floor beside me, so I wrap myself in it. I lie on my side to watch a content Matty thrive in his childish world where a smile can make everything okay again. Preston throws his brother over his shoulder as Matty shrieks with laughter, and for a moment, I feel a little uneasy. As wonderful as it might be to push everything aside and become somebody else, you can't run away forever. You just can't.

CHAPTER 12

I wake to rap music. It takes a while for my mind to properly surface as thoughts, feelings and memories swarm my head, and it takes me even longer to realise where I am. I'm still at Preston's squat. I don't remember leaving it, anyway. I open my eyes, but I can't see anything except white because I'm wrapped up in a bundle of blankets, as if I'm floating on clouds spritzed with aftershave. Once I manage to sit up, I'm momentarily blinded by the sunlight streaming through the room's windows, and I can't help but desire the candlelight from last night to return.

I recognise the rap song as a Kanye West one just as I recognise Preston's figure above me. He hands me a glass of something clear. Water, I assume.

'What time is it?' I ask, still a little dazed. 'How long have I been asleep?'

He bites a chunk out of an apple in his hand as he sits onto the floor next to me. 'Well, you slept the whole night through, and it's now approximately.' He pauses as he glances down to his phone. 'Quarter to one in the afternoon.'

I widen my eyes. Is he serious? I'm all for a Sunday lie in, but bloody hell, I've been asleep so long that I've basically died and resurrected. I take a sip of the water Preston handed me as I sit up, and it clears my mind as it clears my throat. With the clarity come the questions. Has Dad tried contacting me? Where's Matty gone? Is he home? Does Mum know I ran out on Dad? Will I go home to find Gwen in the house? I begin with the only question Preston can answer.

'Has Matty left?'

He leans back and places his elbows onto the floor behind him for support. He nods. 'I drove him home when you were asleep last night.'

'You drive?' I ask before he can continue.

The first time I visited what I originally thought was Preston's house, he was walking home from college. Since then I've assumed he can't drive, or at least that he doesn't have a car. In fact, how on earth could he afford to keep a car? Per usual, Preston catches onto my confusion.

'I share a car with Robbie. He has it the majority of the time, but I'm insured on it. I help towards its MOT's and petrol, so he lets me use it occasionally. I have it for the weekend.'

I nod slowly. I guess that makes sense. But then let's face it: it's Preston, and nobody knows when the hell Preston's being completely honest. I don't even think he knows himself.

I take another gulp of water as I scramble around the mattress for my phone, and find a text from Dad. I have four missed calls from him too, and as I stare at his name on the screen in front of me, all I can think about is how I don't want to go back home and face him. Not yet. As I'm texting him back, a message from Mum comes through. I haven't seen her in days.

'We're in Miskin Street, right?' I ask Preston as he stands up. He nods. 'D'you know how far Roath is from here? My mum's staying with a friend there, so I was thinking I might go and see her.'

'It's about an hour walk,' he replies thoughtfully. He doesn't say anything else as he takes my empty glass and heads towards the kitchen area. He bites into his apple again. 'I'll drive you, if you want. It's barely ten minutes by car.'

'You sure?' I ask, a little surprised at his offer. 'If you don't mind, then yeah, that would be great, thanks.'

Preston shrugs with indifference. He drops my empty glass onto one of the units, and it's only now I question how he got the water. Is the plumbing working despite this place technically being unoccupied? There's a sink installed into one of the units, so it must be. I try not to question it any further because questioning is all I ever seem to do around Preston, and I'm beginning to wonder if I should just start accepting things for what they are.

By two o'clock, we're on our way to Roath. I've borrowed a jumper from Preston to pair with my jeans, and with his inability to wear clothing his size, it's absolutely enormous on me. I used to think he used practiced precision to achieve the I just rolled out of bed but it's blatantly obvious I spent at least two hours on my appearance look, but it turns out I was wrong. Five minutes before we left, he threw on whatever the hell he found first, then shoved his hair off his face, and it all just seemed to miraculously work in his favour. It sort of pissed me off. Of all people, it would be that easy for him to look good, wouldn't it? People would become physically ill at the sight of me if I put that little effort into my appearance.

The winter sun beams through the car windows as we drive through Cathays, and silence surrounds us. It's not an awkward silence, but one that makes me appreciate the sound of my own breathing. It's me who eventually breaks it.

'Sorry for last night. Y'know, with the whole breakdown thing,' I joke, but I say it a lot more meekly than intended.

Preston's eyes shift to me briefly, and he shrugs. 'It's better to talk about things. 'Unexpressed emotions will never die. They are buried alive and will come forth later in uglier ways'.'

'C'mon, who said that one then?'

'Freud.' We stop at a red light, and Preston turns to me. 'Just a pre-warning though; that one may lack accuracy, alongside the majority of his theories, so don't hold me to it.'

The light turns green, and we speed ahead. Preston's paisley patterned shirt is so baggy that it's hanging off his left shoulder. I've never noticed before, but he has a script tattoo beneath his collar bone, and as I tilt my head to read it, I realise it's written in another language. Gwasgara'r ofnau cyn daw'r wawr. I have no idea what it means.

'Banish my fears before the dawn.' Preston's voice catches me off guard. 'That's what it roughly translates to. It's from a Welsh song.' He glances at me before turning back to the road, and wavers slightly. 'My mum's favourite.'

'How do you pronounce it?'

Preston glances at me again before reciting the lyric as it should sound, and in that moment, I would give anything to be able to speak the language myself. I sometimes forget Preston can speak it as I only ever hear him do so when he refers to mathematical terms during our lessons. I wonder if his mum's first language is Welsh. This is the first time he's ever acknowledged her existence, and this may be my only chance to ask about her. Just as I'm about to do that, the house Mum's staying in comes into view.

'Oh, that's it!' I announce as I point at the small house in the corner ahead of us, and Preston nods before pulling up onto the pavement outside it.

As the car comes to a halt, I remember why I haven't seen Mum in so long, and a wave of uneasiness crashes through my stomach. That look. The expectant look she gives me every single time I see her, the look that's waiting for me to break down. To show any sign of emotion.

'Mia, hey, are you going in? If you'd rather just observe its bricks, then--'

'Oh, sh!' I smack Preston. 'Yeah, I just...' I clear my throat. 'I feel bad about inviting myself to yours and making you drive here and--Well, y'know what I mean, but yeah... Um, I mean, my mum's a killer baker--she makes the best Welsh cakes--so you're welcome to join. Y'know, as a thanks for bearing with me last night. Y'know, if you want.'

I am a shocking liar, aren't I? The reality is that I want him to come with me because if he's there, he'll distract Mum enough to make her forget about my recent coldness. It's painstakingly obvious that what I just said isn't true--in fact, I may as well have the word bullshit tattooed onto my forehead--but Preston nods at me as if I'm the most cunning liar ever to set foot on earth.

He can clearly see right through it but he doesn't question me, and I don't think I've ever appreciated anything so much.

I haven't seen Mum smile so broadly in months. The second she spots me entering the kitchen with a male specimen by my side, she jumps up from her chair and introduces herself to Preston before even looking at me. Once she's done with him, she wraps her arms around me and squeezes tightly. She's still smiling when we sit beside the kitchen table. Cerys, Mum's friend, offers us some tea or coffee, and coincidentally, some homemade Welsh cakes.

Mum starts Preston's interrogation the second she gets the chance, and for the first time ever, it doesn't make me want to bang my head against a lamp post until I lose consciousness. It's like she's herself again, like the situation with Dad never happened.

'You're a different lad to the one Mia met in town a while back, aren't you?'

Most mothers would probably say that with uneasiness, with an underlying worry of their daughter being the kind of girl who has a name for herself. Not Mum, though. She's thrilled.

'Uh, yeah, it's not like that though, we're just friends,' I say before Preston gets a chance to answer.

'Oh, okay,' Mum replies slowly. 'Of course you are. Sorry.'

She's as bad of a liar as me, with a huge grin slapped onto her face. Quite frankly, so long as it keeps that expectant look away from her eyes, I couldn't care less if she believes me or not. Mum winks one of her hazel eyes at me as Cerys squeezes between my chair and the dishwasher to hand me a mug of black coffee.

'I love your shirt, by the way,' she says to Preston as she hands him his mug.

'Cheers.' Preston leans back in his chair, and raises his eyebrows with a subtle grin. 'I sort of match your curtains, don't I?'

He nods at the paisley curtains hanging from the square window behind him as Mum and Cerys start laughing.

'Well, you definitely pull it off best,' Cerys replies with a wink, and despite her being at least forty, I think she may be flirting with him. I barf in my mouth a little.

She brushes her hand against Preston's shoulder as she passes him to leave the room, and heads upstairs just as Livvy enters, catching me by surprise. I didn't notice her car here. I haven't seen her in at least a month now that she's back at uni. She's tying her wavy hair into a ponytail as she steps into the room. We used to have the same long, dark hairstyle until I cut mine to just below my shoulders. She always looked so much better with her hair long than I did, so I decided to stop competing.

Livvy's about to say something when her eyes land on Preston, and in an instant, she freezes, her hair mid-ponytail.

'Oh, Olivia, this is Mia's friend,' Mum says as Livvy regains herself, and it's impossible not to notice the emphasis on 'friend'. 'Sorry, dear, what was your name again?' she asks, turning back to Preston.

'Zack,' he fills in, to which I roll my eyes. Here we go.

He lifts his hand up in a wave to my sister, and there's nothing but casual confidence in his manner. Livvy stares back, wide-eyed. Does she know him? She can't do. She was fully out of it when he saw her at the party a while back. She's nodding at me before my thoughts can run on any longer.

'Mia, come outside a sec, I've got something of yours,' she says, gesturing for me to leave the room with her.

'Um, okay...' I reply slowly, completely aware that she has absolutely nothing to give me.

Mum's eyebrows are raised at Livvy, probably because she didn't acknowledge Preston when Mum introduced him, but my sister doesn't seem to notice. I follow her out of the room and into the long hallway. Its walls are painted a dull green colour, and so it's darker here compared to the bright blue kitchen.

'You're not seeing him, are you?' Livvy snaps at me once we're out of earshot. 'Please tell me you're not.'

My sister is the one person who somehow achieves the physical impossibility of shouting while whispering, and it's a skill I've always been envious of.

'What? Why? No, we're just friends.'

I'm about to ask Livvy why she's throwing a hissy fit when I realise exactly what's going on. No one can be this agitated over someone they've not met. She must have met him at a party, a different one to the one we both found ourselves at. When a girl leaves a party this angry at Zack Maddox, there's generally only one explanation. On top of that, based on the drunken misadventures Livvy has told me she's had with boys in the past, the evidence is really quite strong.

'Liv, please tell me you haven't done the dirty with him because if you have, then I swear to God I might actually laugh myself to death.'

'It's not funny, Mia, just--'

'Girls!' Mum shouts from the kitchen. 'Stop yapping in the hallway, it's rude!'

Livvy flashes me another strained look, and heads into the living room. She doesn't even glance into the kitchen as she passes. Preston must have told Mum how he's my maths tutor because as I return to the kitchen, she's making a joke about the time I thought Pythagoras was the flying horse from Greek Mythology.

An hour or so later, once all of the Welsh cakes have been consumed, we say our goodbyes and leave the house. As we step onto the porch, I turn to Preston to ask the one question that's been weighing down my mind for the past hour.

'Have you slept with my sister?'

Neither one of us steps off the porch as Preston starts laughing.

'Don't you mean your acquaintance?' he responds with raised eyebrows.

He recognised her from the party, then.

'I was embarrassed, okay, can you blame me?' I mutter. 'Stop trying to wiggle your way out of my question.'

'Possibly,' he says, holding back more laughter. 'Where did that assumption come from?'

'She sort of told me you had. Well, she didn't deny it when I asked her anyway.'

Preston is silent for a short while, and it looks like he's trying to retrieve something from his mind, which I imagine must resemble a horrifically complex trainwreck. He twirls his car keys around his index finger. A grin explodes onto his face, and he doesn't need to say anything for me to know the answer to my question. I don't know whether to laugh or cry.

'Holy... Livvy's smart. She's doing a bloody Chemistry degree at university, how could she have ever fallen for...' I gesture towards Preston, and it's obvious what I'm referring to. 'No offence, but when you're like that, you're about as endearing as a pint of milk ten years past its expiry date. I mean, I get why the less... gifted girls might fall for it, but geez, not Olivia.'

Preston is laughing even more now, his green eyes glinting so brightly that it's as if there are tiny flames hidden within his irises. His laughter subsides as he steps a little closer to me on the porch, and his breath smells of jam and tea. It runs down my neck, and its warmth soothes my skin. His gaze locks with mine, and as much as I want to turn away, as much as I know I should turn away, I'm like a moth to the fire in his eyes.

I've never realised how profound Preston's cheekbones are, and I have to consciously stop myself from reaching up and tracing them with my fingertips as the space between us lessens even more. We're so close that I can taste his breath on my lips. I blink, except I don't because my eyes stay closed. I lean in even closer. I don't have to be looking to know that his mouth is centimetres away from mine. I part my lips, hold my breath, and--

Preston abruptly turns away.

My eyes ping open, and he starts strolling towards his little black car. I'm left stammering, thirsty for something I'm not quite sure of, as he lightly chuckles into the winter air. What the--Please tell me I didn't just fall for that, holy mother of hell, please tell me I didn't. My cheeks flush, and I kind of want to spew all over Cerys's porch at the realisation that I almost kissed

Zack Maddox. Particularly after what I just discovered about him and Livvy, I mean... Ew. What even just happened?

'Different people fall for different things, and in case you've yet to notice.' Preston presses a button on his keys to unlock the car, and turns to face me. 'I'm quite proficient at adapting myself to become whatever people desire me to be.'

He bows as if I've just witnessed the most admirable performance I'll ever have the pleasure of experiencing, and for a second, I think I might have.

CHAPTER 13

I stay at Preston's house--a term I use loosely--again that night. The thought of going home and facing Gwen is still too much to deal with. I'm merely postponing the inevitable, but the longer I can pretend it isn't happening, the better. Preston drives me to college the next day, and in fairness, anyone with an ounce of common sense would've realised this, but being chauffeured to college at nine in the morning by Zack Maddox is an atrocious idea.

As I make my way to my law lesson, I don't think I pass a single person who doesn't stare at me like I'm some wild, foreign species. As for what they're saying, they could sure as hell do with a lesson in whispering.

'No way, that's not her! She's not even that pretty.'

'Did you definitely see her get out of his car? Ugh, he can do way better than her.'

Whoa, guys, calm down on the compliments.

'You can tell she's a slut, is she even wearing a bra?'

That one had me rolling my eyes around my skull. What whether I'm wearing a bra or not has to do with my sexual endeavours, I do not know. Kind of makes me want to start an anti-rape culture, feminist protest. I'm charging through the library, while planning where I can get some picket signs, when there's a harsh tug on my arm.

'Mia, you sly dog!'

Aiden.

'Please don't start.' I groan. 'Before you even think of asking, I wouldn't touch Zack Maddox's genitals with a barge pole if doing so would grant me infinite wealth and beauty.'

'Holy Mackerel, bit extreme.' He holds his hands up defensively before taking a seat in front of one of the library computers. 'I heard rumours and got excited, okay? I figured you wouldn't have anyway, considering you and Robbie have your thing. Plus you'd be getting on my sloppy seconds, of course, considering Zack and I have shared a passionate kiss in the past. I mean, yeah sure, he wasn't conscious, but I don't think that really matters.'

I groan as I slump into the chair next to him. I'll probably be late for law, but I can't say I really care. The library is packed, but the watchful eye of the librarian is causing all chatter to become monotonous murmurs, not that it helps. I can still hear what everyone's talking about. Is this what it's like to be Preston? No wonder he has a few screws loose.

'Robbie and I don't have a thing,' I mutter. 'Anyway, yeah, if anyone does ask you, please ensure them that I haven't been seduced by Zack's mediocre charm, please?'

Aiden salutes me, which I assume is him agreeing to my request, and so I thank him before making my way to class.

By noon, the majority of the gossiping has died down. I have some bitchy comments flung at me, and the stares are still coming in thick and fast, but it's better. I'm not most pleased with Preston when the time comes for our maths lesson, though. With the exam approaching, I'm now having to endure two hours a week of tutoring. The room is just as disorganised as ever, with paper flung across the only table in there. The walls seriously need decorating, so much so that even sticking some of my maths homework on them would brighten up the place.

As always, Preston is casually sitting on the blue plastic chair beside the table, with the big comfortable chair left empty for me to sit on.

'You're a curse, y'know that, right?'

I cross my arms as I sit down. Preston moves his eyes up to my face, smirks, then moves them back to the papers in his hands.

'I think you'll find that I'm a delight,' he replies innocently. He waves his hand in the air as if brushing away some invisible entity. 'Just ignore them. Someone will get someone else im-pregnated or something, and you'll be an irrelevant being again in no time. Humanity has a rather minuscule attention span.' He sits up straight. 'Anyway, maths. Your exam's only a few weeks away, and if you fail, I don't get don't get my bonus, which is the true priority here.'

Saying something about asparagus or Pythagoras or whatever, Preston hands me some sheets of paper. I don't really focus on anything he's saying, though. I just stare at him. His eyebrows dance across his forehead while he speaks, he waves his hands around as if maths is the most exciting thing on the planet, and even his light hair falls onto his face in a way that makes him look like he has no care in the world. And I thought I was good at ignoring the shit in my life.

Preston is otherworldly.

Watching him now, as his face glows and his light eyes glisten, I'm beginning to question if he actually is a squatter with no parents, and barely a penny to his name. The person I met on the weekend can't be this person sitting in front of me now. It just can't.

As I'm leaving the room after the lesson, I jump at the sight of someone I never expected to see at college.

'Oh, hey Robbie.' I stammer. Robbie laughs at my obvious shock. 'Why are you--What are you doing here?'

There's a jingling sound behind me. Preston stands there, leaning against the closed door as he holds up his car keys--Robbie's car keys.

'This knobhead wants his car back, should've nicked it when I had the chance.' He laughs as he throws the keys to Robbie, who catches them.

As for how Preston manages to jump in and out of character so quickly, I don't even want to try and unravel that.

'Cheers, mate,' Robbie replies. He's about to turn away when he pauses, opens his mouth, stammers, then pauses again. He looks at me. 'You got any more lessons?'

I shake my head.

'Fancy going to Roath Park? It's a nice day, the ducks need feeding, and I have all the bread you could ever dream of.'

I smile. Screw it, why not? I accept Robbie's offer, say goodbye to Preston, and then before I know it I'm in his car all over again, just with a different driver this time round. I suppose I can see why people might be starting to form questionable opinions of me, but I can't say I care much about what other people think. I can't say I care much about anything, anymore.

Robbie and I haven't been at Roath Park for very long when the conversation turns a little awkward. Now that Aiden, Delyth, Samantha, and I tend to hang around with Robbie and Preston as a collective, Robbie and I rarely spend much time alone together. That in itself is something I still find strange--the fact we've suddenly been thrown into Preston and Robbie's friendship group. Then again, they don't exactly have one solid friendship group because they're always surrounded by different people. They might not even consider us friends. It wouldn't shock me if they don't invite us to half the things they do, and have another group of people stored for those instances.

I pick at a slice of stale bread as I gaze at the scene surrounding me. We're sitting by Roath Park's lake, with our legs outstretched on the soft grass. The afternoon sun is gleaming down onto the water, and it looks like someone has crushed a million diamonds into tiny pieces, then sprinkled them gently over its surface. The greenery surrounding the lake is almost too neat and tidy, and I can't help but desire to know what it would look like for the bushes to be wild and unkempt, and for the trees to be left to their own devices.

I lived and breathed this place as a child, and it feels like the only thing that's remained the same throughout my life. I think it's important to have somewhere like this. Somewhere you can come back to year after year, and find that it still looks exactly the same as it did when you were a child. Not just looks the same, but smells the same, tastes the same, feels the same.

It's important to have somewhere that, when you close your eyes, you have the exact same feeling when you're eighty as you did when you were eight. No matter what else is going on in your life, if you can find somewhere to close your eyes and take yourself back to when everything was perfect, then nothing else matters. Nothing else is real. Even if it's only for a second.

'Hey, Mia?'

I bring myself back to the present and find Robbie's blue eyes peering into mine. He's just lit a cigarette for himself, and he's holding the open packet in front of me. I figure he's offering me one. I open my mouth to decline his offer, but hesitate. I've had a drag here and there while I was drunk, but never a full one, and certainly not sober. I glance at the lake, and pause. Something's different. There's a tree missing. I can see where it's been cut down because it's left an empty patch of grass, and a tiny stump. Something churns in my stomach. I turn back to Robbie.

'Sure.'

I take a cigarette from Robbie's packet, and light it up. It tastes stale and burns my throat each time I inhale, but I ignore it.

'We should do this more often,' Robbie says as he breaks some bread off the loaf, and throws it into the lake.

'What, feed ducks? I mean, yeah, I guess, don't want to over-feed them or anything though. I think bread is actually bad for them, y'know.'

Robbie laughs as he slowly shakes his head, his eyes now fixated onto my face. It takes me a lot longer than it should to grasp onto the fact he wasn't referring to feeding the local wildlife.

'You're an idiot, y'know that, right?' Some chuckles are still leaving Robbie's mouth as he speaks.

I shrug as I take a drag of my cigarette. 'Nah, I'm just a bit behind everyone else is all. Takes me a good few minutes to process things.'

My cheeks must be bright red because my face is boiling all of a sudden. For once in my life, would it kill me to say something even the tiniest bit alluring? I throw some bread into the water to try and distract Robbie from my general idiocy.

'C'mon then, what is it?' Robbie asks as he leans back onto his elbows so that he's half-lying on the grass. 'What makes you the one girl who doesn't want to hop into bed with Zack Maddox?'

I shrug. 'I don't know, I just don't. I don't quite understand anyone who does. He's pretty and all that, but nah, not my type.'

'Pretty? You make him sound like a ten-year-old girl. Mentally he's about ten, I'll give you that,' Robbie jokes. 'But yeah, I still find that weird as hell. I swear everyone I know wants to get him into bed.'

Robbie loves chatting about Preston--well Zack--doesn't he? I'm sure we more or less had the same conversation at the coffee shop. I'm not sure what to make of it, whether to find it annoying that our conversations always turn to Zack Maddox, or feel sorry for Robbie for constantly comparing himself to him.

'He's charming, I guess.' I shrug as I realise I still have a cigarette in my hands. I've barely had any of it, but I stub it out because it's burnt down by now anyway. 'By which I mean cocky, really, which admittedly I don't quite understand how anyone can find attract--'

'Mia!'

I turn my head to see a dark-haired boy charging at me from the path above us, and it takes me a while to realise who it is. I trip over my words as he stops at the top of the banking.

'Matty, hey!'

Matty grins. 'D'you have bread? Can I borrow some, please? Paul forgot to bring any, so now all the ducks are gonna starve and die unless I feed them.'

As Matty speaks, I spot a bald man power-walking towards us, who I'm assuming must be Paul. Who Paul actually is is beyond me. Robbie asks me who Matty is as I hand him some bread, and I hesitate before saying something about family friends. That's another thing Robbie has no idea about Preston then--his brother's existence. Robbie nods and stands up, then strolls over to Matty and begins helping him feed the ducks. It's quite sweet.

'Sorry about that,' the man I noticed earlier says as he stops at the top of the banking where Matty was just standing. His cheeks are red and he's breathing heavily. 'I've told that boy all about stranger danger, but it goes in through one ear and out the other.'

'It's fine, don't worry about it! I'm friends with Matty's brother. We've meet before.'

Paul's bushy eyebrows rise, and he looks surprised. He puts his hands into his jean pockets as he nods slowly.

'Preston?' he eventually asks. I nod. 'He's a good kid deep down, thinks the world of Matty, anyone can see that.' Paul sits onto the grass next to me, and his eyes are focused on Matty and Robbie. 'My wife and I can both be a little harsh on the lad sometimes, really. He's hardly the best role model for Matty, but given the situation with his mother, he sure could be a lot worse.'

'Yeah, he's not all bad.' I smile. 'But yeah, definitely,' I say as if I have any idea what Paul is referring to, in the hope of him continuing the subject of conversation.

'My wife hates the idea of Matty visiting the prison, and I know that bothers Preston. I think it's important he does, though don't tell my wife that.'

Curiosity is gnawing at me, and I'm dying to ask a hundred and one questions, but I keep my mouth shut. I can't make it obvious that I've not even known Preston a year, and that every single thing Paul is saying makes little sense with the limited information I have. I feel somewhat guilty for intruding on Preston's life without him knowing, but I can't help it. I'm drawn to him. I want to know everything about him. He's the most peculiar person I've ever come across, and it's as if I have this undying need to know more, to know him completely.

Paul turns back to Matty as he and Robbie start picking at the bread, then eating it themselves. I take the opportunity to think. Who's in prison? Preston and Matty's mum? Why? This is killing me. Paul seems nice though, and there's a warm feeling in my gut knowing that he's Matty's foster dad. While I only met her for a few seconds, his wife seems like an arsehole, so at least Paul's a decent bloke. He laughs beside me, and it's big and loud.

'Right then, we have food waiting at home, so I better collect the young'un,' he says as he stands up.

It takes him a while, but he gets Matty's attention, and they're soon leaving. Matty tells me to say hi to Preston for him, Paul says it was nice to meet us, refers to Robbie as my boyfriend, and then they're gone.

Robbie sighs as he sits down. It was odd seeing him be so friendly with Matty, just as it was odd seeing Preston with him at first. Associating the people I met at Robbie's party with the same people who are so kind to an eight-year-old boy feels wrong, somehow. Knowing that Robbie has no idea whatsoever who Matty really is f eelssomewhat surreal too. Robbie takes a cigarette out of his pocket and is lighting it as he turns back to me.

'Who's Preston?'

'Now that is a very good question,' I mutter under my breath.

'What?'

'Just another family friend,' I reply. 'No one you know.'

CHAPTER 14

Maxxie barks. A knife scrapes across a plate, and Dad coughs. Maxxie barks again. You could cut this atmosphere with a blunt, soggy toothpick, let alone a knife. I gaze at my plate as I cut a slice of overdone bacon into minuscule pieces.

'So... Euphemia--'

'Mia.'

'Oh, sorry. Mia. What lessons do you have today?'

I roll my eyes at my bacon. I'm not having a conversation with it--I've not yet lost it to that extent. It's Gwen who's speaking, but it's so painstakingly obvious that she's trying too hard to pretend she has any interest in my life.

I shrug. 'Law and psychology.'

I'm still not looking at her. Maxxie barks.

'Which one is your favourite? My son takes law, but he can't stand it.'

Gwen laughs as if she's just told the most spectacularly hilarious gag known to mankind, and I glance up to see Dad laughing into his cereal. Did I miss the joke? Maxxie barks again, and I feel relieved that at least he isn't standing for Gwen's bullshit.

It's seven in the morning, and she's dressed like she's meeting the queen for dinner or something. Her red hair is tightly curled and tied to the top of her head, and she's wearing a long pencil skirt with a blindingly white blouse. How good would it be if my sausage accidentally found itself being flung at that blouse? I could blame the dog or something. Say Maxxie barged into my leg, and in a flurry of panic, I lobbed my sausage at Gwen's torso.

'Mia, Gwen asked you a question.'

I snap out of my trance to see Dad glaring at me.

'Uh, I don't really have a favourite,' I mumble.

It goes quiet again. Gwen's been staying here a few days now, but this is the longest period of time I've had to spend with her. It's awful. I pop some egg into my mouth, only to find that it's gone cold. Damnit. Maxxie barks again. I push my food around my plate, and sigh. Gwen's not actually that bad, not really. She tends to stay out of my way, and it's clear she's trying to make some kind of connection with me. I just can't like her. She could save me from getting trampled by a herd of wild elephants, and I still wouldn't be keen on her after what she and Dad have done. Dad keeps forcing her on me though, to the point where I don't even think she feels very comfortable with it.

'Gwen has a job interview today,' Dad informs me, making me want to poke my eyes out with my fork as it requires me to fake enthusiasm.

'Oh, uh, cool. Good luck,' I mutter to Gwen.

She thanks me quietly. Dad wanted me to stay in tonight because Gwen was cooking her apparently famous spaghetti bolognese, so when Robbie invited me out to the city centre tonight, I jumped at the opportunity. All I have to do now is make it through the rest of today, and I'm free to do whatever the hell I want. I put my cutlery down, sit back, and sigh. I don't even like spaghetti bolognese.

As soon as the doorbell rings that night, I'm charging towards the front door. Aiden was meant to get here at eight, but he's half an hour late. I open the door ready to snap at him, but the second I see his big brown eyes and cheesy smile all full of dimples, I just laugh.

'Sorry I'm late, my hair looked like a cow had taken a dump on my head.'

'Could you not do anything to fix it?'

His eyes widen in horror. 'What? Is it still bad? Holy mackerel, I can't go out, I need to cut it. D'you have a shaver? Don't just stand there, woman, this is serious! C'mon Mia, get something befo--'

I elbow him. 'I was joking, you look great.'

'Really? Goddmanit, you shouldn't joke about these things,' Aiden mutters as he steps into my house.

I reach up to give him a patronising tap on the head, and send Robbie a text to let him know we're ready to be picked up. Aiden and I wait on my staircase until he, Preston, and some boy I don't recognise show up fifteen minutes later, and I can't get out of my house quickly enough. Before I know it, we're speeding through Cardiff with music blasting so loudly, I can't hear my own thoughts. Perfect.

Delyth and Samantha are meeting us there, and I've not seen much of Delyth since her Aiden-fuelled outburst, so I'm a little on edge. She and Samantha tend to keep to themselves on group nights out, so with any luck, I'll be able to avoid her. There's a tap on my shoulder, and I turn to the boy whose name I don't know. He offers me a small bottle of vodka and a packet of cigarettes from the plastic bag by his feet, but before I say anything, Robbie speaks up.

'Thought I'd treat you,' he says as he winks at me in the rear-view mirror.

Free alcohol? I'm not complaining. I thank Robbie and take the drink, along with the cigarettes. Might as well. I tend to avoid vodka because last time I had it at a family barbecue, I redecorated my bedroom walls with my own sick. That was six months or so ago now, and since that happened, Dad has refused to let me drink a drop of anything alcoholic until I turn eighteen, so I can't resist. I take a sip. It burns but it's good, like it's cleaning my insides. As I pass the bottle to Aiden so he can have some, I catch a glimpse of Preston watching me with his jaw clenched. It's a look only Preston would be capable of mustering up, not Zack, but I blink and he's back in character.

By the time we've reached the museum, it's almost nine o' clock. I've told Dad I'm having a sleepover with Aiden and some of the girls, so he's not expecting me home at any time. We park in the museum car park per usual, which I'm fairly certain is illegal or something. There's a decent sized group of people here. Bigger than usual, actually.

'Ah, shit,' Robbie mutters. His eyes are focused on the group loitering on the lawn outside city hall, and he turns to Preston. 'That's Jacob Griffiths, isn't it?'

'Who?' I ask, leaning forward. 'What's wrong?'

'Robbie did the dirty with Jacob Griffiths' sister by the fountain like the romantic sod he is, so now Jacob wants to fight him.'

Preston scoffs, and Robbie shoots him the most scathing look I've ever seen. 'It was ages ago but he's still pissed, and Robbie's too much of a pussy to fight him.'

Robbie mumbles something under his breath, but follows it up with a, 'nah, it's cool, we'll just stay out of his way,' as he opens the car door.

'Such a wimp,' Preston mocks as he steps out after Robbie, and we soon follow. 'D'you want me to fight him for you?'

Robbie doesn't respond, just mutters under his breath again. Why must Preston insist on being a complete arsehole to anyone and everyone when he's playing dress-up as Zack Maddox? I realise he refuses to be himself when we're out in a group like this, but there's nothing forcing him to be so vile. Knowing how decent of a guy he can be makes me want to shake him so hard that all traces of Zack are concussed out of him.

We're wandering towards city hall's fountain, away from Jacob Griffiths and his friends, when Preston makes some other immature comment. Robbie ignores it again. I spot Samantha sitting on the fountain, and she's singing to herself as she traces her hands through the still water. I don't see Delyth, but there are some familiar faces sitting near Samantha, alongside some less familiar faces.

'Hey look, it's the love fountain.' Preston bursts into laughter as he nudges Robbie's side.

Robbie halts. 'Shut up, will you?' he snaps, his tanned face inches away from Preston's pale one.

'Jesus Christ, calm down, I'm only joking.'

For the third time in five minutes, Robbie mutters something inaudible under his breath. He goes to turn away, but Preston grabs his arm before he can move.

'What?' Preston gnarls.

'Nothing,' Robbie mumbles.

'What did you just say? At least have the balls to say it to my face.'

'I said.' Robbie speaks slowly. 'Shut up, or next time you can't hack the cocktail of shit you've taken, maybe I won't get help.'

He shoves himself out of Preston's grasp, and stomps towards the fountain. Everyone follows besides Preston, who doesn't move an inch. As I pass him, I give the dirtiest look I can muster up, but he turns away the second our eyes meet. I take another sip of the vodka, and slip a cigarette out of its packet. I'm going to bloody need this stuff at the rate things are going.

The moment I sit beside Robbie on the grass, he apologises in a manic ramble for the whole Jacob Griffiths' sister ordeal, and I have to assure him at least ten times that it's fine. Once his rambling has come to a conclusion, his eyes are plagued with what I guess is hope that I believe what he's just said, and the way his dark quiff has flattened onto his forehead makes him look younger than he is. I smile softly at him when, out of nowhere, he leans forward.

Our lips collide, and I've got no idea what to do. I don't even know if I want to be doing this in the first place. I just shut my eyes and kiss him back. It's not exactly the most romantic thing in the world because he's a little too enthusiastic with the tongue, and there's an irritating house anthem playing in the background, alongside the subtle stench of something rotting.

I found a dead rabbit here once when I was little, so maybe it's that. Wouldn't surprise me. I'm halfway through a cigarette too, so I bet my breath reeks. Can't be any worse than that rotting smell though.

My teeth bash against Robbie's, and I suddenly remember what I'm doing. Why the hell am I thinking of dead rabbits right now? I try to focus solely on Robbie's lips touching mine until he pulls away.

He smiles shyly at me. 'Uh, sorry.'

'It's fine, don't worry, totally cool.' I stammer as my cheeks flush.

Robbie goes to say something else, but as he opens his mouth, someone calls his name. We both lift our heads to see a small group of guys standing on the grass a hundred yards or so away. One of them is motioning Robbie over, so he apologises before standing up and wandering over to the group, while I'm left pondering over how much of a loser I am.

I watch Robbie as he leaves, and as I turn away, I catch Samantha's eyes. One of her eyebrows is raised. She sits down beside me, crosses her legs, and stares at me. I'm never sure of what to make of Samantha. I mean, she doesn't really speak enough to form much of an opinion. I take a long glug of my vodka, probably a little too much because it stings for a while afterwards, and offer some to Samantha.

'No thanks. D'you like Robbie?' she asks with her timid voice.

I stammer a little as I stub my cigarette out. 'Um, I think so... I mean, yeah, I think I do.'

'Hm.'

She doesn't say anything after that, and instead starts humming to herself. Err, okay.

I've barely drunk anything, but I already feel lighter. I haven't eaten much today, I guess. I scan the lawn for Aiden, and when I do spot him, Delyth is unsurprisingly stalking him. I should probably let him know that she's in undying love with him. Preston is with them, and his arm is draped over Aiden's shoulder. He catches Aiden's attention, and when Aiden looks at him, he gives him a peck on the lips and starts laughing hysterically. I clench my jaw. He's such an arsehole.

'Don't feel like you have to like him because he likes you,' Samantha suddenly chirps up again.

'What?' I ask, turning back to her. 'Oh, Robbie. Uh, no, I don't.'

I'm kind of insulted. If anything, I should feel like I have to fancy Preston. I mean, everyone else seems to. If I do like Robbie, it's based on genuine feelings. I'm just not entirely sure I do yet.

'Hm,' Samantha says again.

'Oi, Morrissey!'

As if on cue, a rough voice shouts from the other side of the lawn. I whip my head around to see a short, broad boy storming towards us. Robbie curses loudly a few feet away. I turn back to the short boy, who's getting closer and closer by the second. That's Jacob Griffiths then. Before I can even blink, he's pressed up against Robbie, who now has Preston by his side. They've stopped right next to me, so I've got a front row seat. I stand up, and Aiden hurries over to the kerfuffle, planting himself beside me. His eyes are wide, and my head feels strange.

'C'mon then,' Jacob snorts. 'Let's do this.'

Robbie's stammering, so Preston takes charge. At least he's not a total dickhead when he's Zack. He moves Robbie aside and stands so close to Jacob that they must be able to taste each other's breath.

'How about you get back to your little powwow over there, and stop being such a sensitive arsehole.'

'Piss off, Maddox, it's your boyfriend I have a problem with.'

'One day that'll be me,' Aiden whispers beside me, and without any forewarning, I burst into laughter.

I clamp my mouth shut the second I realise what I'm doing, but it's too late. Jacob shoves Preston aside, and he almost trips over. The next thing I know, Jacob's face is inches away from me. His breath reeks. The half empty bottle of vodka is suddenly feeling heavy in my back pocket, and my hands are shaking. I stammer.

'What's so fun--'

'Leave her alone, it was my bad,' Aiden interrupts from beside me.

He nudges me out the way, so now Jacob's breathing in Aiden's face. Jacob blinks. He shoves Aiden backwards, then grabs his arm. What have I done? I bite down onto my lip, hard. Jacob's grip tightens around Aiden's arm, and he looks between the two of us.

'Someone tell me what the hell is so funny before I break this idiot's--'

'Don't touch them!'

Jacob's harsh grip is ripped away from Aiden, and the next thing I know, Preston has Jacob by the scruff of his shirt. Jacob struggles to free himself, but it's no use, so he resorts to the next best thing.

He pulls his arm back, and whacks Preston square across the face.

Someone shouts as Preston's grip is released, and I've barely had a chance to blink before Preston retaliates by slamming his own first into Jacob's face. Jacob stumbles to the floor, and there's a thin line of blood seeping from his lip. Another shout. My brain feels like it's about to explode, and I can't stop blinking. Someone pulls me back, and when I turn around, it's Aiden. He's okay. Is he okay? He says something over the mass of voices shouting words I can't make out, but I can't understand him.

Everyone is yelling, and now that I've been pulled away from the group, I can't see anything. I try running towards them, but Aiden yanks me back again. Where's Robbie? I try moving again, but I'm pulled back.

'Mia, leave it!' Aiden shouts. 'I swear you have a bloody death wish! If I had any idea you'd impersonate a hyena on acid when I said that, I would've kept my mouth shut.'

'Where's Robbie?' I ask, ignoring what Aiden said.

'No idea,' Delyth, who I hadn't even realised was standing next to me, announces. 'Shouldn't you be off sucking his face somewhere?'

'Oh, piss off. Aiden's gay, deal with it,' I mutter.

Using that astounding revelation as a distraction, I break free from Aiden's grasp and sprint towards the group, who are still screaming and shouting. I shove my way through the crowd to find Jacob and Preston knocking the crap out of each other on the damp ground.

I don't know if it's the alcohol or if it's just a moment of insanity, but I push through the rest of the crowd until I'm right in the middle of the circle. I'm screaming at the boys to stop, but they pay no attention. I scream again. Nothing. Swearing, I grab Preston's t-shirt from behind, and pull him as hard as I can until it occurs to him what's going on. The second he realises it's me grabbing him, he stops. He doesn't struggle, or try to swing another punch. He just stops.

'What's wrong, Maddox?' Jacob yells, his face splattered in bruises and smudged blood. 'You scared?'

'Get over it, Jacob.' Preston's next sentence is an utterance. 'it's not like you can blame your sister for trying to fuck away the reality of you being her brother.'

Jacob looks like he's about to swing for Preston again, but a few of his friends pull him away before he has the chance to do anything. As quickly as the crowd appeared, it begins to disperse. In the matter of what feels like seconds, only a small group consisting of Preston, Aiden, Delyth, Samantha, Robbie and me remains. At least Robbie's finally made an appearance.

By the time things have calmed down, I'm sitting on the fountain by myself. My hands are still a little shaky. Why the hell did I just jump into the middle of a fight? I could've gotten myself smacked right across the face. I'm questioning my sanity when I notice Robbie dragging his feet in my direction. He's staring at the neatly cut grass below him, while avoiding my gaze at all costs. He sits next to me.

'Sorry for that, I--I panicked and, I'm sorry, I should've helped you guys, I just...' Robbie's voice trailed off.

'It's fine,' I lie. 'Pre--Zack helped, so y'know.'

'I'll make it up to you,' he announces, finally looking up. 'Maybe we could go for a walk around Roath or something tomorrow, or get some food?'

'Go for a walk? You going to rub my belly and give me treats too?' I joke.

As always, that's the worst thing I could've possibly said. Robbie turns even redder and starts stammering. Bloody hell, I take stupid to a whole other level. After his disappearing act just now, I'm not sure I want to see him tomorrow. As his big blue eyes shy away from mine though, I can feel myself melting. I sigh. He's not a bad guy.

'Sorry, I was kidding. That sounds good,' I say.

Relief spreads over Robbie's face. 'Okay, great.' He starts playing with his hands. 'I seriously am sorry for earlier, I don't know what happened, I just--I'm not a good fighter, and I--' He sighs. 'I swear I'm not usually that pathetic, I'm not.'

I reassure Robbie that it's fine, and it occurs to me that I spend a lot of time reassuring Robbie Morrissey. I think about what Samantha said, and for a moment, I question if she might've been right.

CHAPTER 15

It's not until I see Robbie pull up on Cerys's driveway that I realise how atrocious this date idea was. The whole boy-girl thing really isn't my forte, is it? I don't have much money, so I suggested we do something cheap, which resulted in the idea of him visiting Cerys's house for food with Mum and me. That's moving way too fast, isn't it? He's met Mum before, but the whole sit down and have a family meal thing could be a bit much. He didn't seem horrified at the idea, but he might just not have wanted to tell me no.

I don't think Robbie's even knocked the door when Mum glides towards it. This was a bad idea. A really bad idea. She yanks it open and welcomes Robbie with the goofiest grin ever, which must either amuse or terrify him. Probably the latter. I flash him an anxious smile as our eyes meet, and lead him into the living room. Livvy's watching TV in there, and when she spots Robbie, she gives me an accusing look. Another idiotic move on my part. If she hates Zack, I can't imagine she's too keen on Robbie.

'Sorry if this is a little... intense,' I say to Robbie quietly as he sits on the sofa next to me. 'I didn't really think.'

He shrugs. 'It's fine, I like your mum, she's funny.'

Funny is one word for her.

As Mum enters the room, she introduces Robbie to Livvy, who couldn't be less welcoming if she tried. She shoots me another glare. Mum still has an enormous smile on her face, and she turns to Robbie armed with every question she could've possibly thought of. My cheeks turn warmer and warmer by the second, and I'm not sure if this is better or worse than the time we bumped into him in Cardiff.

'...had awful rashes as a child, the poor dab even managed to get herpes in her mouth when she was about--'

'Mum, I think the food is burning,' I snap as I realise who she's talking about.

I stare at her with the most aggressive expression I've ever mustered up, and I think she finally gets the message. She apologises, nods at me, and leaves the room.

Once she's left, Robbie starts laughing. 'She's brilliant.'

I'm too busy forging a plan to change my identity and leave the country to respond to him. As his laughter eases off, Robbie gently rests his hand on mine. His palm is a little sweaty, but it's warm. Nice. I slide my fingers in-between his.

'Is he staying for food?' Livvy asks as if Robbie isn't in the room.

'Yeah.' It's Robbie who replies. 'I've met you before, right? At some of my parties?'

Livvy glances at me before turning back to Robbie. 'Maybe, I'm not sure.'

She turns straight back to the TV, clearly in the hope that Robbie doesn't ask any more questions. He's smirking, so he must be completely aware of my sister's misadventure with Preston. The thought makes me want to puke in my mouth.

'Don't take it personally,' Robbie continues, but my sister doesn't look at him. 'He dumps everyone once he's gotten what he wants.'

It doesn't take a genius to figure out who Robbie is referring to. Before anyone can say anything else, Mum calls from the kitchen. Food's ready.

Once we've finished eating, Robbie suggests we go for a drive. I don't think I could've said yes any quicker. Mum continued her intense questioning throughout the meal, and Livvy spent the entirety of it staring at her food. I don't even care where we drive. He could take me to a dumping site and I'd be happy if it meant escaping the embarrassment of Mum, and the awkward-ness of Livvy.

As I watch Mum humming while she washes the dishes, it occurs to me that she seems happy. For the first time since everything happened, the smile on her face isn't forced. If a result of that is telling Robbie I had herpes as a child then screw it, it's worth it.

Robbie and I are about to leave the house when I hear Mum call from the kitchen. Her voice sounds like a song, and I can tell she's still smiling.

'Don't get up to any funny business unless you're being safe!'

Yeah, I changed my mind. It's not worth it.

I shove Robbie out of the house, and quickly slam the door behind me. He's laughing as we head to his car, and he's strolling up the driveway with a skip in his step. He opens the passenger door for me.

'You didn't tell me your sister was one of Zack's victims,' he says as I step into the car.

I roll my eyes as he slots himself beside me. He starts the engine, pulls off the driveway, and begins driving through the suburbs of Cardiff.

'To be honest, it wouldn't surprise me if Livvy's been with more people than Zack has,' I say through a chortle.

'Pfft, I highly doubt that somehow.'

'Hm, yeah, probably not. She's just as bad with guys though, then whines about how awfully they treat her. She had this one poor guy trailing after her for months last year, but loved the attention too much to ever shut him down.' I start laughing. 'You should've seen her face when she saw Zack with me the other week,' I say, shaking my head.

'What?'

'Huh?'

'Why were you alone with Zack?' Robbie's eyes are on my face, as opposed to the road he should be focusing on. 'When was that?'

I suddenly realise what I just said. Shit. I ramble some explanation about how he came to the house to discuss some maths stuff with Mum, but I may as well tell him I beheaded a dragon and sold it to the tooth fairy because that would sound just as believable. Robbie doesn't question it though.

'Have you spoken to him since the fight last night?' I ask, trying to steer attention away from what I just said.

Robbie shrugs as he approaches a roundabout. 'Nah.' He hesitates. 'It kinda pissed me off that he did that. I don't need him to fight for me. I appreciate him standing up for you and Aiden, but he shouldn't have for me.'

'He was just trying to help.'

'I don't need help,' Robbie mumbles in response.

We've been in the car for almost twenty minutes when I realise where Robbie is taking me. The only interesting thing to do near here is to go to Barry Island. I'd usually question why we're going to the beach in late January, but Robbie's face is lit up like he's come up with the best idea ever, so I say nothing.

As we emerge from a narrow street, the setting sun bursts out from in-between buildings, and the light brightens every feature on Robbie's face. His eyes are so illuminated that they look clear, and I've never noticed before, but he has tiny freckles dotted around his cheeks. He has a slight bump on the bridge of his nose where he must've broken it once, and I wonder how he did it. Did he fall when he was little? Did he get into a fight? Maybe he was just born with the bump. All of a sudden, I want to know everything there is to know about Robbie Morrissey.

We stop in the car park that faces the beach, and it's more or less empty. It's not as chilly as it has been on previous nights, so the oversized cardigan I have on is enough to keep me warm. Robbie offers me his jacket, but I decline his offer with a no thanks. He takes my hand and leads me in the direction of the beach, and as we reach the shore, he can't resist stopping at one of the fish and chip shops to buy himself a cone of chips. I raise my eyes at him.

'The chips here are good, okay?' He shrugs as he douses the chips in salt and vinegar.

'No, I get it, you hate my mum's cooking.' I sigh dramatically.

'Shit, you got me,' he replies as he shoves a load of chips into his mouth.

I nudge his side, and he flings a chip in my direction. I squeal as I dodge to avoid it, and jog down the concrete ramp leading to the beach in an attempt to skirt any more attacks. I stop at the bottom to take my trainers off, but Robbie walks ahead of me with his shoes still on his feet.

'You're going to get all kinds of shit in your shoes, y'know!' I call after him.

'All kinds of shit? What d'you think is on the beach besides sand, Mia?'

'Hey, it's Barry, you're guaranteed to find a rotting corpse,' I scoff.

'One's a little optimistic, don't you think? I'd say we're guaranteed at least three.'

Robbie plops himself down onto the sand, and once my shoes are off, I catch up and sit beside him. The stench of vinegar is overriding the salty beach air, and I wrinkle my nose in disgust. The stuff smells even worse than it tastes.

The only sound to be heard is the calm ocean washing onto the beach. I sigh and shut my eyes. I never come to the beach anymore, and I feel insane for that right now. It's beautiful. Now that I've adjusted to the acidic smell of the vinegar, the ocean air is circling my nostrils, and I can taste the sea salt on the tip of my tongue.

By the time Robbie's chips are running low, he's picking at them slowly. His eyes are glazed over as if there are a million thoughts racing through his head, and I want to ask him what he's thinking. He starts chewing at a crispy chip, and his eyes appear as if they're staring at something I can't see in the distance. It's crazy to think how this frequently shy boy is the same person who shouted demands at me as his best friend lay dying in his front garden seven months ago. It's as if he's a different person entirely, and I can't say I've ever met the Robbie I met at that party since that night. I guess he was panicking. I sure was.

Did I ever tell Robbie about Preston mumbling some nonsensical gibberish while half-conscious that night? I don't think I did. As the words Preston spoke try swimming to the surface of my memory, I can't hold my tongue.

'Hey, Robbie, d'you know if Zack was involved in an accident a while back?' I ask.

'What?'

I realise how random that must've sounded. I try to conjure up a clearer way to ask the same question. Should I tell him? I know there's no real reason not to, but it feels intrusive of me to share something no one else knows about. I doubt even Preston remembers.

'I was just thinking,' I begin. 'Y'know, on the night of your party, when you went to get rid of everyone from your house? And I was left alone with Zack?'

Robbie nods.

'Well, he said some stuff... I can't remember what exactly, but he said how something was an accident, and he kept repeating something about someone bleeding.'

Robbie frowns and furrows his eyebrows. He looks just as perplexed as I felt the night I heard Preston speaking those words. I don't need Robbie to say anything to know that he's just as clueless as I am about what Preston, or Zack, meant that night. Maybe that's it. Maybe the words that left his mouth that night were Preston's, not Zack's. That would explain why Robbie doesn't seem to have a clue about it.

'Hm, it's strange, maybe he was just delu--'

'Um, I don't really want to talk about Zack,' Robbie interrupts me mid-sentence.

'Yeah, of course, sorry.' I laugh a little awkwardly. 'We do seem to talk about him a lot.'

'Yeah, everyone does.' Robbie laughs too, but it sounds just as dry as mine. 'Anyway, um, I was thinking... We get along pretty well, right?'

'Yeah, I mean, I wouldn't believe it if you'd told me that this time last year, but yeah, I guess we do.' I smile as I realise how much truth there is in that.

'Okay, cool.' His voice is a little shaky. 'Um, so basically, I was wondering if you'd want to... Well, would you like to, y'know, give things a stab.'

'Give things a stab..?'

'As in us, give us a stab.' He's chewing on his lip.

It takes me a while, but I finally realise what Robbie is talking about. Is he asking me out? Is Robbie Morrissey seriously asking me out?

'Are you asking me to be your girlfriend?'

He nods quickly, and glances down. What should I say? I wasn't expecting this. Does Robbie even ask girls out? Crap, what do I say? I bite down onto my lip as a wave crashes onto the beach. A seagull squawks.

'Yeah,' I say without even realising I've said it. 'Yeah, let's give things a stab.'

Robbie drops me back to Dad's that night, and I have an enormous grin slapped on my face for the entire journey home. I've never had a boyfriend, not really. Aiden and I told everyone we were married when we were eight, but I don't think that counts. And I like Robbie. I never thought I'd even dare say that about Robbie Morrissey, but I do. He's not just the narcissistic sidekick of Zack Maddox, but someone with a heart who might actually be quite complex. It still bothers me a little that he disappeared when Preston was fighting his battle for him. It's not a big deal, though. I don't expect him to be perfect. I can't say I've ever met a person who is.

I kiss Robbie goodbye before getting out of the car, and my lips are still tingling as I step into Dad's house. The hallway is quiet, and the light's switched off. The blank wall where Mum and Dad's wedding photo used to hang is staring at me, so I quickly turn away. The hallway is too empty without it. I shake away the feeling as I quietly slip my shoes off, but as I'm about to go upstairs, I hear a mumbling sound. I hesitate. I think it's coming from the kitchen.

By the time I'm a few yards away from the door, I can hear Dad's hushed voice. He's speaking but no one's answering him, so he must be on the phone. I stop outside the closed kitchen door, and gaze at the painted white wood standing between Dad and me. I try to figure out what he's saying. I can't hear much, but the words I can make out sound like words I'd never imagine

Dad would speak. He's spewing out a load of cliché, romantic bullshit, and it kind of makes me want to throw up. He must be speaking to Gwen then.

Just as that thought crosses my mind, the front door slams behind me. I almost jump out of my skin. I spin around to see Gwen taking her shoes off in the hallway, but she's not on the phone.

What the hell?

The kitchen door suddenly swings open, and Dad emerges with his phone in hand. He seems shocked at the sight of me, but the second he notices Gwen, he ignores me and goes towards her. As he does so, he slides his phone into the back pocket of his baggy jeans. For a while, as I watch Dad warmly welcome Gwen 'home', I'm confused. What just happened? Did I imagine the conversation Dad just had over the phone? Was Gwen on the phone when she walked in, and I didn't realise? I shift my eyes past the space where Mum and Dad's wedding photograph used to hang, and that's when it clicks.

I can't believe him. I actually cannot believe him.

Dad's cheating on Gwen.

Gwen isn't, and never will be, my favourite person. But this is ridiculous. I should be glad she's getting a taste of her own medicine, but right now, I feel anything but glad. Just like he did with Mum, Dad is cheating on Gwen. He has to be. Does he even have a heart?

It's only now I realise my entire body is clenched, from my jaw to my fists. I shove my way past Gwen and Dad in the hallway, and charge upstairs. Dad calls after me, but I ignore him. Does he not learn? I collapse onto my bed, and for a moment, I swear

I'm going to cry. Why do I feel like crying? Dad cheated on Mum and I couldn't feel a single thing, but he cheats on Gwen and I want to explode. No, this isn't right. No, no no. My mouth is dry, my head aches. What is wrong with me?

CHAPTER 16

I'm at Cerys's house a few days after the revelation of Dad's latest screw up, and I've spent the entire time staring into space. As she and Mum chat among themselves with mugs nestled in their hands, I pick at an orange I don't even want to eat. I don't know why, but I feel like I should tell Mum what I overheard the other night. They may not be together anymore, but it's like she deserves to know. Since I was born, my parents always came as a pair, and now that they don't, it's as if I can't comprehend the idea of them being individual people.

I still catch Mum's eyes glazing over every now and then, and I know she's thinking about him, but it's getting better each time I see her. She's becoming herself again.

'You sure you don't want any tea, Mia?' Cerys asks.

'No thanks, I don't really like the stuff,' I reply with a slightly forced smile.

'You've had some here before, haven't you?' she asks as she drops her empty mug into the sink. 'Or am I thinking of your friend?'

'Oh, the lad who was here about a month ago? Mia's maths tutor?' Mum chimes in.

'Ah, that's the one! Lovely boy, he was.' Cerys sits back down at the table. 'Handsome. He had a nice shirt.'

There's a gentle smile on Cerys's lips, and I swear she fancies the hell out of Preston or something, and it's just about the most uncomfortable thing ever. She's old enough to be his mother. As Mum and Cerys start discussing shirts and tea and who knows what else, it suddenly occurs to me that I never thanked Preston for saving mine and Aiden's arses the other night. The whole thing was so hectic that I didn't even think to thank him.

'Hey, Mum, would you mind dropping me to a friend's house?' I pipe up as Mum and Cerys are midway through a conversation.

'Yeah, of course, where to?'

'Cathays, please.'

As we're nearing the squat I spent close to an entire weekend in, I realise I probably should have checked Preston was home first. The houses we pass are beginning to look a little more disheveled, and it's not long until we're in the heart of Cathays. Most of the buildings here are student houses, so the front gardens are all a little worse for wear, but I think they're quite charming. It's as if you can tell exactly who lives in each house based on the bricks they're built with.

The house we pass with a pile of clothes dumped on the garden wall belongs to a protesting student who swears to walk around the house butt-naked until his housemates stop stealing his milk, and the house with ivy crawling up its walls belongs to a lonely old woman with a garden resembling a rainforest, who thinks nature should be left to its own devices. Of course, I've got no idea if any of this is true, but in my mind it's as clear as day.

'So, Mia,' Mum says, drawing my attention away from the window. She hesitates. 'How are things at home?'

I stammer. I'm not sure what to say. I mean, do I just respond with a casual 'fine'? Do I tell her everything about the phone call I overheard the other night? As I lift my eyes to Mum's almond-shaped ones, I notice the look she's not given me in a while. The look that's waiting for me to break down. I quickly turn away.

'Yeah, fine, good,' I mutter as a response.

Mum nods, and we don't really say much after that.

The door to Preston's squat is open when I get there, which is hardly a surprise. I wasn't sure how Mum would feel about me requesting to be dropped off outside an abandoned house, so I convinced her to drop me at a small park where I said I was meeting this friend who, for some reason, I decided to name Delyth.

I let myself into Preston's house and quietly make my way up the dusty stairs, and in the matter of seconds, I know he's home. I can hear music. I think it's classical. The steps creak, and even at the top of the staircase, there's a faint musky smell from the dusty abandonment of the ground floor. Once I'm in the hallway upstairs, the smell is replaced by something sweeter. He must've bought an air freshener or something. As I near the room the music is emanating from--the only room Preston seems to use in this place--my legs begin to wobble a little. I can't help feeling like I should've called in advance.

I open the heavy door to see Preston lying on the double mattress in the middle of the massive room. His arms are outstretched with his legs laid out straight in front of him as if he's mid-crucifixion, and he balances a cigarette between his lips. He's surrounded by sheets of paper with black scribbles all over them, once of which is lying on his chest. I'd almost forgotten how weird the boy was. His eyes are shut, and I'm not sure what to do.

There's classical music seeping out of Preston's stereo, and I consider waiting until the song's finished before I say something. Then I remember how far too many classical songs can last half an hour or more, so I figure that may not be a wise idea. I notice his eye is slightly blackened, and there's a small cut on his left eyebrow. It must be from the fight. I open my mouth to speak, but clamp it shut before anything comes out. Preston's eyes are still closed. Maybe he's sleeping. Ah crap, I really didn't think this through. Maybe I should just--

'Moonlight Sonata, Beethoven.'

Holy mother of shit. I yelp, almost jumping out of my skin at the sound of Preston's voice. He's not asleep then.

'Hardly an original choice, I am aware,' he continues as if he didn't almost give me a heart attack moments ago. His cigarette is now balancing between his fingers. 'But I'm limited for space, and Euphemia, I must confess that I like it a rather lot.'

What on earth is he on about? I shake my head as I stroll over to the mattress, and by this point, Preston has opened his eyes. He sits up. How the hell he noticed me in the doorway, let alone recognised that it was me standing there, I don't know, but I take it for what it is. I sit next to him on the stained mattress.

'What are you doing?' I ask, gesturing to the papers dumped around the room.

'A list,' he replies absentmindedly as he glares at the sheet in his hand.

'What?'

He waves his hand in the air. 'Best songs--Well, favourite songs. The arts cannot be judged objectively, and what not.' He frowns as he hands me the sheet in his hands. 'I can't settle on a tenth. I keep deciding on ones, and then replacing them with others, but then I return to the old ones and conclude that I prefer them. Then I begin doubting that choice, and I'm back to where I began.'

I read the list he's handed me.

The tenth song is unclear because Preston has scribbled all over it. I can see where he'd written Moonlight Sonata though, among other song titles and artists.

'Why do you have to decide?' I question him. I glance at the list again. 'They're all a bit... depressing, least the ones I recognise.'

He doesn't reply. Instead, he watches me with innocence buried deep in his big eyes, and tilts his head. He looks confused. In that look, I see someone else. Not Zack, not Preston, but someone else entirely. Then as quickly as it appeared, it's gone.

'Hey, anyway, I came here to say thanks,' I say, handing him back the paper.

'For what?'

'For not letting me get my arse kicked by Jacob Griffiths a few nights back,' I reply as if he's dumb.

'Oh, yeah, that. It's fine.' Preston gives his list one last look over, sighs, then drops it onto the worn wooden floor.

'Have you spoken to Robbie recently?' I ask, curious to find out if he knows that we're officially an item.

'Yes, you're screwing him now, right?'

I open my mouth wide and I must resemble a gormless fish, but before I can hurdle an insult at him, Preston is on his feet. He heads on over towards the makeshift kitchen.

'No,' I state matter-of-factly, 'we're going out, not screwing. I mean, I've never, I mean... y'know.'

Preston doesn't respond. He doesn't even ask me if I want a drink. He just stubs out his cigarette on a countertop, and gets me one regardless. Most people would ask first. Even he usually asks first. The Beethoven song finishes playing, and an unrecognisable Welsh song replaces it. Preston quickly skips it. Something by The Smiths or Morrissey starts playing, rather amusingly.

'You'll never guess what,' I mutter as I take the can of cola from Preston. 'My dad's cheating on the woman he was cheating on my mum with, with some other woman.'

Preston nods. Again, he says nothing. He soon pipes up though.

'How long have you known Aiden?'

'What?'

'Aiden. How long have you know him?' he repeats.

'Uh, well we've been friends for, like, ten years. Why?'

Preston nods for what feels like the hundredth time today. It's becoming a little annoying now. I'm about to ask him why again when he answers me.

'He seems sad.'

'What?'

Aiden isn't sad, he's the bloody happiest guy I've ever met. Disturbingly happy, if anything. So that's what I say to Preston.

'Have you ever asked him?' Preston responds.

'Asked him what? If he's happy?'

'Yes.'

I stammer. 'Well, I've never just randomly asked him if he's happy, no.'

'How do you know he is then?'

Preston's beginning to irritate me now. 'Because he's the most confident person I've ever met, and I just do, okay? He's my best friend. I mean, I guess I see how the whole gay thing isn't always easy because our neighbourhood is hardly diversity central, but it doesn't mean he's unhappy.'

Preston sighs. 'See, that's it. That's the problem. Why would you measure his happiness, or unhappiness, based on something like his sexuality? People shouldn't be defined by one aspect of who they are; that entire concept is ridiculously one dimension-al. Every single problem a gay person has doesn't revolve around the mere fact that they're gay. We're more than the narrow perceptions of ourselves invented by others.'

Where the hell did that come from? Why is Preston getting all deep on me for no reason? He's starting to piss me off.

'Well okay, maybe if he is unhappy--which I'm certain he isn't anyway--it isn't about his sexuality, but if you think you're so attentive, tell me why Aiden is unhappy.'

I can hear my own agitation. I don't like Preston thinking he knows Aiden better than I do, I really don't.

'I can't tell you why because I'm not him, I can only propose a theory.' I nod my head for Preston to continue. 'Perhaps it's more than his sexuality, more so his identity beyond that--or as an extension of that, maybe.'

'What do you mean?'

'To the majority of people, Aiden is the flamboyant, excited gay kid, right? Well, maybe he's played that role for so long he's scared that if he stops, he won't be anyone anymore. He'll just be Aiden, that guy.' Preston shrugs. 'And then he'll leave college, and go to uni, and get a house and a car and grow old and rot and die, and no one will really care all that much because he's just Aiden, that guy.'

I'm frustrated. I'm really frustrated. Why does Preston always spew all this pretentious dribble? He assumes he knows best, but he doesn't. There wasn't even any need to bring Aiden up; he just saw an opportunity to show off and sound clever, and grabbed it while he could. He lights another cigarette from his pocket, but doesn't put it anywhere near his mouth. He just stares at it in his hand as it begins to burn down.

'I don't mean to devalue your friendship with him,' Preston continues, 'it's just that I've been noticing it lately--that he seems lost--so it got me thinking.'

I hadn't noticed him pick it up, but Preston is writing some-thing down on the piece of paper he handed me earlier. He stubs the burnt down cigarette out on the mattress, which nearly gives me heart palpitations, then scribbles out what he's written on the paper almost immediately. I'm about to scold him for stubbing his unused cigarette out on the flammable fabric I'm sitting on, but before I have the chance to criticise him, Preston swears loudly, crumples up his list, and lobs it across the room.

He turns silent and stares at the wall in front of him as he tries lighting another cigarette. He swears when he can't get the lighter to flicker on, then gives up.

'Are you okay?' I ask quietly.

'Yes.'

No, there's definitely something wrong, but I know the odds of getting anything out of him are painstakingly low. Anyway, after him telling me I don't know my best friend, I'm still a little too pissed at him to show much sympathy. It wouldn't shock me if the sole dilemma he's facing is the fact he can't think of a tenth favourite song.

'D'you think I should tell my mum that my dad's cheating on his new girlfriend?' I say, turning the conversation back to one I tried starting earlier.

'No,' Preston replies with a shrug.

'Really?'

'Some things are better left unknown. Regardless of who your dad is screwing, now your parents are separated, it won't affect your mother either way. No need to open doors that have already been closed.'

I guess he's right. Except for Livvy and me, nothing connects Mum and Dad anymore. Livvy's still refusing to see Dad, so that connection might not even fully be there. It's just difficult for me to grasp sometimes.

'I guess, but I don't--'

'I don't know, Mia,' Preston suddenly snaps. 'I don't bloody know. If you're going to oppose everything I say, then stop asking me for advice. Do you know what I think? I think you're going out with Robbie for the sake of it, I think you need to abolish this irrational belief that your parents' issues are yours to solve, I think you need to grow up and accept that the world doesn't function on righteousness, and I think you've changed recently, and I don't like it.'

I stare at Preston with my eyes wide. He jumps to his feet and stomps back towards the small kitchen area. Where the hell did that come from? He flicks the tap and water comes rushing out of the nozzle. He's muttering as he fills a cup. Why is he being so horrid to me? No, I'm not standing for this.

'How have I changed?' My voice is full of venom.

'You're drinking, you're smoking, you're making stupider and stupider decisions by the day.' He takes a massive gulp of the water in his hand. 'You jumped into the middle of a fight a few days ago, for Christ's sake!'

'Don't you dare criticise me for making stupid decisions, not you of all people,' I hiss. 'All you do is make stupid decisions! You drink, smoke, get into fights, ride bloody trolleys into walls! Hell, you almost got yourself killed last summer from getting so wasted!'

Preston doesn't say anything. Instead, he watches the half empty cup of water in his hands with his jaw clenched. He sighs as he drops it into the sink, and leans back against one of the mismatching kitchen units.

'Sorry,' he mutters so quietly that I'm surprised I even hear him. 'Sorry.' It's louder this time.

He drags his feet back towards me, and drops himself onto the mattress. The afternoon sun highlights the bruise on his face, and it's like an artist has dabbed the most vivid purple colour they could find onto his eye with a tiny paintbrush. Preston glances down, then turns to face me.

'Sorry,' he says again in a hushed tone. 'I'm being cruel.'

'What's wrong?'

I inwardly pray for an honest answer this time. Preston shuffles on the mattress.

'Matty's moving.' His voice comes out in a mumble. 'His foster parents are moving to Norwich, and they're going to take him with them.'

I soften my eyes, and the guilt spreads over me like a rash. I barged into here uninvited, spewed out a load of problems at Preston, and talked on and on about myself without even considering there might be something wrong in his life. I thought he was upset over picking a song, for God's sake.

'Can't you stop them? Speak to them about how you feel? I mean, that can't be good for Matty, he can't just be taken away from yo--'

'You don't think I've tried? They hate me, or at least Julia does. This is probably all her idea, and it's solely so that Matty's far enough away from me to stop caring.' Preston shakes his head and picks up one of the sheets on the floor. 'I just need one more song.'

'Stop worrying about a silly song.' I try to sound reassuring, but I just sound timid. 'Look, you're the only family Matty has, and no one with a single brain cell will let them just take him away. It can't be as easy as that, I'm sure.'

'What do you think of Fleetwood Mac? Do you like them?' Preston asks, ignoring everything I said while simultaneously avoiding anything resembling eye contact.

'Preston, it's okay to talk abo--'

'I've always really liked Dreams, but I'm not sure if I'd put it in my top ten, y'know? I think Landslide is brilliant too, saying that.'

Preston continues rambling on about finding a tenth song for his list, but I stop listening. I'd almost forgotten about meeting Paul in Roath Park, almost forgotten what I'd learned about Preston's Mum. As I watch Preston's expressive face while he babbles, I want to hug him. I want to grab him and wrap my arms around him so tightly that I have to make a conscious effort not to squeeze all of the air out of him. I want to tell him it's going to be okay. So that's what I do.

Halfway through one of his sentences, I force him towards me and grab hold of him as if letting go would cause the building to collapse around us. It shuts him up, anyway. Preston is stiff for a few seconds, but he slowly begins loosening up as I feel a small lump form in my throat. I may not know what the hell he's talking about half the time, but I've never wanted life to work out for anyone as much as I do for Preston. I really haven't.

CHAPTER 17

One hour to go. I chew my lip and tap my fingers against the table. I can't do this. I'm going to fail. I'm going to screw everything up, fail, and never get into university. I'll leave education at eighteen, never move out, buy a cat and an annual prescription to Knitting Weekly until I'm eighty-years-old, where I'll die alone in my sleep with nothing but the crumbling carcass of the cat I adopted sixty-two years ago. I finally look up from the mock exam paper in my hands.

'Eleven...?'

Preston clicks his fingers, and flashes me a smile. 'See, you'll be fine!'

'No I won't,' I mutter. 'It's not fair, I don't even like cats.'

'Huh?'

'Nothing.' I sit up straight. 'I can do the questions you give me, but it'll be different in the actual exam.'

'Believe it or not, Euphemia, I have actually been teaching you the syllabus. I wouldn't put you through this torture as some elaborate joke, as tempting as that may be.'

'Mia,' I stab back.

Preston throws an eraser at my face, which I narrowly dodge, then hands me another question. My maths resit is in under an hour, and I am bricking it. I really need to pass this. I'm still yet to see the relevance of the subject in my life. If the syllabus was all about paying mortgages and managing bank accounts, then fair enough, but instead we're required to know how to measure the angle of a triangle.

Next time I look at the clock, there's only fifteen minutes to go. Crap, now I'm nervous. Preston must be able to tell, as he always seems to, because he suggests we call it quits and relax for a bit. It turns out he does know what he's doing when it comes to teaching mathematics: the guy had eleven A*'s and one A in his last round of exams, which astounds me considering I've never seen him do any school work, ever. He can't possibly do as well in his final exams, which he'll be taking a year later than most due to his Zack-induced exploits. I shake my head. Why am I thinking about Preston's educational performance? I'm about to take an exam in--I glance at the clock--just over five minutes. Shit.

Before I know it, I'm making my way into the exam hall. Preston says something before I go in, but it doesn't process in my mind. The doors shut behind me, and I find my assigned seat. There's a slip of paper with my college photo on it for me to sign on my desk. I sign it. The large hall is silent, with the occasional disruption of a cough or a sneeze, and every single one makes me jump. The examining officer announces the usual rules: no talking, phones to the front, hand up to use the toilet, blah, blah, blah.

We're handed our exam papers. I stare at them. I bounce my leg underneath the desk. Five minutes until we start. Someone coughs. I close my eyes and take a deep breath. Another cough. Two minutes. I trace my finger along the front of the paper, and then click my knuckles. Thirty seconds. Shit.

'You may begin.' The examiner's voice booms and echoes around the room, and as I open my exam paper, I think I might be sick for a few seconds.

Here goes nothing.

It went well. I can't believe it, but it actually went well. Heck, it went brilliantly. I answered every single question, and even had time to read over my answers afterwards. Granted, I've probably just misjudged the entire test and failed miserably, but screw it. It's done, and I'm just glad to be rid of it. Who needs maths anyway, right? It's this sense of euphoria that made me agree to go out with everyone tonight; I need to celebrate. Aiden did inform me of what the group were actually doing, but I was too busy basking in the sweet, sweet joy of leaving a maths test and not having the desire to stare at the sun until my retinas incinerate to take any of it in.

That's why when Robbie utters the words Boys' Village as he lifts the handbrake of his car five hours later, a sense of nausea hits me like a boot to the face. Boys' Village is an abandoned holiday camp in Barry that was built almost a hundred years ago, and while I'm certain nothing horrendous happened there, rumours of ghosts and demons haunt the place. Regardless of how nonsensical these rumours are, I've refused to go anywhere near the place for seventeen years, and in no way was I planning on breaking that tradition today.

It's Easter that did it. I just remember being, what, four years old when this enormous fur-covered anomaly burst into my room at eight in the morning with its hands full of eggs, and eyes as cold as glass. It was quite obviously Dad dressed as the Easter Bunny, but in my childish mind, it was some bloodthirsty demon cradling its spawn. Looking back, I was an idiot, and still am an idiot for letting that bother me to this day. I can't think of ghouls and demons without feeling nauseous, and Easter is hardly a blast.

Everyone in the car is chattering away excitedly, but I stare at the sunset and calculate the likelihood of me dying if I leaped out of the car as Robbie speeds along the motorway. It's probably not the wisest idea. Mark Ronson's Uptown Funk is blaring from the car radio, and my stomach drops at every beat. Robbie, Preston, Aiden and Delyth are in this car, while Samantha and a few of Robbie and Preston's friends are in a car behind us. Delyth is, as always, practically climbing over Aiden. How he's yet to notice her enthusiasm is a mystery.

Preston's oddly quiet, and it momentarily distracts me from how much I don't want this journey to end, and how much I don't want to face Boys' Village. The group haven't been out since Prestom told me about Matty moving to England, and Preston is noticeably far less Zack-esque than he's ever been before. Aiden lets out a deafening laugh, and I remember what Preston said about him being unhappy. I glance at Preston, then back to Aiden. I don't know. I really have no idea anymore.

My mind is still burning when we stop for Aiden to relieve himself. Unlike every other guy, he believes peeing at the roadside is filthy and won't partake in such crude behaviour. Unfortunately for him, Robbie has the patience of a child in the middle of a sweet shop, so Aiden is forced to suck it up and leave the car to relieve himself just off the side of the motorway. He assigns me as his guard to make sure no one sees him, which sends Delyth into an internal fit of rage.

'Can people see me from here?' Aiden asks when we're what feels like miles into the shrubbery. 'Holy mackerel, look, there's a hole in that bush, everyone can see me. Everyone knows what I'm doing, I'm disgusting. I disgust myself. This isn't natural, I'm not meant to do my business in the middle of a bush. Everyone can see me, Mia, can everyone see--'

'Aiden, I swear we're practically in Scotland, okay? You're covered.'

Aiden nods. He takes a sharp breath, shuts his eyes, and when I turn away, I hear the sound of his flyer unzipping. Once he's done, for the first time ever, I ask Aiden if he's happy.

'Don't get me wrong, I've pissed in a bush before, but it just makes me want to scrub myself all over afterwards, and then take an ice bath to wash away my sins, not that there's enough water in the world to wa--'

'No, I don't mean now, I mean in yourself. As in you, the person. Sorry to spring this on you randomly, I just... I--' I close my eyes. 'Aiden, are you happy?'

He mutters something, but it fades away into the air. I open my eyes to look at him, and see uncertainty on his face.

'Aiden, please, if there's something that's making you unhappy, no matter how stupid or embarrassing or scary or whatever, please tell me. I don't even need to know what it is that's wrong,

I just need to know if you're okay. Are you?' I sound like I'm begging him.

He's staring at me. His brown eyes have never looked so dark, and the way they're bulging makes him resemble a small boy lost in the middle of a crowd. Aiden shrugs. He says nothing as his eyes turn misty, and it just gets worse from there.

I return to the car numb. Aiden leaps in and begins blabbering away as if everything is perfect and the world is a playground, and if I hadn't been with him as he broke down five minutes ago, I would never believe it if someone told me it had happened. How could I be so damn selfish? How the hell could I not notice how Aiden was feeling? If he can't show himself to me--really show himself--and me be none the wiser, then I am a poor excuse of a friend. I hate Preston for being right. I hate him.

'Cider or whisky?' Delyth's high-pitched voice pulls me out of my trance. She's looking at me, and we're driving again. 'Hello? Mia?'

'Uh...' I mutter as I notice her holding up a can of something, and a bottle of cheap bourbon.

'You all right, Mia?' Aiden cuts in. 'You kinda look like you want to decorate the car's interior with some puke.' He laughs, but he can't look me in the eye. 'Not that it wouldn't be an improvement.'

'Oi!' Robbie interjects, showing his middle finger to Aiden via the overhead mirror.

My thoughts flash from Preston's secrets, to Aiden's happiness, to Boys' Village within the space of seconds, and it feels like my skull is caving in on itself. Delyth asks me what I want to drink again, and I turn my gaze back to her.

'Bourbon, please.'

I sure as hell need it.

By the time we reach our destination, the earth's light has been switched off, and I'm swimming. The blackness engulfs me, and I greet it with arms wide open until I'm drowning. My throat still burns from the whisky, but my fingers are numb and my head is weightless, so I barely notice it. Preston glared at me throughout the entire journey, and it was so funny. Like, really funny. So funny that I've started laughing my arse off in the passenger seat, and I'm even snorting a little.

'Bloody hell, Mia, that shit has gone straight to your head.' Robbie laughs over my own uncontrolled giggling, and I snort as another laugh flies out of my mouth.

'That was attractive,' Delyth mutters under her breath.

'Oh shut up, Delyth, Aiden doesn't fancy you.'

I start laughing even harder.

I have no idea why I was so depressed earlier. I mean, come on, I need to get a grip. Aiden's a sixteen-year-old kid, of course he's going to have mood swings. As for this haunted boys' camp crap, I need to stop being such a whiny little bitch. Nothing can hurt me now, I'm invincible.

As everyone steps out of the car, someone taps my arm and leads me to the side of the road. Preston. Oh God, here we go. Whine, whine, whine. He snatches the whisky from my hand.

'Hey!' I roar.

'Stop.' His voice is quiet, but stern. 'I don't know what this is about, but whatever it is, drinking yourself senseless won't help.'

'You were right! Oh, Holy Preston was right again! I bet you feel really goddamn good, don't you? Well done! Aiden isn't happy, and once again, Preston proves Mia wrong!'

'Pardon?'

I snatch my arm away from his grasp, and spin around. I'm not letting him ruin my buzz, and I don't need anymore of that whisky right now anyway. I'm swimming.

It turns out Boys' Village is a load of bullshit. As I stare at the crumbling ruins in front of me with a cigarette burning in my hand, I want to laugh again. It's located in the midst of some country lanes, and we're not technically meant to be here because it's private property, but there's not an ounce of fear stirring inside of me. There's a worn down war memorial in the middle of the site, and surrounding it are several grey buildings illuminated by the moonlight. Overgrown plants crawl along the floor and scale the walls as though they're clinging to life, and every inch of the concrete has amateur graffiti sprayed onto it. It's pathetic, really. I almost laugh.

As everyone heads onto the site, I waver because I'm scared--terrified, but not of this ruined holiday camp. What used to shorten my breath at the mere thought of now makes me reek of indifference. That's what terrifies me. I catch up with the group and slot myself between Robbie and Aiden, and Robbie entwines his fingers with mine. He raises an eyebrow at me and says something, but I'm trying to figure out how he raises one eyebrow without the other, so I don't hear him.

'Mia?'

'How d'you do that with your face?' I ask, my eyes wide.

Aiden bursts into laughter, leaving me even more confused. What's funny? Seriously, how the hell do you move one eyebrow without moving the other? I contort my face in an attempt to do it myself. Aiden laughs harder.

'Mia, what the hell are you on about?' Robbie asks as he suppresses laughter through a smirk. 'I asked if you were cold.'

'No, why? Is it cold?'

'You okay? We're battling sub-zero temperatures here.'

It's not cold, is it? It's only now I notice that everyone else is wearing a jacket, while I'm strolling along with mine in my hand. Weird. Preston, who's miles ahead, is the only other person without a jacket on. Why he's so far ahead, as opposed to being a pain in the arse with Robbie, is beyond me. He'd usually have unleashed Zack by now, but there's no sign of anyone but Preston so far. Maybe the personality disorder's subsided.

People are saying things and tip-toeing into the blackness of the buildings surrounding us, but none of it is interesting me. I want to explore. I don't want to hesitantly peek inside a building, and then come back after a few seconds; that's shit. I want my legs to shake until my knees buckle under me, I want all of my organs working on overdrive, and I want fear to choke me until I have to scream. I don't just want to see things, I want to feel them.

I let go of Robbie's hand and run ahead. I pass everyone without a second glance, and keep running until I reach what used to be an outdoor swimming pool. Robbie calls my name, but I ignore him. I'm about to head into the old gymnasium when I spot Preston. He's sitting inside the otherwise empty pool, but I don't think he's noticed me. I jump in next to him.

The pool, just like every other inch of this place, has graffiti plaguing its walls. Opposite us is a steep slope which I figure used to be the deep end, but it's filled with rainwater now.

'You're unusually Preston-esque tonight,' I say. 'Oh hey, d'you still have the whisky? I think it's wearing off, and I don't want to stop swimming.'

'Do you believe in luck?' Preston responds, ignoring everything I said. He's holding something in his palm, but it's too dark for me to make out what it is. 'Walking under ladders, black cats, breaking mirrors. Crap like that?'

'Ugh, not really in the mood for an episode of Preston's Profound Musings on Life right now, to be perfectly honest.'

Again, he ignores me. He may as well be talking to the graffiti. He probably was before I came, to be fair. I dip my hand into a puddle beside me, and flick my fingers so that the water splashes onto Preston's face. He doesn't even flinch.

'Okay, okay, fine.' I hold my hands up and sigh. 'I don't know, not really.'

'Hm.' Preston nods. He hands me something, and I squint at it to see that it's some reflective glass. 'I used to have a thing for breaking mirrors.'

As if that was a perfectly competent way to end a conversation, Preston stands up and lifts himself out of the pool. Okay then. The glass is cold in my hand, and I examine it to find my own blue eyes staring back at me. I toss it to the ground, and gaze at the night sky. I can't tell if it's the stars that are spinning or my head, but it's making me feel faint, so I look back down.

I spend the next hour or so wandering around Boys' Village trying to terrify myself. I find the darkest corners of each building, and climb as many rickety stairs as I can, but not even the abandoned church makes my heart rate rocket. I bump into people occasionally, but am determined to continue on my own each time. Still nothing scares me. Having given up, I return to the group, who are all gathered on the large grassed area in the centre of the site. The alcohol has worn off a lot by now, and all I really feel is discontent.

I'm sitting cross-legged on the grass with Aiden and Delyth, and as every second passes, I'm becoming more and more irritated. Delyth keeps shamelessly flirting with Aiden, then glancing at me each time as if she's trying to rub it in my face. When she starts suggestively massaging his thigh, I've had enough. I shoot her a glare, and as if she'd been waiting for that all along, she turns away from Aiden, stands up, and faces me.

'Will you please stop staring?' she scoffs.

I shift my eyes away from her in an attempt to not take the bait.

'Mia? Hello, I'm speaking to you!' she snaps.

'Delyth,' I begin as I stand up. 'I. Don't. Want. Aiden. He's gay. If I have to say this one more time, I might literally implode in on myself, okay? Aiden is gay.'

Robbie has picked up on our confrontation, and he and some others are watching. Samantha is staring at me wide-eyed, and I think she's trying to tell me something. I shake my head and turn to Aiden. He's bright red. I gaze at him pleadingly to once and for all end this ridiculous dispute Delyth and I have.

'Aiden? Tell her, please, for the love of God.'

He stammers.

'Aiden?' Delyth asks this time.

'I'm gay, yeah.'

A grin bursts onto my lips as Delyth's face drops. Everyone is watching, and the guilt slaps me in the face. I've just embarrassed the crap out of her, haven't I? As Delyth storms off the site and towards the cars, I consider running after her, but I don't have the guts. Samantha follows her instead. Why can't I do something right, just for once?

'Uh, anyone fancy some food?' Robbie suggests in an attempt to add noise to the awkward silence.

A few people nod in agreement, and everyone heads back over to the cars. This isn't fair. Tonight was a chance to have fun, but all it's been is miserable. I need to relax, cheer the hell up, and stop being such a bitch. Robbie offers me a cigarette, which I take, and when I notice him holding the bottle of whisky, I ask for some.

CHAPTER 18

By the time everyone's eaten, I'm tipsy again. I'm not in the state of euphoria I was in earlier, but I feel invincible, and that's enough. Robbie's asking me if I've had any driving lessons yet, so I tell him I haven't, but my uncle lives on a farm so I've driven a tractor. He finds that hilarious, and almost chokes on his soggy burger. He keeps bragging about his car, and when I tell him it resembles a shed on wheels, he dares me to drive it. So I agree.

We're back in the country lanes. Robbie doesn't think it's safe for me to drive on any main roads, so he's pulled up outside Boys' Village again. Most people have left, so it's just Aiden, Robbie and Preston with me in the car. After Robbie explains the whole clutch-accelerator scenario to me, he opens his car door and gets out. Before he can get very far, Preston jumps out from the backseat, and grabs Robbie's arm.

'You're not actually letting her drive, are you?'

He sounds angry. Really angry.

'Nah, I just drove us here for a laugh, and now I'm going to drive right back to where we came from.' Robbie laughs, but Preston sure as hell doesn't. He needs to relax.

'She's not driving.'

'Yes, I am, screw you,' I snap, peeking out the window at them.

Robbie and Preston start arguing and it's really damn loud and annoying, so I leave the car. I don't think they notice because they're still arguing when I step back into it, this time on the driver's side. I fasten my seat belt. See, I'm responsible.

'Uh, guys,' Aiden says, distracting Robbie and Preston.

They turn to him, and it takes a few moments for them to realise where I'm sitting. Once they do, Robbie cheers and laughs as he heads towards the passenger side. My palms are sweating a little as I grasp the steering wheel, and for the first time tonight, my heart is pumping. I smile. This is what I need, this is exactly what I've been craving. When I turn to my left, it's Preston sitting in the passenger seat, not Robbie.

'Mia, don't do this. You've been drinking, you can't drive, it's dark, and these lanes are a death trap.'

Does Preston do anything but whine? Where's Zack? I can't believe it, but I actually want him to be Zack right now. Why hasn't he been drinking? Everyone else has.

'I'm fine, just leave me be.' I make sure to say the next sentence loudly enough for Aiden and Robbie to hear. 'Deal with it, Preston.'

He doesn't say anything in return. He clenches his jaw, clips his seat belt in, and stares straight ahead. I'm pretty sure Robbie and Aiden weren't even listening, but I think it's fair to say I win.

I return my focus to the car. The engine is making a quiet humming sound, and the steering wheel feels heavy in my hands. I can sense every breath I take, really sense it, and my hands are shaky.

I'm terrified. It's perfect.

Remembering what Robbie said about feeling for the bite, I press down on the clutch lightly, lower the accelerator, and lift the handbrake. The car jolts, then stops dead. I gasp, and the boys in the back take it as their cue to mock me.

'Mia stalled!' Robbie announces.

I shake my head as I flush.

'Don't remove the handbrake until you feel the car drop slightly,' Preston mutters beside me.

Oh, so now he's helping me?

I do as Preston says, and much to my dismay, it works. It doesn't last long because I stall again. Another shot of adrenaline races through me. Robbie makes another joke, and I turn to Preston pleadingly. I want more. I need fear to engulf me. He sighs before telling me to lift the clutch more slowly as the car begins rolling. Finally, I begin driving.

I start slow, and if I may say so myself, I'm not too bad at this whole driving thing. I've left the responsibility of gear changes to Preston, who keeps glancing at me. As the car creeps through the narrow lanes, I can sense my pulse all over my body, and there's a buzzing in my head that's getting louder and louder each minute. I speed up. Preston tells me to slow down, but I don't. I speed up a little more. I keep going faster and faster until nothing is real anymore.

Robbie leans forward from the back of the car, and switches the radio on. A classical song fills the small space, and Aiden and Robbie shriek with laughter, but Preston promptly turns it off, so Robbie complains and fights to turn it back on again, but I don't care. I don't care about any of them, or what they're doing. They're not real, not now. Only I'm real in this moment. The radio is on again, Robbie and Aiden are laughing and singing, Preston's hand is on the bottom of the steering wheel, and I'm smiling like a maniac.

I'm barely going thirty, but it feels like I've stopped the world, like we're moving faster than time itself. I can feel nothing, but sense everything. The booming laughter that fills the car, Preston's looming presence beside me, the trees and bushes swishing past. Preston is yanking at the wheel, and I'm giggling. He keeps pulling it towards him, over and over again. He's shouting, so I turn the wheel away from him, but he just shouts even more, and so I laugh even more.

Then Robbie shouts, and everything is real again.

There's a turn in the road, but the car's facing straight ahead, and Preston is pulling the steering wheel one last time but it's too late, so all I see is darkness and all I feel is my heart in my throat.

And then nothing.

This nothing is different though, this nothing is numb. Empty. Preston isn't real and Robbie isn't real and Aiden isn't real. I'm not real. We're all just pretend people in a pretend world. The nothingness doesn't last long because within moments, a feeling of nausea overcomes me. I can smell metal, my forehead is wet, and there's a shuffling sound. Something touches me and I want to push it off, but I can't open my eyes, let alone move. Why can't I open my eyes? I'm scared. I'm not scared like I was when I was driving; I don't welcome this fear, I repel it. I'm moving, how am I moving? Is something moving me? I want to be sick.

What's happening?

CHAPTER 19

I wake up to a brightness that's far too white, so consider the possibility that I might be dead. My mouth's dry and my head is aching, and it doesn't seem like I should be able to feel that if I'm dead. So I assume I'm not. It doesn't take me long to realise where I am and why I'm here because the last thing I remember is driving the car. The fact that I've not been on a bed this hard since my tonsils were removed eight years ago is another giveaway.

'Mia?'

Mum?

'Mia, darling, are you okay? Can you hear me?'

Wait, no, Dad? I lift my eyes to look beside me, and for a moment I swear I'm going crazy because my parents are standing there, together. I've not seen them together for months. I try to speak, but all that comes out is a squeak. God, my mouth is dry. Mum grabs a jug of water from the cabinet beside my bed, then pours it into an empty glass before handing it to me. I sip it lightly.

'Uh, yeah, I'm good, it's cool. Really cool, honestly,' I blabber.

Probably not the most normal response to give your parents after waking up in hospital. They both start fussing and fluffing my pillow as if it'll make any difference to anything, but all I can focus on is how awkward this whole situation is. Neither of them are acknowledging each other in any way. Dad's in his scrubs, so he must be working tonight. The thought of him working here has always been strange to me, but watching him now as he mumbles a load of jargon and strokes my hair makes the idea of him having a life outside this place unnatural.

I want to ask them where everyone else is and if they're okay, but my throat keeps drying up. I take a long gulp of water, cough to clear my throat, and try again. Mum tells me that everyone's fine, and I don't think I've ever felt more relieved in my life. Preston was the only other one who had to come to hospital, and he's been discharged already. I ask for more detail on that, but Dad just mutters something under his breath while Mum refuses to elaborate. My parents glance at each other, and Dad nods.

'Mia,' he begins. 'We're so relieved you're safe, but we're both extremely disappointed in you.'

That's when it hits me. I was driving. While slightly drunk, I drove a car I'm not insured on without a licence, and I crashed it. I landed someone, as well as myself, in hospital. I'm about to speak up and apologise when Dad continues talking. Mum sits silently with her ankles crossed and head down as he prepares to lecture me. Just like old times.

'You're only just seventeen, and you were drinking. You got into a car full of other drunk people on private property in the middle of the night, and didn't once consider the consequences.

You've never done anything remotely like this before, so why now?'

Why now? Is he kidding? I want to jump out of bed and slap him, and if it wasn't for the IV line in my hand, I swear I would. I glance at Mum to see a sour look on her face, and I'm almost certain my expression mirrors hers. She doesn't say anything.

I turn back to Dad. 'Guess,' I mumble.

'What?'

'Nothing, I just... I'm sorry.'

Why are they pussyfooting around? They've not even mentioned the fact I was driving yet. Maybe that's what this is building up to. I mean, there's no way in hell I'm getting away with it because what I did was illegal. Really bloody illegal. I purse my lips together. I'm in trouble. I'm in a shit load of trouble.

'The police want to speak to you, but we've told them you won't talk to them until you're ready,' Mum pipes in, as if she can read my thoughts. 'Just be honest, darling, don't worry about getting anyone into trouble.'

Dad's waist starts beeping and I'm momentarily perplexed, but when he lifts his pager to his face, the confusion fades. He apologises about a hundred times before we say our goodbyes, and he's soon out of the room. The second he leaves, all of the awkwardness disperses.

I chat with Mum for a while, but I can tell from the bags under her eyes that she's shattered, so I don't keep her long. She says Livvy sends her wishes, and promises to cook me my favourite meal as soon as I get out of here. Once Mum's said all she can possibly say, I tell her that I'm tired and that she should head home. It takes a good half hour of convincing, but she eventually listens to me and leaves. I'm finally alone, so I take a deep breath and shut my eyes. The peace doesn't last long.

'Euphemia, what a pleasure it is to make your acquaintance.'

I snap my eyes open and jolt up in the hard bed, and I'm stunned my heart monitor doesn't think I'm having a heart attack. Leaning against the closed door of my room is Preston, his left eye a deep purple colour and his bottom lip lined with stitches. He's wearing his infamous smirk, along with the same plain white t-shirt he was wearing last time I was conscious. I'm both extremely pleased and extremely irritated to see him. I'm kind of craving some time to myself.

'Hey,' I say quietly.

'Your name kills me, it really does. Has anyone ever told you it sounds like an STD?' he asks me for the umpteenth time, and the amused look on his face tells me that he knows exactly what he's doing. He sits at the end of my bed, despite there being a chair inches away. 'Suits you. Does it hurt?' he asks, nodding at my forehead.

What? I lift my hand up to it, and feel a large bandage tapped to my skin. As I trace my fingers along the rest of my face, it's sensitive to touch, and I have a row of stitches above my right eyebrow. I don't know why, but I'm surprised to find physical damage from the crash.

'Oh, uh, not really,' I mutter in reply, then chew the inside of my cheek before continuing. 'Listen, I'm so sorry about what happened. I know driving was really goddamn stupid and dangerous, and I was just a general knob all night, so I need to apologise because you put up with a lot of shit, and I definitely didn't mean to land you in hospital.'

Preston shoos away a non-existent entity. 'What? You weren't driving. I didn't realise you had a concussion.'

He takes a bite out of an apple. Wait, what? Where the hell did he get that from? Did he bring it in with him? Hell, maybe I am concussed. He grins at me like a teenage girl who's just told her best friend which boy she fancies. What on earth is going on?

'Where did you get that?' I nod at his apple before shaking my head. 'I mean, what? I was driving, I remember it clearly.'

'A nurse gave it to me. Her name was Linda; a charming lady, she was.'

'I was driving,' I repeat.

He takes another chunk out of his apple, and rolls his eyes. 'No, I was.'

'What? No... Preston, I'm fairly sure you're the one who's concussed.'

He looks at me expectantly, his light green eyes dulled down by the clinical lighting of the room. I tell him that I was driving while he demands he was driving, and this conversation lasts at least five minutes until it finally occurs to me what the hell is going on.

'You lied to the police and told them you were driving?'

'Llongyfurchiadau!'

'Huh?'

Congratulations,' he translates for me. 'Hit the nail on the head, bingo, however you want to say it.'

'Why the hell did you do that?' I snap.

'Mia, think: I was sober, you sure as hell weren't. I'm insured on the car, you're not. I have a license, you don't. I--'

'Okay, okay, I get the point,' I mutter. 'I just...I don't get it. Wouldn't they have found me in the driver's seat?'

He shrugs as he chomps on what's left of his apple. 'We may have repositioned you slightly. Don't worry, I'm assuming you can't remember it but you were conscious at the time, and we made sure you weren't critically injured beforehand.'

'Oh, okay...' I say slowly. I'm not missing any limbs or anything, so I guess that was the right decision. 'Thanks, seriously. That's... That's incredible of you.'

The way my parents reacted makes complete sense now, everything from the expressions on their faces at the mention of Preston's name, to their lack of panic at my imminent arrest.

'Don't,' Preston interrupts my thoughts, and his playful manner has vanished completely.

'What?' I ask.

'Don't ever thank me for anything; it'll conjure up expectations in your head that I can't fulfill.' He suddenly perks up, then says, 'bear in mind, I'm doing something monumentally illegal here, so I probably shouldn't receive praise. You're such a negative influence.'

I roll my eyes at him, but struggle not to smile. Preston explains how he ensured Aiden and Robbie said it was him driving, and how they lied about an animal jumping in front of the car, which caused Preston to panic. No one was seriously injured, so he shouldn't get into any real trouble, and even if there was any doubt, his fingerprints are all over the car's steering wheel. It's all as easy as that, he assures me, and I really hope it is. I'm sure not going to press any charges, anyway.

I wonder if Preston's been here since he was discharged, and I guess the fact he's wearing the same shirt as earlier suggests he has. The left sleeve is slightly bloodstained, so that should've probably given it away. I'm not the most observant right now, am I?

'Are you sure you're not going to get into any trouble?' I ask, struggling to stop the niggling in my mind.

'You have my word. I turned the wheel pretty aggressively right before you planted the car in the shrubbery, which was a vast improvement on that beat up old thing, if you ask me, so the way the car crashed validates the story we've given.'

I dread to think what would've happened if Preston hadn't turned that wheel. We would have smashed headfirst into the bushes, and at the speed we were going, we would've hit something a lot harder eventually. He kind of saved my life. He kind of saved all of our lives. Bloody hell.

I watch him as he places what's left of his apple down onto his shoe as he dangles his leg off the bed, and balances it there with an amused look on his face. That's not the first time he's stopped me getting torn to shreds by a car.

'I know you don't want me to say it, but thanks,' I say again. 'Seriously, thank you. You kinda saved my life.'

'Dw i mond yn ddychwelyd ffafr.'

His voice is barely audible as he kicks the apple into a bin in the far corner of the room, not that I'd have any clue what the hell he just said anyway.

'Huh?'

He laughs at my confusion. 'The less you reveal, the more people can wonder: Emma Watson.' Preston pauses. 'Granted, that was said in the context of sexual attraction, but let's disregard that minute detail.'

'Preston, what the heck are you blathering on a--'

'What are you doing here?'

I snap my head towards the doorway to see Dad standing there with a clipboard in his hands. He's glaring at Preston.

'Mia needs to rest, please leave.'

Preston doesn't argue. He smiles at me, stands up, apologises to Dad, and promptly leaves the room. Dad remains still as he stares in my direction. He starts fussing again, and I'm really damn pissed off because if he had any idea what Preston has done for me, he would be kissing the guy's feet. Why do people keep assuming I need rest, anyway? I'm fine.

'He was just making sure I was okay,' I mutter as Dad sits down on the bedside chair. 'It wasn't his fault, what happened. We were all distracting him and something jumped in front of the car, so it's a miracle things aren't ten times worse.'

'I just don't want you hanging around with him, Mia, you don't understand.'

'Yes, I do, he's my friend. You've never met him,' I argue.

'Yes, I have.'

I'm about to argue again when I process what Dad just said. Dad's never met Preston, has he? He's picked me up from Matty's house before, but they've never actually met.

'I was a nurse on a ward he was admitted to last summer. He came in after some party. You might've even been there, I can't remember.'

Every bone in my body freezes because I know he's talking about Robbie's party. Dad was around the night Preston almost died. Why am I only finding this out now? After all the months of wondering, of rumours, of wanting an explanation. And I could've just asked Dad.

'You were his nurse that night?' I ask with my eyes wide.

'Not specifically, but I dealt with him briefly, yes, which is exactly why you being his friend makes me nervous. I don't like it.'

I slowly shake my head, then sigh. 'I know it must look bad, but please believe me when I say he's changed. I mean, that's not really him, he doesn't do drugs or anything usually.' Preston doesn't anyway, not too sure about Zack. 'He's not a bad person, I swear.'

'Drugs? What?'

I narrow my eyes. 'Didn't he take some dodgy drugs or something that night? Like, some kind of illegal something or other, I don't know. I assumed...' My voice trails off.

Dad's scanning me as he rubs his chin. I've seen this look before, so I know he's deliberating something. I don't know if he's going to tell me it wasn't an overdose that landed Preston in hospital that night, but he's definitely implying it. Dad sighs as he rests his head in his hands. He sighs again, then looks back up at me.

'How did he seem earlier, Mia? When you were out with him? Did he behave in any way that would've implied the crash wasn't an accident?'

'Are you suggesting he crashed on purpose?' I don't even try to act like I'm not offended. 'Why would he do that?'

Dad sighs, and it's starting to irritate me now. He needs to do less sighing and more explaining. I know the whole patient confidentiality thing is a big deal, but I'm his daughter, and he sure does owe me a lot. He finally speaks again.

'Look, you can in no way repeat this to anyone, okay, not even to Preston. If anyone finds out I've told you, my job is on the line, but you need to know because he's... he's not stable.' His voice is stern, and I promise I'll keep quiet. 'That boy didn't overdose on any illegal substances that night, and he was barely drunk. Mia... Preston overdosed on painkillers. He tried to kill himself.'

CHAPTER 20

I've lost track of how many days have passed since the crash. I've not really done much or seen anyone besides Aiden, and since him admitting his unhappiness to me, things have felt fragile between us. Me almost killing him while illegally driving a car may play a part in that too, I guess. Robbie's called a few times, but I've not had the stomach to answer. I sent him a text instead; one suggesting we take a break. I know what happened was entirely my fault, but I'm annoyed at him for daring and encouraging me to drive that night.

I'm somewhat grateful for this lack of human contact because it's presented me with the ideal opportunity to mull things over. I can't get what Dad told me about Preston out of my head. I don't understand it, and I'm not sure I want to understand it. All I know is that I need to convince Matty's foster parents to keep him in Wales. That's why I'm standing here right now with my chest tight, and my nerves shot. I knock the front door of Matty's house, and wait. It's probably barely even ten seconds, but it feels like hours until the door opens, and I see Paul standing where it used to be.

'Oh, hello,' he says awkwardly.

'Uh, hey, I know this must seem a little strange, but could I possibly speak to you for a few minutes?' I pause. 'It's about Preston.'

Paul nods and gestures for me to step into the house, and for some reason, I can't help feeling like I'm intruding without Preston here. I follow him through to the living room to find his wife huddled up on a puffy cream soda. The television is showing one of those crappy antique dealer programmes where people seem to continuously lose money instead of win any, but Julia has her eyes clasped on me as we enter. She narrows them, and I already know my chances of changing her mind are near enough impossible.

'Julia, this is one of Preston's friends...'

'Mia,' I fill in, and Paul apologises. I say it's fine.

'Yes, I think we've met.' She hesitates. 'What do you want?'

Paul glances at her disapprovingly as he offers me a seat, and he puts the television on mute. My mouth is dry and I'm twiddling my thumbs to hide my nerves, but I doubt I'm fooling anyone. I'm surprised I was let into the house so easily, but then I get the feeling Paul wants the issues with Preston resolved.

'Mia's here to talk about Preston,' Paul answers for me. His wife opens her mouth, I assume to protest, but he hushes her. 'Please Julia, give it a chance.'

Julia has the same greying hairstyle she had when we first met, only the grey of her roots has slithered downwards to reach the crown of her head. She looks tired, and I find it difficult to imagine her dancing like a maniac with Matty in the way

Preston does. She turns away from Paul to look at me, and nods subtly. She apologises.

'Okay,' I start. I take a deep breath. 'I know this has nothing to do with me and I don't mean to intrude, I really don't, but Preston told me about you moving to England with Matty, and...'

I clear my throat as I realise I have no idea what to say or how to say it. The light from the TV is flashing against Paul and Julia's faces, and the large living room I'm in is getting narrower and narrower by the minute. Paul is watching me expectedly while Julia looks a little bored, and that annoys me. That really annoys me. She sighs.

'We chose to foster Matty, not Preston. I don't mean to sound harsh, but he isn't really any of our concern.'

'He should be though,' I reply, frustrated. 'Whether you like it or not, Preston is Matty's brother, and you can't just ignore that. And y'know what, yeah, he can be the most frustrating human being to walk this earth sometimes, but so can I. So can everyone. You can't judge someone based entirely on their flaws, you just can't.'

'We've given him chances, and every single time he's thrown it back in our faces,' Julia retorts. 'The language he uses is vulgar, he's rude, and the one time we let him stay here overnight, he stole our alcohol and snuck a girl into the house. We can't be expected to tolerate that.'

She's describing Zack. I always assumed Preston was himself around Matty's foster parents, but if he's Zack around them then, quite frankly, I understand. Would he really be that stupid though? Preston is a lot of things, but he's not stupid. Maybe it's not about stupidity, maybe it's something deeper than that.

'I can't defend what he's done, but that's not him. I can't... It's hard to explain, but please take my word for that. When Preston is with Matty, he's not that person.' I try one last time. 'If not for anything else, please just give him a chance because of what happened last summer. Matty doesn't deserve to lose him.'

'What?' Julia asks impatiently. 'What happened last summer?'

I tilt my head. Julia and Paul must know about Preston's overdose, there's no way they can't. They would've been informed of him being in hospital at least, right, with him being Matty's brother? It's only now that I'm watching Paul and Julia together, Paul silently fiddling with his hands and Julia staring me in the eye, that I realise they're a mirror of my own parents. I hope things work out better for them.

'Mia? What happened last summer?' Paul asks this time.

'Do you really not know? When Preston was at a party and... and he ended up in hospital?'

They shake their heads. I kind of can't believe this. I know I should tell them, but I don't want to. I already feel guilty for knowing all these things about the life Preston's so desperate to hide from me, so sharing that information with other people doesn't sit right. If I have any chance of convincing Julia to give him another chance though, I have to say something.

'Preston,' I try, but my voice is quiet. I speak up. 'Preston's not well.'

I have to clamp my mouth shut before I let anything else slip out. While Julia stares back with raised eyebrows, an expectant expression on her face, Paul's brow is furrowed.

'What?' he questions. 'I don't--In what way? Will he be okay? He never said anything to us, why--'

'Mia!'

All three of us turn to the living room doorway, and standing there with an enormous grin on his small face is Matty. I think about Preston at Robbie's party, and see him lying on the moist grass with transparent skin and dry lips, and then I see Matty again, and my heart sort of breaks.

'Awesome, let's go upstairs, I have to show you my dinosaurs. I bet Preston's told you all about them, he gets really jealous.'

'Matty, what have we said about barging into rooms without knocking?' Julia speaks with her eyebrows raised.

'Mia doesn't mind.' He waves his hand in the air, the same gesture Preston often makes. 'C'mon Mia, I wanna show you!'

I glance at Paul and Julia, and while Paul nods, Julia doesn't look sure. She eventually gives me a strained smile, which I take as permission. There's nothing else I can say to try and convince them now, so I follow Matty upstairs to his bedroom as he grabs my arm and pulls me behind him. And hey, I do like dinosaurs.

As Matty bounces around his room excitedly, his dark curls bounce with him. He's blabbering about who knows what, and he reminds me a little of Aiden--not just because they look a little alike. I sit myself onto his bed and smile at the memory of the first time Preston brought me here, when I was soaked from head to toe.

'Matty,' I say, interrupting his rambling. He turns to me with his dark eyes wide. 'Were you listening to me talking with your parents just now?'

'They're not my parents, they're Paul and Julia,' Matty corrects me, and I'm secretly glad. 'No, grown up talk is boring and dumb. You all always talk about the weather and how you've been doing, and everyone always says they've been doing fine, even if they haven't. If you've been bad, you would never actually say that. It's all dumb.'

'It is,' I agree wholeheartedly. 'I don't really count myself as a grown up just yet, though.'

'Really? You're kinda old.'

I laugh. I half listen to Matty as he begins a detailed lesson on the names and personalities of every toy dinosaur he owns, but I'm distracted by the same photo that caught my attention the first time I was in this room. It's sitting on the bedside cabinet, staring at me. I realise who's in the photo now: Preston, Matty, and their mum. It must be. I wonder if it was taken before or after she went to prison, and it feels like my eyes are locked into hers. I can't comprehend a woman so small and fragile doing anything worth landing her behind bars.

I shake my head and turn back to Matty, who's now explaining why he has a triceratops named Alan.

'Hey, Matty,' I say once he's finished. 'Is that your mum in the photo there?'

I point to the photo, and he nods. He doesn't say anything else, and he remains silent as he begins lining up his prehistoric toys at the end of his bed. Once they're placed neatly, he turns back to me.

'Can you take me to see her?'

'Pardon?'

'I was meant to go with Preston on Tuesday but he can't take me now, so can you take me instead? To see my mum?'

I stammer. 'Uh, I'm not sure if that's a good idea... I don't know if I can, or how--'

He rolls his eyes as if I'm a complete imbecile. 'Of course you can, you just need to know her name and stuff, and I know that.'

Is it really that easy? It sure would be the perfect opportunity to make sense of Preston, and if it's that easy, then... No. No, I'm getting carried away. I can't visit Preston's mum in prison, for Pete's sake, it's not any of my business. Then again, I don't know how many more chances Matty will get to see her before he moves.

'Please, Mia!' Matty pleads. 'Preston takes me all the time, and Paul and Julia never find out 'cause they think I go to after school club on Tuesdays, and I won't even tell Preston either, if you don't want. Please, please, please.'

I'm biting on my lip so much that I'm practically chewing it apart. I can't just visit someone I don't know in prison, it's stupid. I want to, though. I shouldn't want to, but I do. I blink slowly, and sit back on the bed.

'Okay,' I say quietly. 'Okay, I'll take you.'

I spend the rest of the day at Cerys's house with Aiden and Samantha. Mum hasn't seen Aiden in a while, so she's ecstatic when she spots me letting him in through the front door, which leaves Samantha sporting the most bewildered look I've ever seen. As Aiden starts talking, I desperately want to tell him everything about the prison visit I've agreed to, but I resist. He finally knows about my parents' break up, and I hoped that would mend the awkwardness between us, but it's not really worked. I need to speak to him, and today seems to have a theme of me trying to fix things, so I figure now's a good call.

We spend the afternoon huddled in Cerys's tiny living room with hands wrapped around mugs of hot chocolate, and when

Aiden and Mum leave so she can show him her new dress, there's a nudge on my arm.

'I'd take him into the kitchen if you want his attention for longer than five minutes. He tends to stick around if there's food on offer.'

Samantha's voice is as quiet as ever, and it's the first thing she's said since she got here. I've been trying to get Aiden alone since he arrived, but with him being him, I can't keep him still for long enough.

'Is it that obvious?' I ask.

She just shrugs with a soft smile on her pale face. Neither one of us says anything else, and Samantha begins plaiting her red hair into a braid as she hums an old Disney song I can't put my finger on. The inevitable silences that occur in Samantha's company aren't uncomfortable anymore, but a relief. Sometimes it's nice to be with someone and just exist without having the need to make noise.

Once Aiden and Mum return, I suggest grabbing a bite to eat, and he jumps at the chance. I ask Samantha if she wants anything, and she shakes her head with a knowing smile. I've got no idea why I didn't think of this sooner. After handing Aiden some chocolate from the fridge, I open my mouth to speak, but he gets there before me.

'Listen, Mia, I'm sorry about having that dumb breakdown before Boys' Village, and the whole thing with Delyth, and--'

'Aiden, you have nothing to apologise for,' I interrupt him. 'I was a raging arsehole that night with everything from Delyth to the crash, and you should never apologise for feeling low.'

Aiden scratches his head, and he's looking anywhere but directly at me. I guess this has been on his mind as much as it has mine. I edge closer to him, place my hand under his chin, and gently lift his head up. We need to talk about this, properly.

'I mean it, Aiden, it's okay to be unhappy, and if I can help you with whatever it is that's making you unhappy, then please let me.' He tries to look away, but I pull him back. 'Please Aiden, it's me you're talking to here. Nothing you say to me will change anything between us.'

I let out a long breath once I've finished, and Aiden says nothing. He's not turned away from me this time though, so I'm clinging onto hope.

'You know me, just trying to throw in some comedic relief,' he mumbles as an echo of something he said a while ago plays in my head.

'Aiden, I--'

'It's fine, it's nothing--I mean, I don't know what it is, it's like... It's like I want people to like me, y'know? I know it's not cool to admit that, but I do. It scares me that all this is going to end, and that no one will remember me. I want to be someone, and I know that's stupid because we're all going to end up obliterated by the sun anyway, but I can't shake it off.' He swallows. 'I mean, if I stand out then I've got a chance, y'know? If I can be someone people like, someone who doesn't disappear into everyone else, then it'll take longer for the world to faze me out. I know it's dumb, but it just makes me feel really damn sad sometimes.'

Aiden's eyes return to the floor the second he finishes speaking, but I lift his head back up again. There's a smudge of chocolate on his chin that's ever so slightly darker than his skin, and I snigger as I rub it off. A small smile breaks onto his lips, and I giggle a little more. Before we know it, we're both in hysterical fits of laughter. Aiden points at Cerys's kitchen curtains and says they're ugly as hell, and I tell him Zack Maddox has a matching shirt, and we laugh even more. It's perfect.

'Just don't feel like you have to play some character, okay? Least not around me,' I say once we've regained our composure. 'I'm pretty sure everyone our age is stuck in the shitstorm of figuring out who the hell we are, but just know that whoever you figure yourself out to be, he's enough.'

'Way to get soppy, Mia,' he jokes in response, but there's a bashful look in his eyes as he speaks, and he follows it with, 'but thanks. Voicing this shit has made me feel less crazy.'

I smile at him in response, to which Aiden grins, displaying a mouthful of melted chocolate, most of which is stuck to his teeth.

'You're so gross,' I say, laughing again. 'How's Delyth, by the way?' I ask as I steal a cube of chocolate from Aiden's bar. 'I should probably track her down and apologise for being a shameless bitch to her.'

'That you were.' Aiden shrugs. 'I've not spoken to her since you two fell out, and I think she's annoyed at me for the whole gay thing. I know I should've told her from the get go, but I liked it. It was nice not having someone assume, and I think I just fed off it.'

'Well, in any case, I'm sorry I embarrassed you with that. It wasn't my place to announce it to Delyth and force you into telling her you weren't madly in love with her.'

He shrugs, and I take that as him telling me it's okay. Before we make our way back into the living room, I pull Aiden into a tight hug, and we just stand there for a minute with our heads nestled into each other's shoulders. We're still hugging when I whisper into his ear.

'I can't make any promises about anyone else, but I can promise you that I think you're bloody brilliant. And that's worth more than anything any stranger thinks.'

CHAPTER 21

Now that I'm stepping off the bus, I'm beginning to question my sanity. Matty hums beside me as he skips along the pavement, and my stomach is churning so loudly that I'm surprised he can't hear it. It's Tuesday afternoon, and as my application to visit Matty's mum was accepted, I'm headed to the prison. I now know her name to be Anwen, and that she's thirty-seven, but nothing else. I decided not to look her up online beforehand because I want to form my own opinion of her based on the woman I meet today, not on cold facts. I think I at least owe Preston that.

I returned to college last week, and I was instantly propelled back into normal life. Aiden and I were fine, and it was as if the crash had never happened. The only difference was the lack of Delyth, and it was strange not having any maths lessons with Preston. I've not seen him in college a great deal, and I was beginning to get a little worried, but he's been out with the group a few times, apparently. I'm still clinging onto the hope that Paul and Julia will change their minds about moving.

The prison is only a short walk from the bus stop, so it's not long until I'm faced with it. It's an ugly building, and an even uglier thought to live in it. Its red bricks have faded to a dull pink, which wouldn't be so awful if it wasn't for the nauseatingly high walls blocking the much needed sunlight. The inside isn't much better. Matty and I wait in a queue of people with vacant stares, and the woman at the desk we're lining up to doesn't smile back at me when I give my name and visitation details.

Once we've both been frisked in the next room, we're finally allowed into the visitation centre, which basically consists of rows upon rows of tables with women wearing the same blue aprons. Some have people with them while others don't, and the off-white walls in here are just as drab as every other wall in this building. There are stacks of chairs dotted around the room, stacks of tables, stacks of paperwork, stacks of everything, with each stack looking just as forgotten as half the women in here. Matty seems entirely oblivious to it all.

I spot her almost immediately. Her dark-blonde hair is pulled up into a loose ponytail, and she has eyes I've seen so many times before on somebody else. They suit Preston better, but that might be because I'm used to seeing them on him. Despite wearing no make up, she's undeniably beautiful. I take a deep breath, grab hold of Matty's hand, and follow one of the prison officers to the table Anwen sits beside. As we near her, I notice she's barely aged since the photo I've seen of her, and I'm desperate to know how long she's been here. Anwen smiles lightly as we sit down, and within that single gesture, all of my nerves rush out of me.

'Hello.' She sounds how she looks--warm and gentle. 'You must be Euphemia.'

Her North Wales accent is notably strong, and I'm too mesmerised with it to correct her. I almost reach out to shake her hand, but quickly remember physical interaction isn't allowed. It's to prevent friends and family members providing prisoners with contraband, apparently.

'No, she's Mia. Preston says they're not boyfriend and girlfriend, but I think they are,' Matty replies to Anwen before I have the chance to say anything.

I laugh and roll my eyes, and Anwen looks at Matty in the same doting, almost desperate, way Preston does. She's barely said anything, but I want to know everything about her. I want to know how such a delicate woman can live in such an ugly place, I want to know why she's here, where she grew up, what music she likes, her favourite food. It's as if she's the key to Preston, but another mystery altogether.

'Thank you for bringing him,' Anwen says as she delicately flicks her ponytail off her shoulder. 'I'm surprised Preston was okay with it, though I suppose it's fair to assume he doesn't know.'

I nod before realising I'm yet to say a word to her. She speaks a lot like Preston, only with a far richer accent.

'It's nice to meet a new face,' Anwen continues. 'I can't recall the last time I met somebody new. Everyone has a tendency to blend into one in here.'

'I can imagine,' I reply quietly.

As Matty and Anwen begin chatting about anything and everything, from what Matty had for breakfast to why the leaves change colour in autumn, I sit back and simply listen. Matty is speaking at a pace so fast I can't keep up, and it takes me far too long to realise he's speaking another language, and it's even more shameful how long it takes me to realise he's speaking Welsh. Anwen stops him and apologises to me, but I just smile and shake my head to tell her it's fine. They both occasionally slip back into Welsh, but I don't say a thing. It's fascinatingly beautiful to listen to. Words flurry out of their mouths, while I listen in wonder at the sounds I don't understand.

There are about fifteen minutes left of our allocated visiting time when Matty asks Anwen about a play area, and only now does it click inside my head. The photo in Matty's room, the one where Anwen, Preston and Matty are posing in front of a play area. That was here. She really has been here a long time, hasn't she? Anwen rolls her eyes, but can't stop a smile forming on her lips as she gives Matty permission to play. She calls one of the straight-faced guards over, and when he begins leading Matty towards one of several doors, I'm surprised she doesn't follow him.

'I'm rarely allowed to interact with him physically,' she explains, as if sensing my question. She watches as Matty disappears through the door. 'It's difficult. Sometimes it's easier to just leave him to it.'

It's impossible not to notice the sadness in her voice, but she follows it with another smile to cover it up. I nod, and I sort of want to hug her. It's just the two of us at the table now. I'm a little nervous, and I'm not sure why.

'I can't say Preston has ever mentioned you to me. Then again, he rarely tells me much of anything about himself, so I can't say I'm surprised.'

'Yeah, he's... something.'

Anwen laughs, and it's as if that one laugh is telling me she understands what I'm saying perfectly, as if she's been right there beside me throughout all of my bizarre encounters with her son. Her smile soon fades into something more strained.

'I've been a little... I've been worrying a rather lot about him recently, especially with Matty's foster parents moving him away. I was just wondering how he seems with you because he never tells me a thing about how he's feeling, and you probably know far more than I do.'

I fiddle with my hands as I quiz myself on how to answer this question. I'm not sure what the answer even is, in all honesty. I mean, what's normal for Preston? Does Anwen know about last summer? She must do. It seems like she wouldn't be asking me this if she did, though. Does she know he was in a car accident just a few weeks ago? I turn to her and lock my gaze into hers, and all I can focus on are her green eyes. I can't lie to her, I just can't.

'I don't know. Honestly, I've been worried too. What has he told you?'

'A lot less than what you know, I can assure you of that.' Anwen sighs. 'The most detail he's ever given me about anything since he was about fifteen, maybe, is when he told me some of his exam results almost two years ago. He used to talk about everything, but over the years it's like he's gradually been closing himself up more and more. He never talks about friends, school, aspirations, jobs, or anything he gets up to outside of that. I don't even know where he's living.' Her voice cracks at the end of her sentence.

'Do you know about last summer?' The words have left my mouth before I even realise.

Anwen stares at me with her big eyes, and it's as if the greyness of the room we're in is filtering into them. She shakes her head.

'Right, well he's got plenty of friends, so don't worry about that. He was my maths tutor for six months, so he can't be doing that badly in school, and I guess that covers his job too. Aspirations... I honestly have no idea. He has a small place in Cathays, in a house he's done up quite amazingly, really.' Once I finish, I take a deep breath. 'And about the summer... Ask him. It's not my place to say, but please do just ask him.'

I've barely told Anwen anything, but she gives me the most satisfied look I've seen, ever. I worry for a moment that she'll insist on me telling her what happened last summer, but she doesn't. She merely nods and thanks me as if I've just done the kindest thing anyone has ever done for her.

'I don't mean to sound presumptuous,' Anwen begins as I notice Matty returning through the door he disappeared into a while ago. 'But I'd love for you to visit again. It's just that it's been so wonderful speaking to someone new, and you're the only link I have to Preston other than Matty. He tells me nothing, and Matty's far too involved in his own world to be much help with it.'

'Of course.'

'Are you sure? I don't want to put you under pressure, it's rude of me to ask, it truly is, and it is a lot to ask as--'

'It's fine, Anwen, I'd love to.'

Anwen opens her mouth to say something else, but is interrupted by the guard returning with Matty. His facial expression still resembles that of an angry gorilla.

'Your hour is over. Wrap it up, please.' His voice is cold, and it takes a hell of a lot of effort not to smack him.

Anwen says her goodbyes to Matty, and I've never seen a woman so desperate to wrap her arms around her child when she has to resist all urges to do so. As we say our goodbyes, I can even sense her desire to pull me into a hug. I glance at the guard, then at Anwen, then back at the guard, and turn to Matty. He flashes me a knowing grin and yanks the guard's sleeve.

'What's the most chairs you've ever piled up in one go, ever?'

Matty points towards one of the stacks of chairs on the wall opposite us, which makes the guard turn around. He grunts something, clearly disinterested, and I take my chance while it lasts. I squeeze Anwen's hand, flash her a subtle smile, stand up, and make my way out of the building with my arm linked in Matty's. Now that is what I call teamwork.

I leave the room so chuffed with our performance that I almost don't recognise Samantha in the prison's waiting room. It makes me look twice. At first, I assume I'm simply imagining the flash of red hair and pale skin, but when my eyes meet hers and I see her big brown orbs staring back at me, I know I'm not mistaken. I don't know why, but I feel a little embarrassed. Samantha waves and smiles a toothy grin as she jumps out of her seat and heads towards me. She pulls me into a hug, which feels wrong in some way after being disallowed to even touch Anwen moments ago.

'Oh, Mia, hello!' Samantha says as she finishes embracing me.

I'm awaiting the inevitable question of what I'm doing here, and I'm not sure how I'll answer. I expect that to be the next question, but it isn't.

'I'm so glad you and Aiden sorted things out!'

'Yeah, uh, yeah, same.'

I wait for her again to ask me why I'm here, who I'm visiting, who Matty is, but she never does. Instead, Samantha simply strolls back over to her seat, and begins tapping her feet as she hums to herself. She gives us one last wave as Matty and I leave the building for good.

As we make our way to the bus stop opposite the prison, I'm plagued by the curiosity of why Samantha was there. I was so caught up in worrying about her questioning me that it didn't occur to me that she was waiting to visit someone herself. I have no idea who, and maybe I'll never find out, but you know what? That's okay. I don't need to know, and it's certainly not important. Everyone has their secrets, and it's nobody's business to know what they are.

I go to bed feeling happier than I have for a while that night. I can't really be sure why. Part of me feels like things are beginning to make more sense, but they're not, not really. If anything, I'm more clueless than I ever have been. Maybe I'm just accepting it, maybe that's the secret. I've always been so desperate to make sense of everything, but I don't care for that much anymore. I don't need to understand every single thing.

There is one thing I can't resist doing as I wrap myself up in my duvet that night, though.

I take my phone from underneath my pillow, and for a moment, the screen's light makes me wince. I turn the brightness down as I open the web browser, and begin typing 'Anwen Maddox' into the search bar. The first search doesn't retrieve much, so I try searching her name alongside 'Cardiff'. Still nothing. I click my tongue as I consider any other possibilities. Having no better ideas, I search Anwen's name again, this time typing 'prison' after it. I'm mainly bombarded by unrelated web pages, but one catches my attention. It's an article from six years ago.

As I click onto it, a photo of Anwen pops onto my screen. I'm so intrigued by the image of her in a summer dress with her fair hair falling gracefully to her waist, her eyes glistening and her cheeks blushed pink, that minutes pass until I notice the title of the article. 'Mother of Two Sentenced to Twenty Years in Prison For Manslaughter'.

CHAPTER 22

It's a Wednesday morning, and I'm in the college library when I bump into Preston for the first time in weeks. Aiden and I are trying to make sense of the law assignment we've been given, although admittedly, we're spending more time watching videos of dogs wearing fancy dress than we are researching contract law. I hear someone shuffling about next to us and turn to see Preston, which turns my entire body cold.

I think of his secret Dad told me, my visit to his mother, finding out why she's in prison, visiting Matty at his foster parents' home, and just about everything else I know about him that I shouldn't. And I feel awful. He's straddling one of the blue library chairs as he chews on something.

He grins, then says, 'hey dickheads, how's it going?'

I roll my eyes, and my guilt is replaced by pure frustration over his compulsion to play the role of Zack when in public.

'We're doing work, would you mind bothering someone else?' I mutter.

'C'mon, that's not a nice way to greet the guy who saved your arse a few weeks back.' He pouts his lips. 'Ain't you missed me?'

'No.'

'Y'know,' Aiden begins. 'I can't tell if you two have the most intense sexual tension I've ever witnessed, or if you just legitimately hate each other.'

I elbow him hard in the ribs, and he lets out a disturbingly high-pitched screech. Preston laughs and gives him a high-five, which makes the plump librarian at the main desk scowl and tell us to be quiet. I groan as I shoot her the most apologetic look I can muster up in an attempt to make her realise that this is a lot more painful for me than it is for her.

'Hey, Aiden, be an absolute legend and ask that whiny bitch behind the counter if they have this book for me, yeah?'

Preston delves into his jeans' pocket to find a crumpled piece of paper, and hands it to Aiden. Aiden, being the lapdog he is, nods enthusiastically and trots over to the main desk. Preston watches him until he's out of earshot, then turns back to me. He's still chewing on something.

'Mia, I require a monumental favour from you.'

'Oh, hey Preston, fancy seeing you here.'

He smiles sarcastically. 'Matty's foster parents have a rental home in Pembrokeshire, where they spend most weekends. Have I mentioned that before? Apologies if I have. But yes, well, I've no idea what form of chronic illness has overcome them, but they've proposed I join them with Matty this weekend.' He's speaking at a record-breaking pace, and I can barely keep up. 'I understand if you immediately refuse because it would be incredibly awkward, I'm aware, but this might be my final opportunity to fix things, and I fear I'll mess it up.'

'What do you mean? You've not asked me anything?'

'Oh, sorry. I was wondering if you would come along.' He stammers a little. 'I've already asked them about you joining us, and they had no objections.'

Preston's chewing harshly on whatever is in his mouth now, his cheekbones more prominent than ever as he does so, and there's desperation in his eyes. I'm ecstatic. Does this mean Paul and Julia are giving him another chance? Would they go as far as to consider staying in Wales? I don't even have to think about it. I grab Preston and squeeze him into a hug, which he clearly hates, and take him up on his offer.

Paul and Julia pick us up straight from college that Friday, which means I've had to lug a weekend bag around with me all day, and given Dad's negative view of Preston, also means I had to lie and tell him I was staying with Mum over the weekend. It's not like he'll check with her.

Preston has somehow crammed all his essentials for the weekend into his college backpack. He couldn't stand still while we were waiting in the college reception to be picked up, and he kept asking me if it was boiling in there or if it was just him. It was just him. Five minutes or so before Paul and Julia pulled up, he asked me for advice, so I gave him the only advice I could.

'You can in no way pull the Zack card this weekend because the second you do that, it's over.'

He said nothing after that, and hasn't since.

It takes us just over an hour and a half to reach a large white cottage at the end of a narrow road. Minutes ago, we were driving through a small village filled with houses painted in primary colours until we took a harsh left turn at the top of a hill, and began weaving through country lanes. Rows upon rows of trees surround us, their height verging on threatening, but as we reach the front of the house, they begin dispersing, and what remains is stunning.

There's a large wooden gate in front of the property, which Paul leaves the car to unlock, and the traditional cottage resembles something from an eighteenth-century romance novel. Rose bushes in the midst of blooming frame the house's porch, and when I step out of the car to peek around the building, I can see the smooth ocean through a gap in the trees. I know Paul and Julia live comfortably, but this must have cost a fortune.

Matty grabs my hand and pulls me towards the cottage as he hums a tune, while Preston helps Paul with the bags. We follow Julia into the house, and it's just as beautiful on the inside as it is on the outside. The ceilings are notably low, and there's a strong smell of wood and ember. It wouldn't surprise me to discover that the décor hasn't been meddled with since this place was built. The kitchen and living space is one large room, and the kitchen area is filled with old-fashioned fittings and utilities. There's an enormous oak table in the middle of it all, decorated with a large vase of colourful flowers.

The modern appliances stick out like a sore thumb, from the microwave underneath one of the small square windows, to the silver fridge in the corner of the room. The living area is as equally traditional, though as with the kitchen, the twenty-first century has crept in via the small television placed upon a wooden coffee table. Matty's about to continue with his tour of the ground floor when Paul interrupts us to show me to my bedroom. It's enormous. Against the back wall is what I'd guess to be at least a queen-size bed layered with blankets and fluffed up pillows, and beside it is a large wardrobe with swirls of patterns carved into the top. There's a traditional dressing table adorned with a rectangular mirror placed against the left wall, and the floor is made from perfectly polished wood.

In-between the bed and wardrobe is another door, which I'm assuming is an en suite. The only disturbance is Preston, who's lying on his stomach on said floor as he looks under the bed. I don't even want to know what he's doing.

I narrow my eyes. 'Why are you in my room?'

Preston turns his head to me and flashes a grin, but he doesn't get up off the floor. He lifts himself up to rest his weight on his elbows.

'Our room, Euphemia, don't be so rude.'

'I will rip my eyes from their sockets before I share a bed with you, I can assure you of that.'

'Please stop with the romantic insinuations, I can't handle the flattery.'

I sigh and let out a groan. 'There must be at least four bedrooms in this place, why have they put us in the same one?'

Preston shrugs. 'They must assume we're an item.' He laughs as I frown in disgust. 'In credit to them, I'm stunned they'd allow us to share a room with such an assumption, let alone grace us with a double bed. You should appreciate it.'

'Yeah, well, don't get your hopes up,' I mutter under my breath.

I wander towards my bag on the bed, stepping over Preston in the process, and unzip it to begin unpacking. As I do so, Preston remains on the floor, and transporting my clothes from the bed to the wardrobe is proving difficult considering I have to step over his goddamn carcass each time I make the journey. I notice his bag remains unopened.

'You better not be expecting me to unpack for you,' I mumble.

'I don't like unpacking, it's too definite. I'll take things as I need them.'

'Right, okay. Are you going to stay on that floor all night?'

'Possibly.' He pauses. 'Are you ever going to tell me if anyone's commented on the fact that your name sounds like an STD?'

'Shut up.'

Preston doesn't end up spending the night planted on the wooden floor because when I've almost finished unpacking, he announces he's going to take a shower. He jumps up and pulls his shirt and jeans off so quickly that I'm half expecting him to rip his boxers off along with them. As much as it physically pains me to admit, it'd be plain stubborn of me not to acknowledge that he is kind of sort of maybe really attractive.

He's humming an unrecognisable tune as he runs his hands through his hair, and I think of him the night we found him slumped over a bin in Robbie's front garden, and it doesn't seem real. I think of him sitting alone in an abandoned terraced house in Cathays, I think of his timid mother in prison for killing a man, and I think of him swallowing those painkillers knowing that he's taken too many, and none of it seems real.

'You okay?' Preston leads me out of my trance. He's leaning against the bed frame with an expectant look on his face. 'You look like you may be about to projectile vomit.'

'Oh, no, sorry,' I stammer. 'Just zoned out, sorry.'

Preston bends down to remove his tattered socks, and the second he lifts them up and starts aiming towards my face, I stop him.

'Don't you dare.'

He rolls his eyes. 'Ugh, you're so beige. Think red!'

As he always does, as if anything he just said made sense, Preston elaborates no further. He disappears into the door between the bed and the wardrobe.

It's undeniable that the next few hours are plagued by awkwardness. Paul and Julia clearly don't know how to speak to Preston, and Preston is even worse. He must be sensing it fairly well because after a few hours of saying practically nothing, he asks Paul about his job as an area manager for some retail company, despite clearly having no interest in it whatsoever. What I'm finding even more bizarre is how much he's dumbed himself down.

He's not being rude and boisterous like Zack, but he's speaking like him. I can't understand why he's not just being himself, albeit a toned down version because I'm not sure what Paul and Julia would make of gibberish talking, floor lying, Kurt Cobain quoting Preston. I call him into the kitchen when the awkwardness peaks, and ask him just that.

He groans. 'I don't know. In this sort of situation, I always resort to Zack, and I'm trying desperately to do anything but that.'

'You just need to find some kind of common ground with them. I mean, did they grow up in the same area as you? Can they speak Welsh? What films are they into? What do you know about them, d'you get what I'm saying?' I soften my voice. 'Just be yourself, Preston, even if it means doing some of the weird shit you do because that's better than being Zack, believe me.'

'Be myself,' he mumbles with a quiet laugh, seemingly to himself considering he's staring at the floor as he says it.

I shoot him a questioning look when he lifts his eyes back up, not quite grasping what he means, but he doesn't say anything. Instead, he nods, inhales a sharp intake of breath, and we head back into battle. I'm not sure what, but I must have said something right because as we sit back onto the leather sofa, Preston loses the Zack-like traits he was grasping onto previously. It takes him a while to settle into it, but he begins speaking with relaxed confidence, and becomes the most charming human being known to mankind. Occasionally some of his nonsensical, slightly bizarre sentences slip out, but if anything, Paul and Julia seem fascinated by them.

Within the next hour, he and Julia discover their shared passion for an artist I've never heard of, and he jumps on the revelation of Paul's love for The Smiths. Even I discover things about him. His current plan is to study engineering at university to become an aerospace engineer, but if he had money to afford the lessons, he'd become a pilot, hands down. He doesn't have a favourite colour because he doesn't understand the necessity of pitching one above the rest, he's never had a girlfriend, he once dyed his hair dark and then immediately dyed it back light, and his first job was as a cashier at a charity shop.

When Matty suggests lighting the fireplace, the discovery of no firewood becomes the perfect dilemma as it leads Julia to suggest the boys head outside to find some, while she and I prepare food. A little on the sexist side, but hey, whatever helps. While Julia begins pulling ambiguous ingredients from cupboards and the boys head out, I spend the next half hour trying to blend into the furniture in an attempt to stop Julia asking me to cook, and inevitably incinerate, any food.

By the time it reaches eight o' clock, the fireplace is crackling, and I'm stuffed up to my neck with some unknown pie dish, Mediterranean vegetables, and the creamiest mash potato to ever grace my taste buds. Julia is a good cook, I've got to hand it to her. She's now running a bath for herself while Paul cleans the dishes, and Preston, Matty and I have spread ourselves over one of the large sofas. Everything is going swimmingly. That is until midway through a conversation entailing Preston and me trying to convince Matty that we're not madly in love, Matty announces something he really shouldn't have.

'Well, I told Mummy that you're boyfriend and girlfriend and it made Mia all embarrassed, so you have to be!'

'Pardon?' Preston replies before Matty has even finished the sentence.

Matty's eyes widen as he realises what he's done, and before I know it, he's staring at me pleadingly, as if I have the ability to erase what he just said. He stammers as Preston asks him again. He shoots me another pleading look. Preston turns his gaze from Matty to me, and now it's my turn to stammer.

'What is he talking about?' I've never heard Preston's voice sound so flat.

'Please don't be angry,' Matty pipes in. 'I really wanted to see Mummy 'cause I hadn't in ages and ages, and I asked Mia, and she said she'd take me. Don't be angry, please, Mummy really liked Mia, and we even tricked one of the guards so--'

Preston swears, stopping Matty in his tracks, and within seconds, he's left the room and stormed into the main hallway. I hear the front door open and close with a slam, and Paul looks up from the dishes he's cleaning. He turns to me questioningly, and I apologise before chasing after Preston. Shit.

It's beginning to get dark outside, and the tall trees' limb-like trunks are menacing, but I'm focusing on the shadow passing through them. We're probably a hundred yards or so into the forest when I catch up to Preston, but as I reach out for his arm, he smacks me away and finally turns around.

'Et tu, Brute?' He says it like a joke, but nobody's laughing.

'Preston, I--'

'You are exactly what is wrong with me,' he mutters. 'I thought you were different, I just had this feeling, you know? Why does everyone have to lie all of the time? It's exhausting, it's so exhausting.'

He kicks a tree behind him, then slumps onto the ground. His head is in his hands, and he's muttering to himself. It's freezing, and nighttime seems to have crawled into the forest within the past few minutes. I sit down onto the moist ground in front of Preston, and for a while, I say nothing.

'I'm sorry,' I whisper. 'I--I didn't mean to visit your mum behind your back. Matty asked me and... and I don't know, I just never told you. I know I should have, but I didn't want you to be angry at me for going.'

Preston doesn't respond. His head is still resting in his hands, but he's no longer mumbling under his breath. It's silent for another short while, bar the occasional rustling of bushes and the tweeting of birds. It feels like a century has passed when

Preston finally lifts his head. His eyes are facing me, but they're empty. He's not looking at me, not really.

'Do you know why she's there?' he asks, and I nod. 'He was Matty's father. He wasn't good to Mum. He wasn't good to Matty, he wasn't... he wasn't good.' Preston focuses his gaze on me, and he's never looked so childlike. 'Why did you have to go behind my back?' I open my mouth to reply, but he continues. 'You know what? I don't care that you went--I'm astounded by how little it bothers me, but I don't. I just wish you hadn't lied to me.'

Preston reaches into his pocket to bring out a squished packet of cigarettes and a lighter, and ignites one with it. He stares at it as he holds it in-between his fingers. He's only wearing a t-shirt, and he's shivering, but I don't think he's noticed.

He closes his eyes for a few seconds, and sighs. 'I'm not angry at you, I'm not. Just please don't keep anything from me again, please.'

I nod. 'Look, I need to tell you something. It's--Robbie's party, the one last summer, I--I know what ha--'

'There you are!' Julia's high-pitched voice interrupts me mid-sentence, and we turn in the direction of the cottage to see her standing above us. 'What on earth are you two doing?'

Preston lifts his hand to flash his cigarette, and Julia pulls an expression dripping with disapproval.

'Ah, right,' Julia utters in response. 'Well, don't be long.'

She's about to turn around when Preston announces he's fin-ished, dabs his unused cigarette against the ground, then shoves it into his pocket.

CHAPTER 23

I spend the first night sleeping in the cottage with a fortress of pillows between Preston and me, just in case. To my relief, he doesn't try anything, and I wake on the Saturday feeling refreshed. The sunlight seeping in through the open window gently rouses me, and for the first time since I can remember, I'm up and around before nine on a weekend morning. Preston isn't in bed when I wake up, so I check the en suite, but there's no sign of him. Before I begin getting ready, I close the window and partly cover it with its thick red curtains. Preston can't sleep with closed windows, apparently, which I ensured to inform him was abnormal, but I humoured him regardless.

Matty's the only one in the living room when I enter. He has tomato ketchup splattered over his face, and all that remains of what once was a bacon sandwich are scraps of fat and a few crumbs on his plate. He leaps up from the kitchen table and gives me a hello as Preston wanders in from the main hallway. He turned fairly quiet again after Matty spilled the beans last night, and as I watched the brothers for the rest of the night, I got the feeling it was Matty Preston was most upset with, not me. He seems okay now, at least, based on the extremely predictable joke he makes about my name the second he spots me.

'We're going to the seaside today,' Matty informs me as Preston hands me a bacon sandwich. I thank him as Matty continues. 'It's sunny and it's not really cold, but kinda cold so maybe have a jacket just in case. We're gonna get fish and chips too, so I hope you like fish.'

Preston plops himself down onto the sofa next to me with a cheese toastie. 'You can't only get fish at fish and chip shops, pal.'

'Yeah you can,' Matty argues. He turns to me and jabs his thumb at Preston's food. 'He's greedy, that's his second one.'

'I'm a growing boy.'

'No, you're not, you're like thirty.'

'I only turned nineteen last week, Matt.'

'Same thing,' Matty mutters, having clearly lost interest in the conversation.

It was Preston's birthday last week? Since when? I stare at him as he inspects the inside of his toastie, and I anticipate an explanation, but as always, I get nothing.

'Why didn't you say it was your birthday?' I question.

Preston shrugs. 'I don't celebrate it.'

'Why not?'

'It doesn't matter.'

As expected, I receive no elaboration.

It's a lot colder, and certainly a lot windier than Matty made it out to be. We spent the morning and early afternoon wandering around the local town, and while the most fascinating shop here is a Tesco Express, it was surprisingly a lot of fun. The five of us are currently crammed onto two small benches as we snack on the fish and chips Matty promised. The fish debate occurred again, so I got some battered cod in support of Team Matty. I'm surprised the hurricane that's currently sweeping West Wales hasn't blown my food from my lap, mind you.

Matty's been bugging us all about going to the arcade since we got here, and while Julia was reluctant at first, I can tell she's being worn down. It only takes another five minutes of persuading to convince her, and Matty is thrilled. Preston is rather giddy too, which is quite amusing. Both boys charge ahead as we stroll towards the flashing lights in the distance, and Preston has already given Matty ten pounds worth of tokens by the time we catch up with them.

For such a small town, it's an impressive arcade. Lights glare all around us, and there's so much noise coming from so many different places that I'm not sure where to look. Every gaming machine imaginable is here, from claw machines to epic action simulators. It smells of popcorn and copper, and even I'm finding myself feeling like a child again. Paul and Julia sit aside while I follow the boys. Matty sits himself inside a spaceship simulator, and from the corner of my eye, I can see Julia watching Preston like a hawk. He and I glance at each other, and I can tell he's noticed it too. He rolls his eyes and I laugh quietly.

We've moved onto the coin pusher machines when I notice Julia heading towards us, and I wonder if she's going to join us. It turns out I was being far too optimistic. She taps Preston on the shoulder, who looks surprised to see her when he turns around.

'I don't want him playing with real money,' she says in a hushed tone.

'It's only for fun, he's aware of that. We're just using up the change I have, I don't need it.'

'Yes, but it's gambling. It's dangerous, and extremely addictive.'

'Yes, well, he's not extremely stupid.'

'Preston!' I hiss quietly enough for Julia not to hear me.

'Sorry,' Preston corrects himself, realising his mistake. 'We'll move on to something else.'

The rest of the day passes with no arguments. Julia questions Preston every ten minutes or so, but he bites his tongue and remains polite. If that was me, I would've snapped at her constant pestering by now. He deserves a medal. There's some horrendous reality TV talent show on tonight, so we've bought a whole car full of snacks and drinks to help us endure it, or at least help me endure it. There's just something uncomfortable about watching grown men weep while they have their dreams shattered within a two-minute time frame.

The show has been on for over an hour when, in my popcorn and cola induced coma, I realise how happy Preston is. It occurs to me that if this is him happy, then this is the first time I've truly seen it in him. And that's really quite sad. Matty is sprawled out over his lap as he chortles at one of the show's contestants, which makes Preston crack up like crazy. He starts tickling Matty, to which Matty retaliates by throwing popcorn at his brother's face. Paul and I start laughing at them, and even Julia cracks a smile. I turn back to Preston, our eyes meet, and in this moment, he's as far away from Zack as I've ever seen him, but he's not Preston either. He's another entity all together.

The only bad thing about Preston being so happy is that when we settle down for bed that night, it's like trying to calm down a puppy with ADHD. I begin making my pillow fortress, only for Preston to throw each one of them back at me while announcing vive la France! every time he does so. When there are no signs of it ending after fifteen minutes or so, I finally give up and leave the pillows discarded on the floor in a messy heap. Preston, in glee over his victory, then begins singing the Welsh national anthem. It starts out loud and irritating, but after a few rounds it becomes much softer, and before I know it, I've fallen asleep.

I awaken to darkness.

I'm briefly confused because the moonlight seeping in through the open window casts distorted shadows over everything in the room, and then I feel movement. I hear a voice. I wonder if I'm dreaming, but once my eyes adjust to the light and I see a shadow above me, I know I'm not. It's Matty.

'Mia, I can't sleep.'

I sit up and glance to my left to see Preston fast asleep beside me. I turn back to Matty and notice that he's holding a blanket to his face, and in his other hand is a soft toy. He looks terrified.

'How come?' I ask as I fully adjust to my surroundings. I yawn.

'I had a nightmare, and I don't wanna go back to sleep now,' he mutters. 'Can you wake up Preston for me? I tried, but it didn't work. Can we go outside?'

'Uh... I'm not sure if outside is a good idea,' I reply.

With no attempt to be gentle, I nudge Preston, which prompts a groan from his sprawled body. I nudge him harder, and he swears. He smacks me away, so I nudge him some more. This continues for five minutes or so until he's sitting up.

'Outside?' Matty says simply once his brother is fully-functioning.

'Yeah, of course.'

As if he's just woken from an undisturbed twelve-hour sleep, Preston jumps out of bed, throws a jumper on over his t-shirt, and pulls on a pair of jeans. He's not actually going to take Matty outside, is he? It's cold and--I look at my phone on the bedside cabinet--almost two in the morning. Nonetheless, he wraps his brother up in his blanket, picks him up, and leaves the room. I throw on a hoodie, then follow them outside.

Preston carries Matty, who's huddled under layers of blanket, through the forest until we reach the edge of a small cliff, where the ocean sits at the bottom. The night's breeze is cold on my face, and the infusion of salt water and pine creates a sensationally fresh aroma. The three of us sit down at the edge of the cliff. Matty is still shaky, and so Preston points into the distance, which makes us both look up. I'm amazed. The sky is clear, and I have never seen the stars look so bold. There are millions of them, some glaringly bright, while others are faded, as if someone has struck an eraser over them.

'There are so many of them,' I mutter quietly.

Despite my lack of explanation, Preston nods. 'You don't really notice until you bother to look up.'

Neither one of us says anything for a few minutes, and I assume it's because the boys are as overwhelmed by the beauty of the sky as I am. The distant sound of the ocean lapping against the bottom of the cliff permits total silence, and it's Preston who eventually interrupts the natural world.

'Over four billion years ago, we were all stars.' He's whispering to Matty, but I grasp onto every word he says. 'All of the oxygen, nitrogen and carbon atoms inside our bodies were formed from stars that died a long, long time ago. They die in a vicious explosion, one that's so colossal it propels an enormous cloud of dust and gas into the atmosphere. If the explosion is big enough, that one star can shine brighter than a whole galaxy of stars, and as it fades, its material scatters into interstellar space. All of this material--this stardust--is part of what formed our planet, our trees, our animals, our people. Everyone and everything.' Preston's voice is briefly replaced with silence. 'Imagine that. Something that died billions of years ago is the reason you're right here, right now.'

'No way,' Matty whispers back as he stares at his brother in awe.

Preston nods, and once again, the only sound to be heard are the waves gently splashing the rocks below us. We sit in silence for what feels like the rest of eternity, and I wouldn't want anything different. I'm barely noticing the cold by now, and the simplicity of this moment is intoxicating. I begin to notice another noise, and as I turn to the boys, I realise that it's Matty's shallow breathing. He's fast asleep on Preston's lap.

'His nightmares were frequent when Mum left,' Preston explains quietly as I lift my eyes to his. 'He remembers things occasionally, and he was too young to understand them at the time, so I think they scare him. He likes to get outside whenever he has them. Nothing else works.'

I nod slowly. It's as if I'm afraid of speaking, afraid of even the smallest chance of disturbing Matty. It's silent again for another few minutes.

'What happened?' I whisper. I'm not sure I should be asking this. 'Between your mum and Matty's dad?'

Preston turns his gaze away from me. A pang of guilt erupts inside my stomach, and I apologise. I get no response, so I apologise again. Another short while passes.

'He was shouting at her, he always did. I've never referred to what they did as arguing because all it ever entailed was her taking it with no retaliation. I don't... I don't know what happened, I suppose...' Preston's voice trails off. He clears his throat. 'I suppose she'd endured so much that she snapped. She wanted to stop him, so she hit him, and he fell awkwardly. It was an accident. She didn't intend on doing anything bad, not... not that bad.' He glances down at Matty. 'She didn't mean to kill him.'

I struggle to think of a response, if there even is one appropriate enough. A question burns in my mind, but it takes me a while to ask it.

'Were you and Matty there?'

'I was.'

'Did you...' I try to stop myself, but curiosity takes control of me. 'Did you see it happen?'

He nods.

'How old were you?'

'Thirteen.'

Preston stands up, and is careful not to disturb Matty too much as he lifts him from the ground and holds him close. I take this as our cue to head back inside, and so I stand up and follow Preston back towards the cottage.

The door is unlocked when we arrive, which is odd. Preston notices, but doesn't seem to think much of it, but I'm more suspicious. I remember him locking it. The silence of the hallway is reassuring, and we remove our shoes as I open the door into the living area. The moment I do, I want to slam it back shut. I want to close it, and tell Preston to run as far as he can and to take Matty with him because the moment Julia's hard stare meets mine, I know it's over.

'Where the hell have you been?' she hisses. She charges towards us, and pulls Matty from Preston's arms. 'It's almost three in the morning, why in God's name have you taken him outside? Are you stupid?'

Matty, who has been startled awake, looks over Julia's shoulder in a daze. Preston and I are lost for words as we stand in the doorway. I stammer. Preston doesn't say or do anything, he just stares blankly at the wall.

'We had to call the police,' Paul, who I hadn't even realised was here, mutters from one of the cream sofas hidden in the darkness. 'There was no sign of either of you, no indication that you'd gone, no attempt to tell us. Not even a note.'

Disappointment seeps from Paul, and it hits me hard. To lose Julia's faith is one thing, but to lose his is shattering. Julia swears under her breath as she shoves past us to enter the main hallway, and she doesn't return for several minutes. I hear her apologising on the phone, to the police I assume, and when she returns, she no longer has Matty in her arms. Paul hasn't said anything else.

'Well? Aren't you going to say anything?' Julia asks, standing in front of Preston.

He doesn't respond.

'Anything could have happened. He could've run off, you could've bumped into someone dangerous, you could've gotten lost... He could've frozen half to death! This is exactly why you do not deserve any more second chances. I'm so tired of trying to help you when all you do is throw it back in my face!'

Finally, Preston looks at Julia. He inhales deeply, nods, and leaves the room. Julia shouts after him, but he never returns, so I apologise, and hurry towards our room. As I'm about to enter our bedroom, I hear a slam, and walk in to find the ensuite door locked shut. I knock on it quietly, but get nothing in return. I begin knocking louder and louder until the sheer repetition of knocking forces Preston to respond. He tells me to fuck off.

My breath is heavy, my palms are sweating, and I'm clouded in an intense sense of urgency as I call Preston's name because I'm terrified he's going to do something stupid. When I can no longer hear him pacing, I begin panicking. The lock is loose, and so I fiddle with it in an attempt to unfasten it from the outside. It takes several attempts and leaves me with my fingertips feeling raw, but I eventually manage to unlock the door.

An entire ocean, let alone a wave, of relief spreads over my body as I walk in to see Preston sitting on the bathroom floor with his back against the bathtub, but it's short-lived. His forehead rests on his knees, and he's pulling at his hair so aggressively that I can see small chunks of it have fallen out into his hands. He's mumbling hastily but his words are inaudible, and his breathing is harsh and shallow.

'Preston?' I try to force his hands away from his head, but he's far stronger than am I. 'Preston, listen to me. It's okay. Look at me, just look at me.'

I'm not sure he can even hear me, let alone process what I'm saying. I try to force his hands down again, but I can't even budge them. He's still pulling his hair, and his body is shaking. His breath is even shorter now. This time, I try to lift his chin, and while at first he resists, I eventually manage to lift his head from his knees.

I take a deep breath and soften my voice. 'Preston.' I lift his chin up again but his eyes are fixated onto the wall. 'Preston, hey, look at me.'

When he eventually does turn his attention to me, the mumbling stops. I keep saying his name until his breathing calms and he stops yanking at his hair, and it takes a while, but he eventually lifts himself up. He says nothing more to me, leaves the room, and gets into the bed that's so enormous, it swallows him up. Exhausted by this point, I join him in silence, and rest my head on the cold pillow I left an hour ago. Before everything was ruined.

I don't know how much time has passed--it could be five minutes, but it could be an hour--when Preston's arm drapes over me and he shuffles closer. For a moment, I'm unsure of what to say, what to do, whether to move him. A few seconds pass, and I decide to leave it because I want to make everything okay, but I can't, and this is the best I can do.

Chapter 24

Preston doesn't say a word to Paul or Julia on the way home from the cottage, and they say nothing to him in return. He's not spoken to me since last night, either. He's just sitting in the car, silently staring into space. I attempt to get dropped off at Preston's, but he doesn't let me, and so that Sunday afternoon I find myself sitting alone in my living room as I listen to Dad in the hallway begging his other woman not to dump him. Gwen is out with friends. I consider visiting Mum at Cerys's house, but honestly, I don't think it would make me feel any better. I'm not sure anything could right now.

I spend a lot of time over the next few weeks calling and visiting Preston, just in case. I've lost count of the amount of days he's not shown up to college, and every time I trek to his place, the front door is closed and I get no answer. The one time I did manage to get inside, all he did was sit on his mattress and gaze into the mirror opposite him. It was there I asked him to send me a text every day saying something--anything--so that I knew he was okay. He didn't respond to anything I said to him that day, let alone that specific question, but every night since, I've received a message from him. All it ever contains is a comma, and I always reply to it with something, but he never replies.

I'm working on a presentation for my psychology class in the room where Preston used to tutor me when there's a knock on the door, and for a moment, I think it's him. As it opens, Robbie's face emerges. I've only spoken to him in passing over the past month or so, and I think our break may have been more permanent than he or I realised. I force a smile at him as he apologises for interrupting, and he mutters something about Samantha telling him I was in here.

As I watch him stumble over his words, I take in his soft features: his dark hair that desperately needs a cut, his small nose and thin lips, and his slightly crooked teeth, as I realise that I've missed him. Maybe not in a romantic way, I'm not totally sure, but I've missed his company. It's this realisation that makes me accept his offer to spend this evening watching films at his house. As I sit in the car, which now has a mismatching bumper after the accident, I shut my eyes and let the sounds of Tupac Shakur dance around my ears.

Robbie offers me every food and drink item to have ever existed once we arrive at his house, but I don't want anything, and I'm too distracted to pay much attention anyway. I've not been at this house since the night of Robbie's party last summer, and the mere idea of that party feels surreal now. It's so calm here. It somehow seems bigger as well, and as we stand in his kitchen, I stare at the countertop I last saw with an uneaten pizza lying on top of it. Robbie asks me if I want something to eat again. He's tripping over his words, and he keeps scratching his head as if he's been asked to uncover the meaning of life within the next five minutes. I think he's nervous.

The doorbell rings, and Robbie can't dart out of the kitchen to answer it fast enough. I figure it's a salesman or something, so when Aiden and Samantha stroll into the kitchen, I'm taken aback. Robbie must sense my confusion because he shoots me an apologetic look as the colour drains from his face, and I desperately want to tell him to relax. To be honest, I'm more relieved than anything about this not being a date.

'So Samantha and I have stocked up for the winter, and before you say anything, I know it's currently spring, but you see where I'm going with this,' Aiden announces as we all head into the living room. 'We've bought cheap as shit chocolate from the newsagents outside college, but holy mackerel is it good, and in my trusty bag I hold bountiful sweets that will rot your teeth until you've got none left. And I'm not even going to charge any of you for it.' He drops his satchel onto the gigantic corner sofa to show us evidence of his expenditure. 'I'm amazing, I know, stop with the praise already, guys, geez.'

Within seconds, I am immensely glad that Aiden and Samantha are here because Aiden is like an awkwardness filter. Robbie's parents are away for the weekend so we have the house to ourselves, and in the spirit of taking advantage of that, Aiden demands we collect as many duvets from as many beds as we can to enjoy the array of films we plan on watching tonight. Robbie humours him, and so I keep guard of the snacks while the other three search the house.

Duvets are still being rounded up when there's a loud knock on the door, followed by the piercing sound of the doorbell being repeatedly rung. I call Robbie's name. There's more knocking and more ringing, but no sign of Robbie. I groan in frustration, stomp out of the room, barge into the hallway, swiftly open the front door, and freeze.

'You get lost or something, babe?'

Preston is smirking at me, his slack posture unnervingly arrogant. I expect to see a glimmer of uncertainty, reassurance, happiness, sadness--anything--when he realises it's me who's answered the door, but there's nothing. My presence doesn't even faze him. He remains in character, and barges past me into the house.

'Zack!' Robbie yells as he jogs down the stairs with several pillows held tightly to his chest. 'You're missing all the fun!'

'Clearly,' Preston, or Zack apparently, replies through a laugh.

He yanks a pillow from Robbie's arms, which causes a domino effect as they all tumble to the wooden floor. He throws one at Robbie, who proceeds to throw one back at him, and within moments, the two of them are running around the ground floor of Robbie's house throwing pillows at each other. By the time Aiden has joined in, I'm slumped on the living room sofa, surrounded by duvets and cushions.

Samantha kneels on the floor layering and straightening them all out to make what resembles one giant bed, but all I can think about is Preston, and why he was playing Zack when it was just the two of us. Once the boys have settled down, we all sit on Samantha's creation, and get comfortable. The sheer enormity of Robbie's living room gives us each at least a single bed worth of space, and when Robbie told me he had an eighty-inch television, I didn't believe him, but I sure do now.

Preston hasn't stopped talking since he showed up, and as Robbie hands us the snacks Aiden brought, he can't resist throwing some at me. I snap at him, but he just laughs and throws even more.

'Mate, stop being a dick,' Robbie says to him as he plants himself beside me.

Preston ignores him and throws another fizzy sweet at me.

'Seriously, quit it,' Robbie snaps.

'Careful, Rob, her frigidness is rubbing off on you.'

Robbie's body tenses, and he's about to jump back up, but I yank his arm and tell him to leave it. He mumbles something under his breath, and tells Preston to shut up. What the hell is wrong with him? I get that he must still be upset over what happened at the cottage, but why is he doing this? His comeback didn't even make sense. I look at Preston pleadingly in search of an explanation, but Zack gazes back with a smirk still intact.

I hoped Preston would quit being such an arsehole once the films started, but of course, I was wrong. He talks so much throughout the first one that I can't keep track of what it even is, and as we move on to watch some indie film Samantha requested, it only gets worse. I lose track of the amount of times Robbie tells him to be quiet, and even Aiden shyly asks him to tone it down at one point. Once we're halfway through the second film, I can't take it anymore, so I head into the kitchen to get a drink, but Preston follows suit.

'What a load of killjoys, eh?' His voice is loud and grating as he begins opening random cupboards, and shuffling through them. 'You need to get yourself a boyfriend who ain't afraid of his own shadow. You two even kissed yet? I'm all for taking it slow, but you guys are hilarious.'

'Preston, what the hell is wrong with you tonight?'

'Just telling you how it is, babe.'

Narcissism and self-importance is oozing from him as he pulls a glass out of a cupboard, then winks at me. I mentioned wanting a drink as I left the living room just now, so I briefly assume he's going to hand it to me, but he doesn't. He hauls more cupboards open until I hear him shout bingo, and he reaches in to pull out a bottle of gin.

'Shouldn't you ask Robbie first?' I utter as he begins pouring it into his glass without a mixer. He ignores me. 'Preston, seriously that's really rude, do--'

'For Christ's sake, stop calling me that!'

He downs the drink in his hand, pours another, then slams the cupboard shut and leaves the room. There's something seriously wrong here. I don't know if this is some warped coping mechanism of his after what happened at the cottage, but whatever it is, it has to stop. It's been over two weeks now. Surely he's ready to talk about it, or just do something other than whatever on earth this is. I pour myself a glass of water and take a long gulp of it before heading back into the living room.

I slot myself in-between Robbie and Samantha, but instead of focusing on the film, my eyes are glued to Preston. He's already almost finished his second drink.

'Did he say anything to you in the kitchen?' Robbie whispers into my ear. 'If he's being a dickhead, I'll tell him to leave, seriously.'

I shake my head and whisper, 'it's nothing, it's fine,' in return.

Preston is soon on his feet again, and returns to the living room moments later with another full glass. I glance at him, then glance at Robbie. Maybe I should say something. As the protagonists of the film I'm paying very little attention to discuss the inevitability of death on a rooftop in the middle of a snowstorm, for some bizarre reason, Preston gets up one more time and disappears into the kitchen. This time, he doesn't return.

The film is nearing its end and no one has acknowledged Preston's disappearance, but everyone must have noticed it, so I'm not sure why nothing's been said. I think we're all just secretly relieved. I begin wondering if he's left the house altogether when a tremendous crashing sound echoes from the kitchen. Robbie swears loudly as he gets up and hurries out of the room, and Aiden and I follow, leaving Samantha with her eyes glued to the film.

We step into the kitchen to see shards of broken glass covering the black tiled floor, and among it is a river of clear liquid. Standing above the mess is Preston, who's in fits of laughter while apologising to an increasingly red-faced Robbie.

'That's my dad's, you prick!' Robbie hisses at Preston before swearing at what used to be a bottle of gin, now lying in a broken mess on the kitchen floor.

'Oh shit, we better watch out, we all know not to mess with Clive Morrissey!' Preston laughs harder.

'Were you drinking it?'

'Dunno if that really matters now, Rob,' Preston replies as he begins to calm down. 'It's on the floor, in case you ain't noticed.'

All attempts to recompose himself evaporate, and he bursts out laughing again. Robbie shouts at him, really shouts this time, and as if a nerve has been hit full-force, Preston suddenly cracks. He stops laughing, his eyes turn cold, and he begins spitting swear words I didn't even know existed at Robbie in a continuous stream. The two boys start screaming at each other, and before I can even try to grasp what's going on, Preston barges through us, leaves the kitchen, and then exits the house with a slam of the front door. Aiden and I turn to each other wide-eyed, and it's reassuring to know that he's just as clueless over what's going on as I am.

It's almost midnight by the time Samantha and Aiden leave, and there's been no sign of Preston since he stormed out of the house. Part of me is furious with him for being so awful tonight, but another part of me is afraid. To pose as Zack around everyone is one thing, but to do so when it's just him and me isn't right, and the uncertainty of what that means terrifies me.

'Sorry about tonight,' Robbie mutters as we return to the living room after saying goodbye to Aiden and Samantha. 'I wouldn't have invited Zack if I knew he was going to be such an arsehole.'

'Don't worry,' I say. 'All you've done tonight is stress over dumb stuff you can't control. It's well established that Zack's an arsehole, so there's no use crying over it.'

Robbie smiles softly, and the look of a lost child that first emerged in his eyes when we had our coffee shop date all those months ago returns to his face. Before I'm aware of myself even doing it, I bring him into a hug. He's wearing too much aftershave and it tickles my nose, but it doesn't faze me.

'Mia, I'm so sorry about the accident,' he murmurs quietly.

I unravel my arms from around Robbie, and scan his face. His light blue eyes are looking anywhere other than mine, and he's biting at his bottom lip. It's odd, really. I was so angry at him for what happened that night, for encouraging me to drive while Preston took the blame for it all, but now I don't care. I'm not sure why or how, but I just don't anymore. It isn't important whose fault it is, and even if it was, it was entirely mine anyway. I chose to drive, nobody forced me.

'I know it was stupid, and I never meant to put you in danger, and I just feel so shit over it all the time because--'

'Robbie, don't,' I interrupt him. 'It doesn't matter. Besides, I'm accountable for my own actions.'

Robbie clamps his mouth shut and nods silently as a look of uncertainty flashes in his eyes, and I have to stop myself from hugging him again.

'Friends?' I try.

'Friends,' he agrees.

I pull him into another hug, and the guy practically deflated with relief. I continue to suggest throwing on another film, one we'll actually pay attention to this time, and Robbie bashfully agrees.

We're both a little unsure of each other at first, and sit apart without daring physical contact, but as the crappy comedy film plays, we slowly nudge in closer on the mountain of duvets. By the time the film has reached its climax, we're sitting side by side in total comfort, and without an ounce of awkwardness. My eyelids are heavy and I'm beginning to drift off when, in my half-asleep state, I hear a sudden bang. I jump a mile and release a sound so high-pitched that it takes me a moment to realise it came from my mouth.

Robbie starts laughing as I realise the bang came from the television. My cheeks flush, and I want to dive under all of the duvets and pretend I'm not here. What the hell was that noise I just made? Robbie must sense my embarrassment because he tries to control his laughter so that it's more of a light chuckle.

'This isn't even a horror. You know that, right?' he mocks.

I try to shoot him a scowl, but am in no way doing a very good job as Robbie continues to try and control his snickering. Eventually, even I have to fight back giggles, and before I know it we're both laughing.

It's just a shame that the moment is ruined by a sudden blaring sound.

The abruptness of it leaves me flustered, so much so that I don't look at who's calling when I answer my phone. I don't even acknowledge how strange it is for it to be ringing at half past one in the morning.

'Mia, I... I don't, I can't... Are you still there? Are you at Robbie's? It's cold and it was raining earlier, did you notice it raining? Are you still at Robbie's?'

Preston.

I spring up from the floor, and press my finger against my left ear to block out the sound of the film in the background. Robbie asks me who it is, but I don't reply.

'What?' I breathe into the phone. 'Where are you?'

'I didn't notice at first, but the ground was wet. Isn't that peculiar? I don't know... I just--My hands are stinging, it feels strange. I don't--'

'Where are you?'

'I'm outside.'

'What? What do you mean?'

'I'm outside, my hands are stinging.'

I open my mouth to say something else, but the phone cuts off, and the line goes dead. I shove my phone into my pocket and hurry to the hallway, then haul the front door open. Sitting on the gravel driveway, his back resting against Robbie's car, is Preston.

CHAPTER 25

I can't formulate my thoughts into words, so I just stare as Preston stumbles into a standing position. As he moves towards me, the porch light flashes on, and is reflected on the wet concrete. His previously limp demeanour has been replaced by a bolder one, and there's an uneven smile on his face. He's wearing a plain long-sleeved top with a graphic tee pulled over it, coupled with a ripped pair of jeans, and he's shivering. The jacket he had earlier is nowhere to be seen. His face is paler than usual, his eyes glazed over, and in no way does he look right.

He's scratching the top of his wrist, and I still can't manage to string any words together, but I don't end up needing to because soon, Robbie is beside me.

'For fuck sake, what do you want?'

'Rob, relax, relax, you're a way too much of an uptight guy. Relax.' Preston, now standing in the porch, raises his hands defensively, which invokes another swear from Robbie. 'Ohhh hhh... Oh shit, sorry, were you two getting frisky? Bit awkward, sorry.'

He starts sniggering, and he can barely stand still. He's still scratching at the same spot on his arm, and he's blinking so much that he's almost twitching. Robbie snaps at him again, but I don't listen to what he's saying because I'm too fixated on Preston. His teeth are chattering, he can't stop sniffing, and he's using one of the pillars of Robbie's porch to keep himself balanced. He's drunk out of his mind.

'Robbie,' I interrupt him mid-insult. 'We need to get him inside, he needs--'

'Dream on, no way am I letting him back in. Look at him!'

'Whoa, chill out, I'm leaving, okay?' For the second time, Preston raises his arms in defence. 'Enjoy your night and, y'know, while you're undressing Venus, dress up your penis and all that. Be safe, kids.'

Preston turns around and begins half stumbling, half sauntering away from the house, so I chase after him and pull him back. He turns around, stops, stumbles for the umpteenth time, and grins at me. He's still scratching the top of his wrist.

'Mia, just leave him!' Robbie, who's now caught up with us, retorts. 'He can't keep getting away with crap like this!'

'I'm lovely,' Preston slurs in response.

'I'm fed up of everyone licking your arse, myself included,' Robbie snaps back. 'You're an arsehole, Zack, okay? You're not cool, or funny. You used to be, but now you're just... you're just mean. Just go away.'

Now it's my turn to argue with Robbie, and we spend so much time fighting that we don't notice Preston's disappearance for at least five minutes.

I run back into the house to check for him, while Robbie circles the house's grounds. Relief floods over me when, as I inspect the kitchen, the first thing I see is Preston flinging open cupboards. He's not laughing anymore. He's swearing under his breath, and kicking the lower cupboards back shut.

'Preston, calm down!' I don't mean to shout, but the panic overcomes me.

He spins around, only now noticing me, and I freeze. His eyebrows are furrowed, his mouth is twitching, and he looks like he's going to snap any second. I stand still, waiting for him to yell, but he doesn't. He stops everything he's doing, and just stares at me as he starts scratching his wrist again.

Eventually, Preston drops his arms to his side, glances at the floor, then turns his gaze back to me. His voice is so quiet that I barely hear him when he opens his mouth to speak.

'Please make it stop.'

Preston's eyes, usually so on fire, have never looked so dull, and in that moment, my heart breaks for him.

Robbie won't quit moaning beside me, but I faze him out pretty easily. I led Preston into the living room from the kitchen, and by the time Robbie returned to the house, he was sitting on the duvet mountain with his legs crossed like a misbehaved child. I'm kneeling in front of him, trying to get him to focus on me, and not on the wrist he refuses to leave alone. At Robbie's return, he reinforces the character he maintained outside.

'Which one of your folks wanted to name you Robert?' he asks Robbie with a snicker. 'I bet it was your old man, only a guy named Clive would propose something as insipid as Robert.'

'Huh?'

'Oh, Robert. Robert, Robert, Robert. Some vocabulary expansion really wouldn't go amiss.'

'What the hell is he on about?'

I think Robbie is addressing me, but I ignore him. The black top underneath Preston's t-shirt has sleeves so long that they're covering his hands, and he's clutching them so tightly that it's impossible for me to even attempt to pull them back.

'Did you guys bone in the end, I can't remember. I wanna say no 'cause you're both frigid.'

'Oh, shut up! God, you're so annoying!' Robbie bites.

'Whoa, rather malicious there, Robert.'

'What the hell are you talking about?'

Poor Robbie is confused out of his brain, and I can't exactly blame him. It's as if Preston is switching between himself and Zack every few seconds, and even I can't keep up.

'Hey, Robbie, d'you have a bowl, or something similarly spherical? I'm gonna spew soon, so y'know, just a friendly heads up.'

I watch as panic engulfs Robbie, and before Preston has even finished the sentence, he darts out of the room. I hear the familiar sound of cupboards hastily opening and closing. Preston bursts out laughing.

'I won't really, I ain't a spewer.'

'Great,' I reply absentmindedly. 'Preston, what's going on? What's wrong? I'm going to take a wild guess and say this has something to do with what happened at the cottage. Have you talked about it with anyone?'

'Look at you getting all serious, how cute.'

'Please quit making a joke out of everything,' I groan. 'What's wrong? Please, just give me something. Anything.'

'What do you want me to do?' he snaps. 'Should I start crying over how shit my life is, wallow in an abyss of sadness, and write some excessively depressing poetry? If that's who you want me to be, then just let me know, and I'll adapt myself accordingly to your request.'

I sigh as I rub my temples. He knows what I want him to do. I want him to cut the bullshit and actually be himself in a situation where he desperately needs to be. He's not stupid, he knows that's what I want.

'Preston, it's okay to ask for help,' I try, to which he scoffs.

'I'm fine.'

As I'm looking down, I notice his left sleeve has lifted slightly, and of the two fingers that are poking out, one of them is turning black. Without giving him a chance to react, I reach out and shove his sleeve up to reveal his whole hand. All of his knuckles are turning a deep purple colour, and I couldn't count the amount of cuts on his hand if I tried. It's covered in blood, most of it dried, and his index finger looks distorted.

'What--How did you do that?'

'Oh, no, it's nothing. Just hit some stuff.'

Just hit some stuff? It looks like he threw his hand into a blender, stamped on it, and then smacked it against a slab of concrete to finish the job. Preston goes to pull his sleeve back down, and I take that as an opportunity to lift the other one. His right hand looks just as awful, and as the spot he keeps scratching is revealed, I see a deep cut surrounded by fresh blood. He definitely didn't hit anything to do that.

'What have you done to yourself?' My voice is almost a whisper.

'Just leave it, it's fine!'

He's trying to sound angry, but he's never sounded so meek. As I grab Preston's arm to force him up, Robbie emerges in the doorway with a plastic bowl. I barely acknowledge him as I drag Preston to the first bathroom I see. Of course, it ends up being the bathroom where we met the night of Robbie's party. Preston is rambling, but I ignore it and tell him to sit himself down on the closed toilet. The one good thing I've learned from Dad is how to treat a wound.

'Do you have any disinfectant?' I call to Robbie, who's followed us to the bathroom.

'What d'you mean?'

I roll my eyes. 'Some antiseptic wipes or something. A first aid kit should have what I need, do you have one?'

Robbie shrugs. 'I dunno.'

'Can you look for me?'

'I don't know where my folks would--'

'Please, just look!' I argue. I breathe in heavily, and speak again. 'Please.'

At last, Robbie does as he's told, although he leaves the bowl he found with us in the bathroom 'just in case'. As I'm washing my hands, Preston repeatedly informs me of how okay he is, and how they're just some small cuts. I pay no attention.

While I'm waiting for Robbie to return, I wash Preston's hands under some cold water, and apologise when it makes him flinch. As I focus my attention on his right arm, where the deep cut is, my stomach churns. He must have literally scratched it into the skin because as I check for any debris inside the wound,

I find nothing. It's still bleeding slightly. I warn him before running cold water over it.

'This is one, right?' Robbie's voice turns me towards the bathroom doorway, and he's standing there holding a small green bag with a white cross on it.

I thank him and take it, and as I zip it open, I want to kiss his parents' feet. It has everything I need, even Savlon. As I begin treating Preston's wound, Robbie doesn't stop asking me questions I don't answer. Preston, on the other hand, has stopped speaking all together, and only makes a sound when I use something that makes his wounds sting. Even then, he's oddly unresponsive to the pain.

After twenty minutes or so, I'm bandaging up the scratch wound on Preston's right wrist, and when our eyes briefly meet, he lowers his gaze in a flash. He still hasn't said anything, and seems far more sober now. Once I've addressed Preston's wounds as best I can, I take him back into the living room. We walk in to see Robbie fast asleep on the sofa with one of the duvets wrapped around him. I flop onto the duvet mountain with a heavy sigh, and Preston silently joins me. He mutters an apology, and it's the first thing he's said for what feels like forever.

Robbie is snoring lightly, and the film that was on has finished, so now all the gargantuan television is showing is a blank, blue screen. I stand up to remove the DVD, then switch it off before slumping back onto the floor. Preston is lying on his back, staring at the ceiling.

'His parents are never home.' He gestures towards Robbie. 'They give him lots of money he doesn't want, so he throws parties they don't want.'

'I can't say I've ever met them.'

'That's kind of the point.'

Preston releases a breathy laugh, and I watch Robbie for a while. I've always found it hypnotising to watch other people sleep. No one has control over how they look or behave while asleep, and in essence, they're a more real version of themselves. They have nothing to hide behind. Robbie looks delicate, as if waking him could break him into pieces.

The clock is edging towards three in the morning now, and the world is eerily silent. Preston is the first to break it.

'Do you believe your life is an outcome of your own actions, or one of an uncontrollable force?'

I didn't think I'd ever be able to say I was relieved to hear one of Preston's pretentious musings, but I am. It feels normal. He's still lying on the floor, and it's as if a calmness I can't even try to grasp has overcome him.

'Uh, I don't know. I guess it depends on the situation.' I shrug. 'Why?'

'I think the world has forgotten me. I do all of these bad things and I never receive punishment for them, and I suppose I should be pleased about that, but I'm not. All my life I've had to resolve the unbalance by taking control of it myself, but no matter how hard I try, it doesn't work. Perhaps that is the world's punishment. I have to watch myself destroy everything and suffer so little for it, and day by day, it kills me. It's killing me.'

'What have you done wrong? All I've ever seen you do, when you're not being Zack anyway, is good. Dedicating your world to Matty, looking out for me with my parents' situation, covering for me with the car accident--'

'Practically assaulting you in Robbie's bathroom last summer.'

I stammer. He does remember.

'That wasn't you,' I mutter.

'Yes, it was. I may give myself a different name, but it's still me. Same flesh, same heart, same brain.' He sighs. 'That's not my point, anyway. I much prefer Zack to... to... me.'

He has to be kidding.

'Well, the Preston I know is ten times the person Zack is.'

Preston shakes his head, then laughs quietly. 'I'm not talking about that, I'm talking about me.'

What? What does he mean? Is he drunker than I thought? Either I'm mishearing him completely, or he's suggesting the person he's been around me since September has been a ruse all along.

'What? So Preston is an act too? What are you trying to say?' I don't mean to, but I sound angry.

'Yes. No. Sometimes. I don't know,' is his response, and the emptiness of his voice makes it sound like he's just ripped his chest open and laid his soul bare. 'I don't know who the fuck I am anymore, I just know it's not good. I'm not good.' I go to interrupt, but he stops me. 'No one can ever know everything about anyone. You need to understand that, Mia.' His voice is an utterance. 'Yes: I am a dreamer. For a dreamer is one who can only find his way by moonlight, and his punishment is that he sees the dawn before the rest of the world.' He takes a long breath. 'Oscar Wilde.'

I'm not sure what to say to that, so I don't say anything. I run over responses in my head, but nothing feels right. It's deadly silent again, and as the minutes pass, the sound of Robbie's gentle snoring is competed with by Preston's heavy breathing below me. He's fast asleep.

At first, I figure I'll just sleep on the duvet mountain, but I'm shattered out of my mind, and with every one of the five beds in Robbie's house free, there's no way I'm sleeping on the floor. I grab one of the duvets and a couple of pillows, and make my way towards one of the many bedrooms. Before leaving the room, I look back, and it strikes me that the two boys I'm watching are Zack Maddox and Robbie Morrisey.

If someone had told me this time last year that I would be in this situation, I would've thought they were insane. Zack Maddox and Robbie Morrissey have always been these characters within an unattainable story, one that doesn't bear a second thought because it's all make believe. As I watch them sleeping quietly in the middle of a living room at three o'clock in the early hours of a Saturday morning, I realise how wrong I was. They're not characters, they're people. They have thoughts and feelings and lives, and the perceptions I had of them are as false as the story I thought they lived in.

As I'm about to leave the room and head upstairs, I realise something. In his restful state, Robbie seems fragile, but Preston looks exactly the same as he always does. There's no vulnerability, no hidden truths brought to light in his unconscious state. It's as if even when asleep, Preston is in complete control.

Preston is gone when I wake up and amble downstairs the next morning, and when I ask Robbie where he's disappeared to, he tells me he left early this morning without saying much. Robbie says something about another party he's throwing soon, but I don't process much of what he's saying because all I can think about Preston, and where he's gone. My instinct is to panic, to assume the worst, but as I'm leaving Robbie's house, my phone vibrates in my pocket with a text from Preston. All it contains is a single comma.

CHAPTER 26

Since he showed up drunk at Robbie's, Preston has been going out almost every night. I've only been out with the group twice myself, but based on what Robbie's shared, Preston has been in full blown Zack mode each time. It's a far cry from the first few weeks after the cottage where he wouldn't set foot in public, and I have no idea if that's a good thing or a bad thing. I try not to ponder over it too much because it makes me dizzy, and so long as he sends me a comma every day, I'm content. I still always send a reply to it, and he still never responds. I visited Anwen again last week. Preston hasn't told her about last summer, and when she questioned him, he acted like he had no idea what she was referring to.

My house is unusually quiet when I enter it. I stayed at Aiden's last night, and he's left all of his assignments until the last minute, so I pretty much left the moment I woke up to let him get on with it. I can hear mumbling, which is odd because Dad's usually blasting some horrendous daytime cookery show on a Saturday morning. As I pass our dining room, I notice that the door is shut, and that the mumbling is coming from the other side. I hear Dad and don't think much of it, but as I'm about to start walking again, I hear a voice so recognisable that it chokes me. Mum.

'... convenient back-up plan, James!'

'That's not what I'm saying, please, just consider it. I'm begging you.'

What are they talking about? Mum hasn't stepped foot in this house since she moved out, so for her to be here now means there must be a good reason. I'm fairly certain they've not even interacted since I was at the hospital after the crash, and I'd barely class what they were doing there as interacting.

'I came here so that we could be adults and talk about the girls,' Mum says from behind the door my ear is now planted against. 'I don't care if you've ended things with that woman, and I don't care how much you claim to still love me because if you did, this never would have happened in the first place.'

Is Dad asking for her back? Has he seriously got the nerve? I have never wanted to applaud Mum so much in my entire life. All she ever used to do was tip-toe around Dad in fear of upsetting him, so hearing her acknowledging her own self-worth makes me want to burst open the door and give her the biggest high-five I've ever given anyone.

'Charlotte, please, come back, I love you. Imagine how happy the girls--'

'Don't try to blackmail me, don't you dare. I don't rely on you anymore, James, I don't need you to make me happy. I can do that alone. You put me through hell after what you did, and I felt like I was worth shit.' Hearing Mum swear stuns me; I had no idea she was capable of it. 'I loved you, all of you, and you didn't even see me.'

My head is spinning. I'm so incredibly proud of Mum for standing up for herself, for not giving in to the easy option of taking Dad back, but should I be? Shouldn't I want them back together so that we can play happy families again? Footsteps grow closer, and as I realise they're heading towards the door I'm leaning against, I panic and slip back out of the house in a rush. I dash up our driveway and out of our street without looking back once, and I have no idea where I'm going. With Aiden unavailable, I pull out my phone and dial Robbie's number because I have no idea what else to do.

Robbie picks me up from the end of my street. As I let myself into his car, he shows me a questioning look as he scans the overnight bag I still have with me from Aiden's.

'Going somewhere?'

'What? Oh, no, it's from Aiden's last night,' I explain as he pulls away. 'It's a long story.'

'You okay?'

'Yeah, yeah, honestly, fine. Good, actually. I--Doesn't matter, I'm good, don't worry. What's the plan?' I ask as I dump my bag onto the backseat.

'Damn, I thought you had one,' Robbie replies. 'I need to go home first, whatever we do. My mum's paranoid after the accident. She thinks it's dangerous to drive this thing, so she's refusing to let me go further than, like, five miles in it.'

'Okay, cool. Hm... I really don't know what to do. Probably should've thought ahead.'

'How about a castle?' Robbie offers.

I raise my eyebrows. 'Where did you pull that idea from?'

He shrugs. 'I like castles. Wales has a lot of castles. It's the obvious choice.'

I grin. 'Sure, why not? Don't want to tarnish my street cred though, so I'll have to wear a disguise or something.'

'Shame you've got none to lose,' Robbie jokes, to which I elbow his side. Probably not the wisest idea while he's driving, but there we go. 'Which one?'

I lean back in my seat as I think. 'I always used to go to Ogmore with my family, but I've not been in forever. Is that a little far though?'

'Whatever you want, I'm easy.' Robbie glances at me, flashing a lopsided smile. 'Ogmore Castle it is.'

By the time we've reached Robbie's house, I've pretty much forgotten about what I overheard at home. I'm glad Mum has refused Dad's proposition. I can't believe I'm actually saying that, but I am. He's my father and in that sense I love him, of course I do, but Mum deserves so much better, and I know that.

As we wander into Robbie's kitchen, there's a dark-haired woman standing over the sink, who I assume is his mother. I can only see her profile, but she's quite a plain woman. Underneath a button nose sits a pair of thin lips, and her small eyes match the icy colour of Robbie's. Her hair is tied up into a perfectly neat bun, and she's wearing an oddly business-like dress to be cleaning the dishes in.

'The car's back, I'm going out,' Robbie states matter-of-factly.

His mum turns to us, and her face lights up when she sees me, and she slips her bright pink gloves off as she smiles.

'Hello, dear,' she says to me with an English accent, while completely ignoring what Robbie said. 'I'm Harriet, Robert's mother.'

'Mia,' I say with a smile. 'Nice to meet you.'

'Lovely! Where are you going? Would you like me to give you a lift?' she asks, finally acknowledging what Robbie said a few minutes ago.

Robbie narrows his eyes. 'Uh, Ogmore. No thanks, we're just getting the train.'

'Don't be silly, I'll drive you.'

'No, seriously, we're fine.'

Harriet ignores him. She shuffles us out of the room and back into the hallway, and I don't think I've ever seen Robbie look more distressed. Considering I was with him as his best friend lay dying in his front garden, that says a lot. He tries to tell his mum we want to take the train one more time, but again goes unheard, and he eventually gives up. We sit ourselves into the family's Range Rover, the price of which I can't begin to imagine, and I drop my overnight bag onto the seat beside me. This is going to be a nightmare to lug around.

I quickly understand why Robbie was so desperate to take the train. I have never experienced a more uncomfortable atmosphere in my life, and I've been in some pretty uneasy scenarios. Robbie and Harriet don't speak for the whole journey, and it's not because they're comfortable in silence. It's as if they simply have no idea how to interact with each other. It's like when a couple go on their first few dates, and they're at that awkward stage of wanting to get to know each other, but not having the guts to make the first move. It's... odd.

Once I ask her a few questions and throw in some conversation starters, it flows perfectly. She asks me all about college, what I'm studying there, where I'm from, and all of that typical stuff. When I mention having a dog, she begins describing how much Robbie used to love a dog they had when he was little, which Robbie informs her is wrong because it once bit his arm, and the car turns silent again. I'm grateful when the journey is over, that's for sure.

'She wanted a girl, in case you didn't catch on,' Robbie jokes as his mum drives away, although I'm not sure how much of a joke it actually is.

I've not been to Ogmore Castle in years, and for something that was built in the twelfth century, it sure has aged well. Its walls are crumbling and it wouldn't fit its original purpose of defence nowadays, but it refuses to fall. There's a river a few hundred yards away from the castle walls, and dotted in an uneven line across it are large stepping stones. Memories of being carried on Dad's shoulders to cross them flash through my mind, and I can't stop myself from running towards the river. Robbie's laughter follows me as we reach the riverbank, and I insist he goes first so that he's there to catch me if I slip and fall headfirst into the water. He thinks I'm kidding.

We spend at least half an hour crossing the river and conjuring up dumb games to play, most of which include having to jump over as many stones as possible in one go. I make a miserable record of two, while Robbie jumps a respectable four. I lose track of the amount of times I almost fall off, but if I don't regain balance, Robbie always manages to catch me. I feel like I'm eight-years-old again, and it's amazing. The only disturbance is the fact that I keep worrying someone is going to steal my bag, which I've plopped onto the edge of the riverbank.

Once we're done with the river and stepping stones, we cross the wooden bridge over the dried up moat, and make our way into what remains of the castle. Once it has been adequately explored, we sit down onto the grass in the centre of it. Children laugh and run around us, and it occurs to me that it's been far too long since I did something like this. I'm trying to explain to Robbie how he had an unfair advantage over me during the stepping stone championship due to the fact he's at least five inches taller than me, when my beanie is suddenly pulled off my head. I fling my arms to my hair in a delayed reaction, and spin around to see a familiar face grinning at me.

'Got ya!'

Matty giggles as he tosses my hat back to me, but I just throw it back at him. He makes a dramatic gesture and holds his hands against his stomach, as if the beanie was a bullet straight to his gut. This is the second time Robbie and I have randomly bumped into him, and having not seen him since we were at the cottage, I'm ecstatic. I had tried visiting him at Paul and Julia's a week or so later, but they didn't answer the door, let alone allow me to see Matty. Considering I can't gauge anything from Preston about what happened as a result of the cottage situation, this is a godsend.

'Are you the same man Mia was with at Roath Park ages ago?' Matty asks Robbie.

'Yes, I am that man,' Robbie replies, clearly satisfied by being referred to as a fully-fledged male adult.

I roll my eyes at him, to which he jokingly puffs his chest out in pride. Matty begins his usual routine of speaking so quickly that I couldn't have any idea what he's talking about if I tried. The only thing I manage to catch is him asking us what we're doing, to which I simply answer with 'exploring'. When I ask him what he's getting up to, he sits down in front of us and leans in as if he's sharing a secret.

'I'm looking for Y Ladi Wen.'

'For what now?' Robbie asks with narrowed eyes.

'Y Ladi Wen,' Matty repeats, but Robbie and I are still clueless. 'The White Lady? Ugh, don't tell me you don't know. She's a ghost. She haunts this place to warn children not to be naughty, and to protect the treasure that's buried under the castle. Preston told me all about her. You're not meant to speak to her if you see her, but I'm gonna if I do 'cause I wanna be a ghost hunter as my job.'

'Ah, I see,' I reply, nodding my head slowly.

I glance at Robbie, unsure of whether I should ask the next question with him sitting there. I may not get another chance any time soon though, so I have to risk it. He probably won't have any idea what we're talking about, anyway.

'Hey, Matty, how's Preston been since the cottage?'

Matty shrugs and picks at the grass as he mutters, 'I dunno, I haven't seen him yet. I think Paul and Julia are angry at him.'

'What, since you got home?'

He shakes his head as he drops a pile of grass from his hands back onto the ground. It's been over a month since we were at the cottage. They've not seen each other since then? Bloody hell, no wonder Preston is behaving the way he is. It must be hell for him.

'Have you spoken to him over the phone or anything then?' I ask.

Again, Matty shakes his head and stares at the ground. I don't know who the hell Paul and Julia are trying to protect here, but it's not Matty. All of this because Preston wanted to make him feel better about a nightmare.

'I don't know what his phone number is, and Paul and Julia say that they don't, but I know they do 'cause they've called him on his phone before. I've not gone to his house either 'cause Julia only lets me play in the back garden now.' He clicks his tongue. 'We're moving soon, so I wanna see him.'

'Hey, Robbie, pass me my bag, please?' I gesture towards the overnight bag I'm suddenly so glad to have had to drag around with me.

Once Robbie hands it over, I begin shuffling through it until I find my college stuff from the day before, and bring out a pen and a scrap of paper. I retrieve Preston's name from my phone, and scribble it onto the paper before handing it to Matty. I wink at him, and he flashes me the toothiest grin imaginable. As I'm about to start speaking to him again, a shrewd voice distracts me.

'Matty! We're going now, come on!'

It's Julia. She must have noticed me speaking to him because she won't stop calling his name and manically gesturing for him to return to her. I pretend I don't see her and say a quiet goodbye to Matty as he subtly shoves the paper I just gave him into one of his trainers. Preston has trained him well.

I watch him as he's retrieved by a frenzied Julia, and struggle not to laugh. You'd swear I was Satan himself. I get the feeling that once you're on Julia's bad side, there's no turning back. Preston was doomed from the beginning, really. As I turn my attention back to Robbie, he raises his eyebrows at me.

'Seriously, who is this Preston guy?'

CHAPTER 27

As I scan myself from head to toe in the long mirror opposite me, I smile. I rarely think I look good, but tonight is an exception. I've had a much needed haircut, and for once, my typical black ensemble looks intriguing, not depressing. Aiden's rambling on the bed behind me while Preston, or currently Zack, blasts some horrendous dubstep remix of an ABBA song through Robbie's stereo. I feel like the Preston trapped inside of him is trying to send out an ironic message.

Robbie is throwing another party, and Aiden is enthusiastic to say the least. He keeps mentioning how far we've come since the last party as if we've unveiled the meaning of life, when in reality, the only difference is that we've made some new friends. Minus a few other details, I suppose. Robbie has disappeared somewhere; he said he was going to grab us some drinks, but that was about fifteen minutes ago. Preston ensured to mock the fact I asked for water instead of alcohol, and when I reminded him that the last time I drank resulted in me driving a car into a bush and landing him in hospital, he just rolled his eyes.

Robbie eventually returns with a large bottle of vodka, some Diet Coke, and a bottle of water for me, which Preston again ridicules, and I again ignore. The boys pour their drinks while I join them on the double bed. People will begin arriving soon, and if this party's anything like the last one, I'm going to make the most of the calm before the storm. I don't know why, but I feel a little nervous, as if now that I've officially infiltrated 'Zack' and Robbie's friendship group, I have to be more interesting than I am. It's like I'm preparing to put on a show for everyone, and I can't help but wonder if this is how Preston feels every day. If it's how Robbie feels some days, how Aiden feels most days.

'I'm gonna be a bit stricter tonight than last time,' Robbie states before he takes a sip of his drink.

'Ah, c'mon, mate, don't be a buzzkill,' Preston responds with a groan.

'I don't want a repeat of last time, all right? That's all it is.'

'What was wrong with last time?' Preston asks.

'Oh, I don't know, maybe when you almost died in my garden.'

'Touché.'

I glance at Preston to catch a glimmer of uneasiness behind his smirk, which he erases by downing the drink in his hand. He still has no idea I know what actually happened that night, and I'd be lying if I said not drinking tonight had nothing to do with keeping an eye on him. The doorbell rings, and we take it as a sign to leave the certainty of Robbie's bedroom to face what the night has to offer.

For such a big house, it doesn't take long for it to become cramped. Strangers, acquaintances, and friends begin filling up empty spaces, and tonight soon mirrors the last time I was at a party in this house. Teenagers laugh and drink and dance, their faces blending into one, and even the people I know become indistinguishable at times. Robbie and Preston have disappeared somewhere deep into the land of Robbie Morrissey and Zack Maddox, while Samantha and I sit on one of the kitchen counters listening to Aiden blabbering about fifty things a minute.

'Question,' he begins. 'You know how people say something easy is a piece of cake? Why? What does cake have to do with anything? Baking one isn't easy, and people always cut me massive slices--Shit, maybe I should be offended by that. Should I be offended by that? What was--Oh, yeah, I can never finish a full piece, so what about it is easy?'

I'm not sure if he's drunk or just Aiden.

'You should ask them to cut smaller pieces,' Samantha replies absentmindedly.

She looks over Aiden's shoulder and waves, and when I spot who she's waving at, I freeze. Delyth smiles back, and when Samantha begins gesturing her over, I scan the room in a panic as if it'll magic up somewhere for me to hide. My best bet is the sink and it is a big sink, in fairness, so I guess I could squeeze in there if I really tried. I decide against it, though.

Everyone greets each other as Delyth approaches us, and I squeeze out a hello, but I just feel awful. I've not spoken to her since Boys' Village, and I know I owe her an extremely overdue apology for being such a bitch that night. I'm beginning to wonder if Samantha does these things on purpose, especially when she and Aiden begin discussing cake again, which leaves Delyth and me silent in the background.

'How're you?' I finally manage to ask her.

'All right thanks, you?'

'Yeah, not too bad.'

The gigantic elephant in the room is staring me in the face, and I figure I should just get it over with.

'Look, I'm sorry for being so awful to you at Boys' Village,' I say quietly.

'It's okay,' she replies almost immediately. 'I was a bit... dramatic with it sometimes so, y'know, yeah. It's okay, yeah.'

It's reassuring to know she's obviously just as uncomfortable as I am with this. Samantha's dark eyes glance at me, and I spot a tiny smile on her face. I purse my lips. Oh, she so knows what she's doing. I'm about to jump off the cunter to refill my glass of water when my phone buzzes in my pocket, and I'm a little confused when Robbie's name flashes on the screen.

'Uh, hey?'

'Hey, Mia, where are you?' He pauses. 'I've got a bit of a... uh... a situation here. Meet me in my bedroom.'

Before I can reply, Robbie hangs up. I frown at my phone. That was weird. I must be pulling a pretty ugly face because Aiden laughs and asks me what's wrong. With the mention of 'Robbie' and 'bedroom' in the same sentence, his face lights up, and crude jokes pour out of his mouth like a waterfall. I don't even bother reminding him we're not a thing anymore. I leave Delyth, Samantha, and him at the counter to go and find Robbie, but Aiden can't resist following.

'Okay, so I'll go in first. If he's naked, I can give you a thumbs up or a thumbs down. I'll take the bullet for you if it's a thumbs down,' he says as we shove past a couple of girls lingering on the staircase. 'You don't give me enough credit, y'know, I'm such a nice guy.'

'Aiden, I really don't think it's that kind of situation.'

'It won't be with that attitude.'

I sure hope it's not that kind of situation. Robbie's room is always an out of bounds area at his parties, so once we've battled our way through the masses, the door is locked when I try to open it. I knock and let him know it's me, and within seconds it's flung open, and Robbie is ushering us in.

'Hey, what's--'

My sentence becomes jagged stammering as I look behind Robbie because sitting on the unmade double bed, a small backpack in front of him, is Matty. I can't formulate a coherent sentence, so Aiden does so for me.

'Robbie, why is there a small child in your bedroom?'

'Hey, Mia!' Matty jumps onto the floor with an enormous grin on his face, grabs my hand, then pulls me back onto the bed with him. He unzips his backpack and begins showing me everything inside while speaking a thousand miles per hour.

'I'm running away 'cause I don't wanna leave tomorrow, but I had to pack not that much 'cause I had to be like a ninja to escape. I was gonna go see Preston at his house but he wasn't there, but then I saw him walking so I followed him here and I didn't want him to be angry so I snuck in, and then I saw Robbie. It's really loud downstairs, it's probably not very nice for the neighbours.'

'You're meant to be moving tomorrow?' I ask him.

'Yeah, but I'm gonna live with Preston instead.'

I turn to Robbie, who looks bewildered, or it might just be sheer terror. Aiden, on the other hand, looks thrilled. When Matty pulls out one of his toy dinosaurs, there's no stopping him, and he dives onto the bed to join us. While Aiden and Matty are distracted, I turn back to Robbie.

'Robbie, where's Zack?'

'What? There's a random little kid in my bedroom, I don't think his whereabouts are important right now, Mia.'

'No--I, uh.' I glance at Aiden and Matty. 'Right, you guys stay here and keep an eye on him. I'll be back now.'

Without giving him any say in the matter, I rush past Robbie and head back into the crowded hallway. I weave my way in and out of groups of people, but there's no sign of Preston upstairs, so I continue my search on the ground floor. As I enter the living room, there's a circle of people sitting on and around the sofa playing some childish truth or dare game, and their ringleader is just the person I'm looking for.

I try to flag Preston down from the doorway, but he's too absorbed in the stranger's face he's sucking on to notice me. Once he's done, he pulls an expression that makes him look like he wants to be sick, points at the girl he was just kissing, then laughs. How pleasant.

'Aled,' he says, turning to the boy with a shaved head sitting opposite him. 'Is it true your mum--' His eyes flicker to me, and an enormous grin explodes onto his face. 'Hey, look, it's the chick Robbie was screwing. Hey, Mia!'

Again, how pleasant.

'Oh, actually,' he says as he turns back to Aled. 'I dare you to make out with her in front of Robbie.'

I try not to drop-kick Preston as I approach the group, and I notice that half of them have cigarettes in their hands. The stench of it hits me as I near them, and I wonder how the hell I ever hacked smoking any myself. Several of them snigger at Preston's gag as if he's a comedic genius when, in reality, I could've heard something funnier from a cheap packet of Christmas crackers.

'Zack, I need to speak to you about something,' I state as I stand over the group.

'Can't you see I'm busy entertaining the masses?'

It's like he wants me to punch him.

'Do I actually get to kiss her for my dare? She's hot.'

'No,' I snap at Aled.

Preston shrieks with laughter and fist-pumps Aled, while the girls of the group echo their laughter. This is a true reminder of why I avoid these kind of people, and these kinds of situations at all costs. I groan and try to twist my face in a way that tells Preston to stop being an arse, and come with me. He either doesn't notice it, or ignores it.

'It's important,' I try once more as I pull another face.

'Babe, the only way you're getting me to do anything is with a dare, so you're gonna have to join us. You all right, by the way? Your face keeps doing this weird twitchy thing.'

Preston gestures to an empty space on the floor. Fine. If he wants to play this game, then I'll play it. I grin at him sarcastically, and sit myself down in-between two brunette girls, who are still giggling at one of the countless unfunny things Preston has done over the past few minutes. If I wasn't so considerate of his identity crisis, then I would just refer to him as Preston in front of everyone and inform him that his eight-year-old brother has run away from home in the middle of the night, and is currently upstairs hanging out with a drunk homosexual and a distressed party host.

'Okay, my go!' Preston exclaims, despite the fact he insisted on the last dare, and probably the one before that. 'Okay, Mia, is it true that last time you came to one of Robbie's parties, you were so uncool that you knew literally nobody?'

'No. Can--'

'I think you're lying there, babe.'

He nudges Aled and whispers something into his ear, which sends them both into fits of laughter. Again, the girls join in, despite having no way of hearing what he just said. This is starting to annoy me now. I begin tapping my foot against the floor as I glare at Preston.

'Oh, wait, I have another one,' he continues. I get the feeling this game of truth and dare is actually just a game of Preston demanding things from everyone else. 'I dare--'

'How about I have a go?' I snap. 'Truth. Is it true that you use this stupid persona as an excuse to treat people like shit?'

Preston's eyes turn dark. 'Is it true you crashed Robbie's car into a ditch, and then let me take the blame for it?'

'Is it true that you don't actually live in a nice, big house in Pontcanna, but actually a tiny terraced one in Cathays?'

'Is it true your parents are divorcing because your old man can't keep his dick in his pants?'

With that, I spring up from the floor, barge my way out of the patio doors, and stride into Robbie's back garden. Screw him.

Screw him and his stupid multiple personalities and his stupid pretentious attitudes and his stupid life.

'What was all that about?' a voice calls after me, and even over the house music and screaming crowds, I can recognise it as Preston's.

'Go away, Preston, I'm done with you!'

'Oh, you couldn't be done with me if you tried!'

I stop and spin around to see him standing on the moist grass with a smirk on his face. His hands are in his jeans' pockets, and strands of his light hair have fallen down onto his forehead. He's never looked so arrogant. I swear under my breath, then turn back around to walk deeper into the garden until I reach a stumpy tree with an old wooden swing dangling from one of its branches.

As I sit down onto it, I hope not to see Preston when I look back towards the house, but I'm thoroughly disappointed.

'I don't know what the hell is wrong with you lately,' I begin as he stops in front of me. 'But you are awful, you're just awful.'

'Sorry to break it to you, babe, but I did warn you about having high expectations of me. No need to get menstrual over it.'

Why is he still maintaining Zack's character? Can't he give it a rest for five bloody minutes? I begin pushing myself on the swing out of pure frustration, which elongates the ugly smirk on Preston's face. I'm glad this is all such a big joke to him, but I sure don't find it funny.

I'm about to spit another round of accusations, questions, and insults at him when I spot something bright in the corner of my eye. I stare at the house to see fluorescent reds and oranges dancing behind two of the windows of the second floor, and for a while, I wonder if I'm going insane. Then I see the smoke. Bursting out of the crack in one of the windows is black smoke.

'I... Um, Preston, I think the house is on fire.'

Preston laughs. 'What?' He turns around to follow my gaze, and within seconds, he's facing me again with wide eyes. 'Holy shit.'

He begins running towards the house, and I instinctively leap off the wooden swing to follow. Behind the windows of the ground floor, people drink and sing and laugh. They dance in sync with the flames above them without even realising they exist. Things are more hectic back inside the living room. The staircase isn't far from here, and so news of whatever's happening upstairs has spread quickly.

Idiotically, when Preston orders everyone to get outside because there's a fire upstairs, a chunk of the crowd make their way towards the staircase to see for themselves. Music is still blasting around the house, and I can barely hear myself think. Most people just laugh when we tell them to leave the house, and it's making me question what I just saw. Is there a fire? Are my eyes lying to me? Eventually, more and more people come running down from upstairs, and the more panicked they are, the more panicked everyone else becomes.

I follow Preston as he runs to the other end of the house, and I'm desperately wishing it wasn't so enormous right now because it's like trying to herd blind cattle. The further away from the staircase we get, the less panicked people are. Delyth and Samantha are still in the kitchen, so when we explain what's happening to them, they aid us in getting people out. Once we've scaled the entire ground floor, we begin heading back towards the main hallway to get out of the building ourselves, and all of a sudden, the realisation of what's happening hits me. Sweaty bodies barge past me as my heart races in my chest, and my hands are sweating. My chest is tight. All I can focus on is Preston, and I follow him like a lost puppy.

Then the reason why I came downstairs in the first place hits me.

I stop running, and freeze. Preston turns around and yells at me to keep following him, but I don't do as he asks. I open my mouth, but can't speak. He watches me expectantly until I find the words I'm looking for.

'Preston, Matty's here, he--he followed you here.'

Preston's face drops. 'What? Is he still in here? What--Where is he?'

'I--I don't know.'

'What the hell do you mean, you don't know? Where did you leave him?'

I swallow a hard lump that's formed in my throat. 'Upstairs.'

Chapter 28

I don't think I've ever seen anyone run so fast. Preston is darting back into the depths of the house before I can even process it happening. I know I should just keep heading towards the front door, but I don't. I chase after him.

'Preston, don't! Stop!' I can barely keep up with him. 'Robbie and Aiden were with him, he'll be okay!'

He ignores me.

As if on cue, when we're a few steps away from the staircase, I smack into Robbie. We both come to a halt. When I ask him where Matty is, he stammers, and any words he does say are drowned out by the sound of panic. His eyes look wild, and his face is ashen. I ask him again, but he says nothing. He doesn't know.

'You idiot!' Preston, who I hadn't realised had stopped with us, exclaims.

He shoves Robbie, and within seconds, he's running up the stairs against the wave of people running down them. I should just turn back and get the hell out of here, but again, I don't.

I sprint up the staircase behind Preston, and as if entranced, Robbie follows us.

The first thing that hits me is the heat. It gnarls at my skin and burns my eyes, and I don't know if it's the smoke or the running, but my breath is short. The flames have engulfed far more than a few rooms now, so much so that I can't distinguish between doors. The fire is so bright I can barely keep my eyes open, and the smoke is stinging my eyes, itching my throat. The boys begin barging into rooms as I scramble for my phone and call Aiden. It rings but nobody answers. I try again. I'm about to give up and re-dial when he picks up.

'Aiden! Aiden, where are you?'

The other end is muffled, and when he replies, the sound of crackling and shouting drowns out anything distinguishable. I ask again, this time with my finger pressed against my other ear.

'...room. Don't know... one.'

'I can't hear you,' I breathe into the phone. 'Where are you?'

'One of... can't... is jammed... to explain... bathrooms.'

'You're in a bathroom?'

'Yes!' I hear as clear as day.

I keep Aiden on the line as I call for Preston and Robbie, but I can't see them anywhere, and the smoke is turning thicker. I pace up and down the hallway and keep shouting for them until my throat hurts, and eventually, I hear a response from Robbie. He runs over to me from inside a smoke-filled room, and tells me to go downstairs and leave the house. I don't listen.

'They're in a bathroom, where are your bathrooms?' I shout over the roaring flames. 'Where's Preston gone?'

'Uh, there's--there's five of them, I've checked one! Who, what?'

'Zack! Where's Zack?'

Robbie glances around, then shakes his head. I call for him but hear nothing back, and so Robbie and I begin locating all of the bathrooms. After checking two, I'm beginning to lose faith. My head feels light, and my eyes are watering from the smoke. Robbie is on the phone to Aiden now, but he's getting as much sense out of him as I was. As we're heading towards the third bathroom, a deafening banging sound steals our attention.

We run towards the noise until we spot Preston, who's inside the master bedroom, kicking at the door of the ensuite that's slowly turning a dirty brown colour from the fire.

'They're in here!' he shouts as he spots us. 'The door's stuck, it's--it's jammed!'

He kicks it again, and while it bends from the stress, it doesn't open. Robbie throws my phone back to me, and begins hitting the door with Preston. My heart is beating so fast that I feel like I'm going to be sick, and I can't breathe. I really can't breathe. Preston and Robbie's barging and kicking is getting louder and louder, but the door still won't open. I glance out of the room to see tall flames nearing the staircase in the distance. Shit.

'The fire's going to reach the stairs!' I scream, but they don't hear me.

I'm about to shout again when, as Robbie and Preston kick the door in-sync, it gives in and collapses open. Preston darts inside as I dash to the doorway, and staring back at me are two sets of wide eyes. Aiden and Matty. They're here, they're okay. A gush of oxygen rushes back into my lungs, and I can breathe again. What I breathe out, however, are stuttered coughs.

Aiden is carrying Matty, whose backpack is dangling from his hand, and Preston grabs his brother the moment he's able to. With Matty now in his arms, he yells at us to head to the staircase, and we follow him like lost children. I'm so caught up in the glee of finding them that I've forgotten about the flames approaching the top of the staircase, and so when I see them raging even closer to it, I'm shocked. Everyone else must notice because we're all suddenly running faster.

We're too late.

As we reach the top of the stairs, the flames are already devouring it.

'Aiden, go!' Preston shouts at Aiden as he gestures towards the stairs. 'The flames aren't that high yet, but they will be in seconds. You're the tallest, so go! Jump over them, and I'll hand Matty to you!'

Robbie and I are standing behind them coughing our guts out, and the more seconds that pass, the closer I feel to passing out. Every inch of my body feels numb. Aiden hesitates, but when Preston bellows again, he obeys his orders and leaps over some of the shorter flames. He lands a few steps down unharmed, and Preston passes Matty to him over the fire. He yells at him to keep going down, and Aiden disappears towards the ground floor. Preston turns to us.

'Go, quick!'

I'm frozen still, but Robbie doesn't hesitate. The flames have already turned more aggressive, and they've crept further down the banister. I can hear the wood groaning from the heat. Robbie rushes past Preston and jumps over the growing flames, and as he does so, there's an ear-shattering creak. The floor feels as if it's shaking, and it takes me a while to realise that's because it is.

Robbie is reaching out his hand for me to take, but everything is happening too fast and the stairs are creaking so much, and they're--they're collapsing underneath him. I dart my arm out to take Robbie's hand, but I've been too slow. He stumbles as there's a loud creaking sound, and he's disappearing--No, the stairs are disappearing. He stumbles backwards, and within moments Robbie is gone, and so is the staircase. All that's left are its burning remains below us, blocking our path entirely.

Preston calls to him, and Robbie calls back. I can't decipher what he says, but I'm just relieved to hear his voice.

'Shit,' Preston mutters beside me. 'Shit, shit shit.'

He stares at where the staircase used to be and bobs his head around as if trying to make it reappear. He swears again, then turns to me and waves his hands.

'Go back towards the bedroom!'

'I--But, I don't--'

'Go!'

I do as I'm told, and drag my unsteady legs back towards the master bedroom. Once I've reached the en suite, a loud bang follows, and I scream. I spin around to see Preston stripping the king-sized bed of its covers. The bedroom door is closed shut, and I realise that's where the bang came from. Preston is saying something to me, but I can't hear him over my heavy breathing, so I just stare at him. He shouts again. I still do nothing.

'Mia!'

I've never heard his voice so loud, and it immediately snaps me out of my trance. I stutter, having no idea what he's requested of me.

'Mia,' he says calmly as he stops undressing the bed. His voice suddenly turns soft, so much so that it's soothing. 'Grab a towel and stuff it under the bedroom door to stop the smoke, then look for some spare sheets and bed stuff.' He pauses to cough. 'Okay?'

I nod silently. Preston returns to stripping the bed as I grab the white towel dangling over the bathroom sink, and head back into the bedroom to shove it under the door. I didn't realise how much smoke had already gotten in. The walls have started turning a grey colour, and I'm struggling to breathe again. There's a grand wardrobe opposite the bed, and so I fling open its doors and begin searching through all of the clothes for spare sheets. Preston has started tying the ones from the bed together so that they make one long strand, and it finally occurs to me what he's doing.

As I meddle through the wardrobe, he opens one of the tall windows and ties one end of the makeshift rope to the radiator underneath it. When I close the wardrobe doors empty handed, I have to stop myself from crying. I hastily scan the room in an attempt to spot anything to add to Preston's creation, but the towel isn't working as a good buffer, and the smoke creeping into the room is making it difficult to see. My legs are wobbling and every bone in my body aches, but I force myself forward and spot a bright green object in the corner of my eye. It's a laundry basket.

I scurry to the side of the bed and empty its contents onto the floor, and I can honestly say that I have never been so glad to see a bed sheet in all my life. I twist back around with the sheet raised above my head in triumph, but Preston isn't looking back at me because he's slumped on the plush carpet, his back against the wall, with his eyes closed.

'Hey!' I yell as I dive down to him. I tap his check. 'Hey, get up!'

His lips move but his words aren't coherent, and his head is bobbing lightly from side to side. He starts coughing, and he doesn't stop. His makeshift rope is in his hands, and as I continue trying to rouse him, I tie the sheet I found onto it. I tap his cheek again, but get nothing back.

Once I've completed the rope, I throw it out of the window. It's not long enough. I hastily pull off the small jacket I'm wearing, bring the rope back into the room, and attach that to it. All I have left on is my black dress, and that's no use, so I begin unbuttoning Preston's shirt to awkwardly pull it off him, and add that to the rope. Once that's complete, I throw our contraption out the window again, and this time, it's close enough. I turn back to Preston.

'Preston? Preston, listen to me,' I begin. 'I just need you to stay with it for a few more minutes, okay?'

'It's okay, go,' he manages to mutter through coughs. 'I need this, just... just go.'

'No.'

'I'll be okay, I just want... I just need five minutes. I'll be down now.'

'No. We don't have five minutes.'

'Please, I can't... I want to...' He mumbles something incoherent, then words that pierce into me like a blunt knife. 'Please just let me die this time, Mia.'

'I'm not leaving this room until you do, so either get up yourself, or I'm dragging you down this building with me.'

At the realisation that I am in no way going anywhere without him, Preston tries sliding himself up the wall and onto his feet. He stumbles and falls back down. This time, I steady him, and offer myself as a support. He sits onto the bare bed, and he won't stop coughing. As seconds pass, the smoke turns thicker, and if we're here much longer, I'm going to be replacing him on the floor. Now I cough, and I can't stop. As my vision turns blurry, I have to steady myself, and as I trip over nothing, Preston steadies me. He's on his feet again.

I take everything I have left inside of me to stand straight, and follow Preston's orders as he tells me to climb out of the window. I demand he goes first. I don't trust him. He tries to argue, but is quick to realise I wasn't joking about not leaving this house unless he does. He swears under his breath, steps out of the window, and begins climbing down our makeshift rope. My vision is still cloudy, and I slip on the windowsill as I pull myself out of it. The fresh air crashes against my face, and it's like a drug. I inhale deeply and sharply, and it's as if my entire body is being cleansed.

Sirens are blaring, and the sounds of the crowds I hate so much have never been so welcoming. I land on the grass below me with a thud, and its moisture soothes my burning skin. I lay on it with my face towards the black sky. I can't stop coughing, and it feels like there are daggers in my throat, but I smile. It's okay.

It's going to be okay.

I turn my head to see Preston next to me, but before I can blink, he's standing up. Through stumbles, he's charging deep into Robbie's back garden. I stagger to my feet and follow him. I can hear the crowds but I can't see them, so all I can assume is that everyone is at the front of the house. As I toddle after Preston, I check my phone to see sixteen missed calls from Aiden, even more from Robbie, and seven text messages. I ignore them.

Coughs burst out of my mouth in a flurry, and my head still feels light as I chase Preston past the wooden swing I was sitting on when I noticed the fire. He's far ahead of me, and he's walking too fast.

'Preston!' I yell, but he doesn't turn around. 'Preston, wait! Where are you going?'

I know he can hear me because everything is stunningly louder since I escaped the house, and it can't be much different for him. There's a slight buzzing sound in my ears, and their sensitivity has shot up. As Preston's pace quickens even more, I start running, and when I finally catch up with him, I grab his arm, and turn him around. His eyes are glazed over. He stops and stares at me, then starts speaking at a pace I can barely keep up with.

'It was my fault, I did it. I--I... The fire, it's my fault. I don't mean to, I don't, I try but I can't--I--How do I make it stop? It was an accident, I didn't mean to. The fire--I--It was an accident!'

'What? No, Preston, you were downstairs, outside. You were with me outside, remember? You didn't do anything, the fire started upstairs,' I try to reason, but he aggressively shakes his head.

He starts pulling at his hair. 'It's my fault, it's my fault, it's my fault!'

'Stop it, you're hurting yourself!' I reach out to pull his hands from his head, but he shoves me away. 'You were downstairs all night, Preston, whatever started it wasn't you! You had nothing to do with it.'

He stops muttering and lowers his hands so that they're limp by his side. His big green eyes gaze at me emptily, and I stare back into them. I offer him my hand in the hope that he'll take it and we can return to the crowd, but he doesn't. He just looks at it. He opens his mouth and I wait for him to speak, but he never does. Instead, he collapses to the floor, his knees bent with his forehead pressed against them, just like in the bathroom at the cottage all those weeks ago.

He's mumbling under his breath, so I lower myself to the ground in front of him, and call his name. He doesn't respond.

'Mia, I didn't mean to do it, I didn't mean to, please believe me, I didn't.'

'Listen to me, the fire had nothing to do with--'

'It was an accident, I didn't mean to do it, I didn't. He was shouting and I just wanted him to stop, and he wouldn't. She was crying, and he kept shouting and he wouldn't stop.'

'What? Preston, what are you talking about? I don't under-stand.'

I try to reach for him, but he smacks me away. He starts pulling at his hair again, and as the words leaving his mouth quicken, so does his breathing.

'He wouldn't stop bleeding, I don't--She said it was going to be okay, but it wasn't. It isn't okay, it's never okay.' He balls his hand into a fist, then hits himself on the head. 'It was an accident, I--I couldn't stop him bleeding, why wouldn't he stop bleeding?'

I've heard this before. I have. I know I have. My mind runs a marathon in my head to grasp at the mess of memories stuck inside it, but I can't think.

'Make it stop, please make it stop.'

The last party. At Robbie's house, almost a year ago, when we found Preston unconscious. Right before the crowds started gathering, he was uttering random words and phrases to me. The same words and phrases he's mouthing now, except they aren't random, are they?

'Preston,' I say as calmly as I can. 'You're not making any sense. You need to breathe more slowly and explain it to me, okay?'

He ignores me and continues rambling.

'Preston,' I say more firmly this time. 'Breathe. You need to breathe.'

'I didn't mean to, I just wanted him to stop, I swear I didn't. He just fell, that's all he did, it was an accident. He fell and there was blood and it wouldn't stop, it wouldn't stop. She promised it would be okay, she promised he would be okay, she promised, she pro--'

'Preston!'

As if by magic, Preston stops. He stops rocking his body back and forth, stops mumbling, stops pulling at his hair, stops hitting his head, stops breathing at a hysterical pace. He just stops. Slowly, I reach out to him again. I leave my hand floating in front of him for several minutes until he lifts his head from his knees. His eyes are bloodshot, his hair a knotted mess, and he's doing something I've never seen him do before. He's crying.

'I killed him.' His voice is a whisper. 'I killed Matty's father.'

EPILOGUE

The temptation to rip open these envelopes and devour their contents has been gnawing at me since I got my hands on them. I run my fingers along the edge of the crisp paper as the bus halts at a traffic light, and I take in my surroundings. I recognise an Italian restaurant in the distance, which lets me know I should arrive within the next five minutes or so. I don't really care much about what the contents of my envelope reveal, in all honesty. Of course I want to have passed my exams, but so much other crap has happened recently that it feels like such an irrelevant fragment of my life.

The bus begins moving again, and I turn my attention away from the envelopes in my hands. I'm nervous. I'm not quite sure why because I've made this journey plenty of times by now. I figure it must be the unknown contents of the other envelope that's triggering this anxiety. I want its content to be glowing and perfect, and all things considered, I realise that's incredibly unlikely. I try my best to shake away this feeling of intense uncertainty, and focus on the greenery outside the bus window.

Once I arrive, I undergo the usual mundane, and somewhat dehumanising, routine. I had to declare the envelopes beforehand, and I'd hoped it would mean they'd remain unopened, but they're torn apart and inspected as if they're hazardous, and it sort of pisses me off. I make a poor attempt to close them back up as I enter the large room, and am so focused on doing so that I almost forget where I am as I sit down beside the small table.

'Euphemia, what a pleasant surprise.'

With his wavy hair unkempt and his eyes big and wide, Preston flashes me the uneven smirk I love to hate.

'You know every time you call me that, I hate you that little bit more, right?'

'N'aw, thanks. I've got no idea how I endure this prison without your witty charm as a solace.'

'It's not a prison,' I intersect.

He rolls his eyes. It's not a prison, it's not. It's a Young Offender Institution, which as well as being a bit of a mouthful, makes it sound far less serious than it is. Regardless, Preston never refers to it as such.

All things considered, he's lucky. After he made an official statement, the ball started rolling pretty quickly. I went with him to the police station the morning after the fire, and he wasn't the slightest bit anxious. In fact, I don't think I've seen anyone ever look more at peace in my life. Anwen was soon out, and he was soon in. She fought against it at first, denied what Preston had told the authorities, but it quickly dawned on her that this is something he wanted, something he needed. There were issues with Anwen having perverted the cause of justice, but she'd served so many years already that she was pardoned.

It's incredible, really, how simple it was. One day she was locked up, and the next she had all the freedom in the world. Custody over Matty isn't quite so easy. Preston was sentenced to eighteen months for involuntary manslaughter. Eighteen months. Not even two years, while his mum spent over five years in prison for a crime she didn't commit. Even worse is the reality that if Anwen had been honest in the first place, it's unlikely anyone would've had to spend any time anywhere. I mean, Preston was thirteen. It was an accident. He was scared.

I've found myself constantly questioning what must have been going through Anwen's mind to convince herself that what she did was the best solution, but it's obvious, really. When your thirteen-year-old son shoves your boyfriend after beating you then turning on him, only for your boyfriend to fall, bang his head on the corner of a coffee table, and die instantly, it's diffi-cult not to react badly. She was just desperate to protect him, only she didn't realise that having him lie all these years hurt him more than anything else ever could.

'C'mon then, what did we get?' Preston pulls me from my thoughts as he nods at the envelopes in my hand.

'Oh, yeah, sorry. Should I do mine or yours first?'

'Name a colour.'

'What?'

'I ask a simple request.'

I should really be used to his shit by now, shouldn't I? I whine about how dumb this is, but can't help smiling as I say, 'red.'

'Ah, so predictable. Incorrect, sorry. Beige. Yours first then.'

'Huh?'

'We'll read your results first. Come on, Mia, keep up.'

I try, and fail, to muster up a look of anger. I place Preston's envelope onto the grey desk, and stare at the remaining one in my hand. Now I'm nervous. I try opening it delicately without ripping it more than the guard did earlier, but after a few seconds, I lose all patience and just tear the thing open. I shut my eyes, yank the paper from inside, and hold it out in front of me. The first thing I see when I open my eyes is the letter B.

'I got a B in maths, oh my god!' I shriek, maybe a little too loudly considering the majority of eyes in the room glance at me. I clear my throat and flush, and as I scan the paper properly, I'm even more amazed. 'Holy shit, I got an A. I got an A in law, a B in psychology, and a B in biology!'

'Not even an A in maths?' Preston replies. 'I've clearly failed you.'

Despite his sarcasm, I desperately want to leap from my seat and hug the life out of Preston, so much so that I have to grab the sides of the chair to stop myself. For someone to have the ability to make me produce anything above a D in Maths is award-worthy, let alone a B. I'm thrilled. I'm ninety-nine percent sure my papers have been graded incorrectly, but I'm sure as hell not going to question it. With adrenaline now pumping through my veins, I move on to Preston's envelope. I release a long breath, and swallow hard. I'm far more nervous about this one, and I'm far more gentle with opening it.

I slowly pull the paper out, and I'm wishing for him to have done well so badly, and the likelihood of that not having happened terrifies me. I set my eyes onto the black writing, and release another breath.

I look up from the paper to Preston's expectant eyes, my mouth agape. 'You got an A* in physics, an A* in maths, an A in music, and a B in chemistry.'

'Hm, it'll suffice, I suppose.'

'You what? Are you kidding? You barely turn up to college all year, have a literal mental breakdown, spend four months in this place, take your exams in a juvie, and still get better grades than me--I--You could get into Oxbridge with these results, Preston. I'm legitimately annoyed at you for doing so well, holy--You're such an accidental arsehole.'

'I've never had a B before,' he mutters.

'I actually want to punch you.'

That's incredible, can he not see how amazingly he's done? I know he's critical of himself, but this is ridiculous. As his eyes bore into me, I realise he's not kidding in the slightest. I shake my head at him in disbelief, while Preston leans back in his chair and shrugs.

'Well, at least I've surpassed Robbie; he dropped out before even taking any exams.' He nods at me. 'I'd consider that when a marriage proposal is thrust on you. It's clearly a sign of a commitment complex.'

'Oh, shut up,' I retort. 'You know we're just friends now.'

'Who knows what the future may hold? Love can be rekindled, you know, Euphemia.' He's grinning, and it's pissing me off, and he knows it. 'What are his new digs like? And how are the odds of him burning this one down looking?'

Robbie didn't actually burn his house down. It was a discarded cigarette in one of the spare bedrooms. We've got no idea whose, and we never will, but if anything, he's lucky it's taken this long for something like that to happen. The entirety of the second floor was ruined from the fire, and this was one party his parents couldn't just get over. They gave him a chunk of money and basically told him to get the hell out of the smaller, yet still hugely impressive, house they were renting as a result of the fire.

I don't think Robbie could've been happier to have left. He put a deposit on a tiny flat in the city, and moved into it last week.

'It's a nice place,' I reply to Preston. 'I don't think working as a club promoter is going to let him keep up with the rent payments, though.'

'He should look into event planning,' Preston jokes.

'Y'know what, he genuinely should. I'll suggest that to him.'

'Hey, you better give me credit.'

'Probably a bad idea; if he knows it came from you, he won't do it,' I say, to which Preston responds with a pout. I raise my eyebrows. 'You lied to him about your name, date of birth, address, and general identity for years. The boy has very justified trust issues.'

Preston shrugs and rolls his eyes for what feels like the hundredth time today. He and Robbie didn't speak for a while after the truth came out, but they'd relied on each other so much over the past five or so years that Robbie couldn't keep it up for long. It only took him one visit to Preston, as opposed to Zack, to realise how monumentally better he was in every way.

'Good news,' Preston suddenly chirps up, bouncing in his seat a little. 'It's recently occurred to me that igniting some rolled up tobacco doesn't make you a modern-day Edgar Allan Poe, but in fact, makes you an idiot, so I'm quitting smoking. Only been a month or so, but so far, so good. Only had a few minor slip ups.'

'Oh, good. As well as the whole tarnishing your internal organs with tar thing, your method of storing burnt out cigarettes was going to get yourself set on fire one day.'

Preston shoots me a dumb grin as if he's proud of his past idiocy. As he does so, the sound of a chair scraping against the floor vibrates in my ears, and it's followed by some loud yelling. The inmate a few tables to our right has jumped up from his chair, and is screaming at some poor old woman sitting opposite him. He must be at least six and a half feet tall, and muscles bulge from places I didn't even know muscles could bulge from, compared to the old woman who looks barely five foot. A guard rushes over, and drags him out of the room.

'He asked me if I'd have sex with him this one time,' Preston says once the drama is over. 'Nice bloke, little temperamental, but I turned him down. He proceeded to punch me in the face and knock me out for ten minutes, which I was exceedingly impressed with, and now creatively refers to me as a the f-slur, but a nice bloke nonetheless.'

I can't tell if he's joking. The thought of Preston spending all day with these kinds of people intensifies motherly instincts I didn't even know existed. He has to serve a minimum of six months here, and I'm relying on that to keep me sane, but Preston's constant stream of pessimism makes him doubtful of that happening. He was astounded to have been sentenced to just eighteen months, but to me it seems logical. Preston confessed, pleaded guilty with no question, he was barely thirteen-years old at the time, it was a form of self-defence, a complete accident, and his criminal record is otherwise clean.

I'm pretty sure his poor mental state helped lessen the blow, too. If he showed even half the amount of remorse I'd seen in him in court, that would've been enough to convince the judge into making a generous decision. It's bizarre, really, how this is one of the happiest I've ever seen him. Being trapped in this place isn't the breeze he makes it out to be, I can see that. I'm not a total idiot. He rarely talks about the people in here, and I notice him flinch every time there's a sudden sound. He's told me countless times how much he hates the bland grey ensemble he has to wear day in and day out, and now that his studies are over, he's pretty much dying of boredom.

A month or so after entering this place, I noticed a deep cut in his arm similar to the one he made when he turned up drunk at Robbie's, but he's better. Compared to what he was before, he's so much better. The person I saw for a fleeting moment in the cottage before everything started spiraling is appearing more and more. He's glad his mum is free, and that he's finally received the repercussions he knows he should've faced six or so years ago. More than anything, I think he's just relieved to not have to lie anymore.

'There is one thing I still don't understand,' I say, resting my elbows on the plastic table. 'Why me? You made up a whole other life, and never showed this one to anyone, then one day just decided to be honest with me, or what? I don't get it.'

'I owed you more than that,' he replies simply. 'I knew who you were the morning we met for the tutoring--I knew immediately--and I knew you were the reason I wasn't dead. So I owed you more than that.'

I go to interrupt him, but he lifts his hand to stop me.

'Aiden and Robbie helped too, and I'll be forever grateful of that, but for them it was more complex. Of course they didn't want me to drop dead, but Robbie was terrified of getting into trouble, while Aiden revelled in the excitement of it all. For you, it was simple. Regardless of what I'd done to you an hour prior, you just wanted to help me. Nothing more, nothing less.' He hesitates. 'And honestly, I think I just needed someone--any-one.'

'Sheesh, that makes me feel special.'

Preston flashes a small smile, then glances at his hands before lifting his head back up. His eyes shy away from mine as he utters the next sentence, and he says it as if speaking to thin air.

'You know why I was in hospital that night, don't you?'

I don't say anything, and instead, nod my head. Preston nods his, and I open my mouth in an attempt to talk about it, but he gets there first with a dig on the breakfast he was served this morning. His attempt to skirt the topic is unmissable, but I don't press him on it. He shared his depression and PTSD diagnosis with me shortly after he got it, and if his pained expression was anything to go by when he did force himself to share it, doing so was driven more by some warped IOU thing than a genuine desire to tell me.

This institution is big on reformation, and despite Preston's refusal to discuss it with me, I know he's getting help. Given my many split personality jibes, he's also proudly confirmed his definite lack of personality disorder. Realistically, I knew that was never the case; everything about Zack was planned and intentional. I just wish he'd asked for help sooner, or at all. He's only getting it in here because he has no say in the matter. He won't admit it, but I think he's secretly glad. I don't think he realised how much he needed it.

I sit back in the hard, plastic chair and gaze at Preston, and I realise I love him. I'm not in love with him, but I love him, and I don't think I've ever loved anyone any more than I have Preston Maddox. The quiff he'd placed his fair hair into has almost completely deflated by now, and even in the fluorescent lighting of this bland room, his eyes are striking. He's saying something but I'm not listening, yet his indistinguishable words sound like galaxies forming.

We both have no idea what will happen with custody over Matty, what my final year of school will bring, what Preston will do for work or uni once he's out of here, nor how much of his sentence he'll have to serve. I don't know how Dad will cope with his newly single life, or whether or not I'll have to deal with any step-parents in the future. A year ago, this level of uncertainty would have left me terrified, but now I know that's okay. No one really knows much about anything, and those who think they do probably know the least.

The sound of a bell ringing alarms me, and I'm propelled back to the present. Visitation time is over. We only get forty-five minutes, and while that's barely any less time compared to the regular prison, it feels significantly so. I'm desperate to stay, and despite the fact I've already booked another visit in a fortnight, leaving here always feels like the last time I'll ever see Preston.

We say our goodbyes as the guards start to rush everyone, but as I'm about to stand up, Preston stops me.

'Oh, one more thing!'

'Yeah?'

He leans in slightly as his bright eyes gaze into mine with wonder spilling out of them. What looks like a moment of uncertainty passes through his face as he opens his mouth, and then stops himself. He glances at his hands, then back to me, and leans in further. I wait silently, my breath slow and quiet in fear of missing what he's about to say. He clears his throat, and opens his mouth again.

'Has anyone ever told you that your name sounds like an STD?'